DARK SKY

Also by Carla Neggers
in Large Print:

The Carriage House
Cold Ridge
The Harbor
Night's Landing
The Rapids
Shelter Island
Stonebrook Cottage
The Waterfall
The Cabin

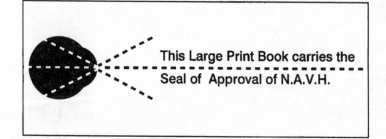

This Large Print Book carries the
Seal of Approval of N.A.V.H.

DARK SKY

Carla Neggers

Thorndike Press • Waterville, Maine

Published in 2006 by arrangement with Harlequin Books S.A.

Thorndike Press® Large Print Romance.

The tree indicium is a trademark of Thorndike Press.

The text of this Large Print edition is unabridged.
Other aspects of the book may vary from the original edition.

Set in 16 pt. Plantin by Ramona Watson.

Printed in the United States on permanent paper.

Library of Congress Cataloging-in-Publication Data

Neggers, Carla.
    Dark sky / by Carla Neggers. — Large print ed.
      p. cm. — (Thorndike Press large print romance)
    ISBN 0-7862-8238-X (lg. print : hc : alk. paper)
    1. United States marshals — Fiction. 2. Revenge —
Fiction. 3. New York (N.Y.) — Fiction. 4. Vermont —
Fiction. 5. Large type books. I. Title. II. Series:
Thorndike Press large print romance series.
PS3564.E2628D37 2006
  813′.54—dc22
                                               2005026937

To Pam and Paul Hudson.

National Association for Visually Handicapped
----------------------------- *serving the partially seeing*

As the Founder/CEO of NAVH, the only national health agency solely devoted to those who, although not totally blind, have an eye disease which could lead to serious visual impairment, I am pleased to recognize Thorndike Press* as one of the leading publishers in the large print field.

Founded in 1954 in San Francisco to prepare large print textbooks for partially seeing children, NAVH became the pioneer and standard setting agency in the preparation of large type.

Today, those publishers who meet our standards carry the prestigious "Seal of Approval" indicating high quality large print. We are delighted that Thorndike Press is one of the publishers whose titles meet these standards. We are also pleased to recognize the significant contribution Thorndike Press is making in this important and growing field.

Lorraine H. Marchi, L.H.D.
Founder/CEO
NAVH

* Thorndike Press encompasses the following imprints: Thorndike, Wheeler, Walker and Large Print Press.

One

~:❦:~

The lake still smelled of summer. Juliet Longstreet, her jeans rolled up to midcalf, stood in water up to her ankles. Its warmth surprised her, although it shouldn't have. As kids, she and her brothers had gone swimming in the small lake into October, not that the water was warm then. But in late September, in the early days of autumn, anything was possible.

She dug her toes into the soft, muddy bottom, looking across the rippling water to the opposite shore, nestled amid the hills of east central Vermont. The leaves were beginning to turn. She could see dots of red, patches of yellow. She breathed in the clean air and suddenly was sorry she had to head back to New York in a few hours. She'd already packed up her tent and rolled up her sleeping bag.

Her work was in New York, if not her life.

But she didn't know that her life was here, either. She glanced behind her and

7

took in the small clearing where she'd pitched her tent, the cluster of granite boulders amid birch trees, the tall pine trees with their dead underbranches, the huge, ancient sugar maple on the edge of the path to the dirt road that encircled half the lake. She could have stayed with her parents just over the hill, in her old bedroom overlooking the barn, or with any of her brothers who lived in the area, but she liked the quiet and solitude of her five acres on the lake.

A family from Massachusetts and a couple from New Jersey owned second homes on the lake, nothing fancy, just ordinary country houses. A private, nonprofit nature preserve owned the rest of the land on the lake. The only structure on the preserve's two hundred acres was an early nineteenth-century barn, all that remained of an old farm.

With the increase in land prices, Juliet could sell her quiet lakefront lot for a sizable profit. But given her itinerant lifestyle as a deputy U.S. marshal, she liked having land of her own, the sense of permanence it gave her. And her roots, at least, were in Vermont.

Spaceshot, the family black Lab, waddled down the path from the road and joined her at the lake's edge, but didn't get too close to the water. "You could use a swim — the exercise would do you good," Juliet said to the dog, knowing he wouldn't have worked up the energy to walk down to the lake by himself. "Who came with you?"

Her niece Wendy followed the dog's route down the path, walking over the matted-down grass where Juliet had pitched her tent. At seventeen, Wendy was the eldest of the Longstreet grandchildren. She was short and slim and had dark hair and dark eyes like her mother, who'd walked out on Juliet's oldest brother fifteen years ago. Susie Longstreet had home-schooled her only child. Wendy graduated a year earlier than her peers but decided not to go straight to college. Then, over the summer, Susie announced she was renting her house and leaving on the first of September to study yoga in Nova Scotia for six months.

That left Wendy with few options, but she chose to live with her Longstreet grandparents and work at the family land-scaping business. She seemed happy with her decision. She was a hard worker, but she was self-conscious, determined to see herself as something of a mutant because she wasn't tall and big-boned — or fair-haired and blue-eyed — like her Longstreet grandparents, her father or her four uncles and aunt.

There were days Juliet would have traded Wendy for her long, fine, straight dark hair. Her own was cut short and filled with cowlicks. She'd never figured out what to do with it.

"Grandma said to tell you lunch will be on the table in twenty minutes," Wendy said.

"Thanks. Who'll be there?"

"Grandma, Grandpa, Uncle Sam and Aunt Elizabeth." Wendy studied the water. "Dad."

For the Longstreets, a small gathering. "All right. I should get moving, anyway."

"Do you think I could visit you in New York sometime?"

"Sure, Wendy. Of course. Do you have something special in mind you'd like to do there?"

"Everything. I haven't been since Mum took me when I was ten. I'd love to go to the theater and see Central Park and Fifth Avenue — and go to museums. Mum and I went to the Met, but we didn't see all of it."

"My apartment's only a few blocks from

the Museum of Natural History. But I'm only there for another month or so. My friend Freda will be back from L.A. then and need her apartment back."

"Maybe I can come before you have to move?"

"That'd be great."

She seemed satisfied. Of Juliet's seven — and counting — nieces and nephews, Wendy was the most difficult to talk to. It wasn't just the divorce, the homeschooling, the tension between her mother and the expansive Longstreet clan — it was the girl herself. She was private, cerebral, defensive and very sensitive. "She's not like all you Longstreet lunkheads," Susie would say. And she'd be right, Juliet thought. Wendy was her own person; in fact, last night over dinner, she'd informed her father, aunt and grandparents that she was going vegan. She'd been a vegetarian for two years, but now she was locking down even further, eliminating all animal products from her diet, including milk and eggs.

Joshua had stalked from the table, telling his daughter she'd dry up on a stick and blow away if she didn't get a grip. In the morning, her grandparents had made her an omelet with cheddar cheese, as if she'd never said a word about her intentions. Of-

11

fended, Wendy marched up to her room and stayed there. When Juliet headed back out to the lake, she'd noticed her niece up in her window seat, scribbling madly on a pad of paper. Her mother said Wendy wanted to be a doctor. Juliet wasn't so sure.

"Come on, Spaceshot," Wendy said, cheerfully clapping her hands at the dog. "Let's go back to the house. Come on, let's run!"

The dog didn't follow her lead and run to the path. He resumed his determined but interminable waddle. But at least Wendy was laughing, and, for the first time since Juliet had arrived in Vermont three days ago, she thought her niece would be okay for the next six months, with her mother in Nova Scotia. At least she'd had the sense not to try to live with her father at his place in town. As a Vermont state trooper, Joshua didn't keep a regular schedule, and he wasn't an easy man — even on a good day. He was the oldest of the six Longstreet siblings, Juliet the youngest and the only sister. None of her brothers fazed Juliet, but Wendy wasn't quite as hardheaded as her aunt — or the rest of the "Longstreet lunkheads."

Juliet rolled down her pants' legs and

slipped into her sport sandals, then joined her niece and Spaceshot on the path. They crossed the dirt road and picked up the wide, grassy lane that put them back on Longstreet land. To their left, a steep dirt driveway shot up to a small hillside cabin that her family used for guests, overflow family, temporary workers or grandchildren's adventures. Juliet, Wendy and Spaceshot stayed on the lane, which wound around the bottom of the hill, passing through a stone wall into open fields. They came to a fork, one branch leading up into the apple orchard, the other back down to the house. They took the latter, amid wildflowers and pine saplings no more than a foot tall.

"Why do you always wear a gun?" Wendy asked abruptly.

Juliet hadn't expected the question. "I'm a federal agent —"

"But not here. You work in New York."

"That's where I'm assigned, but 'federal' means I'm as much a marshal here in Vermont as I am in New York."

"Well, I would think you'd be able to take off your gun for Sunday lunch with your family."

It was a fair point, but Juliet didn't respond. Wendy was accustomed to law enforcement officers in the family. Not only was her aunt a deputy U.S. marshal and her father a state trooper, but another uncle was a police officer in town, and her grandfather was a former state trooper on disability since a shooting had left him with one leg shorter than the other. He'd nearly bled out that night. Juliet was a teenager when the troopers showed up at their door. Wendy was a toddler, her parents on the verge of divorce — she wouldn't remember.

Juliet had no intention of taking off her gun, for one overriding reason that trumped all others.

Bobby Tatro was a free man.

He'd been released from federal prison in late August after serving a four-year sentence on a nonviolent gun charge, but he wasn't a nonviolent man. Juliet had picked him up in a Wal-Mart parking lot in Syracuse, where she had been assigned at the time. She'd been transferred to New York almost two years ago.

As she'd cuffed him, Tatro had vowed to come after her when he got out. *"Your pretty blond ass is mine, Marshal. You can count on it."*

It wasn't Juliet's first death threat nor would it be her last, but it was the most memorable since it came from Bobby

14

Tatro. The gun charge was only the tip of the iceberg when it came to Tatro's crimes. Everyone knew it, but prosecutors needed more evidence to charge him.

In the three weeks since his release, Juliet hadn't seen or heard from him, but still she watched her back. If Tatro was smart, he'd recognize that he'd served his time, paid the price for his mistakes and was now a free man. He'd move on with his life. Leave his past behind him. Get a job, save some money. Be glad he hadn't been charged on any of the violent offenses various prosecutors and investigators suspected him of having committed.

That, however, wasn't what Juliet or anyone else believed Bobby Tatro would do.

As she and Wendy approached the house, Spaceshot perked up, leading the way through a gap in another stone wall and down to the small barn, where spikes of hollyhocks and dahlias with blossoms the size of dinner plates and tangles of blue morning glories grew up against its rough-hewn boards. The barn and sprawling white clapboard house were pre-Civil War, but the three greenhouses and perfunctory equipment shed were added as Longstreet Landscaping had expanded.

15

Her parents and three of her brothers — Jeffrey, Sam and Will, Jr. — worked in the family business. Joshua and Paul were in law enforcement. Juliet was in law enforcement, too, but they all persisted in the stubborn hope that she'd give it up soon and come home. It wasn't that they didn't believe in her. It was that they worried about her.

Wendy stopped alongside the tidy vegetable garden, fat, ripe tomatoes and pole beans dripping off staked plants, and tilted back her head, looking up at her aunt. "We need to bury Teddy sometime."

Taken aback, Juliet managed a nod. Teddy was Wendy's golden retriever, who'd died at sixteen the week before her mother left for Nova Scotia. Wendy had his ashes in a cracker tin in her room. "Sure, Wendy. Do you want to do it before I leave for New York —"

"No!" She seemed almost in a panic, then calmed herself. "No, I'm not ready. I can't do it today. But I think we should before the ground freezes. Unless — I don't know. I've been thinking about spreading his ashes in the lake. He loved the water."

"He sure did. I've never seen a dog love the water as much as Teddy did."

That brought a tug of a smile to her

16

niece's face. "Remember when he jumped in and followed us in the kayak? He didn't want to give up. I thought he'd drown."

"He was a great dog, Wendy."

"Dad says sixteen's a good run for a golden retriever, but —" Her eyes pooled. "I wanted him to live forever."

Juliet put an arm around Wendy's small shoulders. At five-nine, Juliet was half a foot taller. She didn't want to think about how much she outweighed her. "Whenever you're ready, whatever you decide to do with Teddy's ashes, I'll be here."

"Dad almost left them for the vet to get rid of. He said he thought it'd upset me, having Teddy's ashes. It'd upset me more *not* to have them."

"I guess he meant well."

"You know what Grandma says —"

"Yes, I know. 'The road to hell is paved with good intentions.' " Juliet smiled. "We've all had that lecture."

They started down the stone path to the side porch, Wendy sniffling back her tears. When they reached the country kitchen, Sunday lunch was on the long, scarred pine table. Roast chicken, buttermilk biscuits, gravy — but also vegan ratatouille, salad and, especially for Wendy, a little bowl of kidney beans, pinto beans and chickpeas.

The girl leaned into her aunt and whispered, "Don't mention my wanting to visit you in New York, okay?"

Juliet nodded her promise to keep her mouth shut.

Joshua sat next to his daughter. At forty, he was the tallest of the Longstreet brothers and also had the hardest head. He didn't approve of homeschooling, vegans, Wendy's year off, his ex-wife's six months in Nova Scotia — none of it. And he wasn't subtle about it, either.

Sam, two years younger, worked the landscaping equipment and kept it running, and he and his wife, Elizabeth, a nurse, had three kids — two boys and a girl, ages thirteen, ten and eight, all of whom went to public school.

Juliet's father, Will, Sr., almost white-haired now at sixty-five, settled at the head of the table. He smiled at Wendy and asked her about her walk out to the lake. "The leaves are starting to turn," she mumbled, but didn't seem to know what else to say.

Her grandmother set a small pot of hot green tea in front of Wendy's plate. "I read that tea is the healthiest drink there is. We should all drink more of it."

Wendy smiled at her, obviously pleased

with that small hint of approval. Anne Longstreet was in her early sixties, but looked younger, a fair, strongly built woman whose hard work and worries seemed to have made her stronger instead of wearing her out.

Juliet could see a muscle working in her brother's jaw; Joshua wouldn't want his mother or anyone else encouraging Wendy's, to his way of thinking, weird eating habits. But he kept quiet, and that was something. He loved his daughter. No one, including Juliet, doubted it. He just hadn't had much say in how she was raised, and now she seemed almost like a stranger to him.

He also hated tea, especially green tea.

When Wendy heaped ratatouille onto her plate, he relaxed somewhat. Juliet understood — they'd all worried that with her mother's departure and her dog's death, Wendy would lose her taste for food altogether. She was hard on herself by nature. An eating disorder wasn't an unreasonable worry.

Talk shifted to autumn landscaping jobs, the apple and pumpkin crops, and Wendy grew animated, telling how she had an idea for arranging pumpkins out front to sell. Juliet didn't contribute to the conversation but enjoyed it, and pictured herself if she'd stayed — if she came back.

When she got ready to leave, she thought about pulling Joshua aside to tell him about Bobby Tatro, but decided against it. Tatro was her problem. And he wouldn't look for her in Vermont. With any luck, he wouldn't look for her at all. Three weeks had to be a good sign.

But Joshua ended up pulling *her* aside. "You okay, Juliet?"

"Yes, fine."

"You looked preoccupied all weekend. That business last month with the assassin —"

"It's over," she said. "I was never that involved." In light of Tatro's release, she'd all but forgotten about her encounter in August with an international assassin.

Ethan Brooker had turned up at her apartment in New York and swept her into his hunt for what turned out to be a clever, dangerous killer with a long list of targets. Ethan was almost killed. It wasn't the first time — he was a Special Forces officer with a knack, at least lately, for attracting trouble.

"Brooker?" Joshua asked, as if he could read his sister's mind. "What happened to him?"

"He took off once the dust settled."

20

"That's what he did back in May, too."

Juliet tried to smile. "No, in May he took off *before* the dust settled. He's lucky he didn't get himself arrested." Brooker had eventually come back, and he'd told the FBI and the marshals and the Secret Service what he knew about the crazy plot to extort a presidential pardon that he'd helped expose, although not by following the rules. And Brooker had never been that interested in the plot. All he'd cared about was finding out who had murdered his wife and why.

"Juliet, guys like that . . . should be left alone."

"Ethan's gone, Joshua. I have no idea where he is. I couldn't contact him if I wanted to."

Her brother gave her a curt nod. "Yeah. Okay. If you ever want to talk, you know where to find me."

It was as brotherly a comment as he'd ever made, and Juliet had to force herself not to let her jaw drop. "Thanks," she said, meaning it, "but Brooker and me — well, there is no such thing."

For once, Joshua didn't argue with her.

On the five-hour drive back to New York, Juliet kept telling herself that her brother — everyone — was right. For the past year, Ethan Brooker had been a man out of control, willing to do what it took to find his wife's killers and get the answers to her murder, to satisfy himself that he'd left no stone unturned. Juliet thought back to the time she'd first met Brooker, just before they found the bodies of two thugs in the backyard of the Tennessee boyhood home of the president of the United States. It wasn't an auspicious start to any kind of relationship.

He hadn't turned up in her life in August and stayed at her apartment — on her futon couch — out of any romantic pull to her. He'd needed her help.

And when he didn't anymore, he took off.

Just as well, Juliet told herself, and concentrated on her driving as traffic picked up and the New York skyline came into view.

Four hours after arriving back in New York, Juliet sat at a grime-encrusted table on the back wall of a Bronx bar that smelled of stale cigars and, somewhat less strongly, urine. She hadn't touched the coffee she'd ordered. Its color didn't look right, not that she was fussy. She didn't point out to the bartender that there was no smoking anymore in New York's bars. There was probably no peeing on the floor, either.

George O'Hara — his real name, although he himself said he didn't have a drop of Irish blood in him — didn't seem to care as he sat across from her. Dark and hugely overweight, O'Hara was a one-time felon who'd pulled himself together after his release from prison and made a fresh start. He cleaned bars during the day and performed comedy at night. On occasion, he provided Juliet with information. He was selective in what he told her; he had no great desire to tell her anything. But he accepted that some people simply needed to be off the streets.

Juliet fingered the handle on her coffee mug. "What do you tell people who ask about me?"

"I tell them you think I'm funny. You do, don't you?"

She'd seen his act once. "You're very funny."

"Like my federal agent jokes?"

"I'm material," she said. "That's what you tell anyone who asks about me, isn't it?"

He leaned his bulk about a quarter inch closer to her, the best he could do in the cramped quarters. "Nobody asks."

"How's the cleaning?"

"Pays more in three months than you earn in a year as a marshal."

No doubt it did. "You don't clean this place, do you?"

George seemed offended. "It wouldn't smell like pee if I cleaned it."

Juliet breathed in through her teeth. That morning, she'd gone kayaking in a pristine Vermont lake. "The cigar smoke's getting to my sinuses," she said, then looked out at the crowd of loud, happy drunks, a third of whom were as overweight as O'Hara. Without turning to him, she went on. "I need anything you can give me on Bobby Tatro."

She'd given George a heads-up. Her mention of Tatro wasn't out of the blue. George sat back, his chair groaning under him, and when she finally shifted her attention back to him, he sighed. "Word is he's out of the country."

"Where?"

"South America."

"That's a whole continent, George. Can you be more specific?"

He shook his head. "He's hooked up with some vigilante-justice types. He's going to save the world."

"Good. It'll keep him busy."

She picked and prodded some more, but it was all O'Hara had to offer. He promised to keep his ears open — he prided himself on his listening skills. He said they helped make him a better comic. He wasn't after just the content of what other people were saying, but the rhythm of their speech, its syntax and cadences. Juliet had suggested he put together a class for her fellow deputies, and he'd almost choked on his tongue laughing at the idea.

But he wasn't laughing now. "Nobody likes this guy Tatro."

"Smart."

"What does he want with you?"

"Nothing, I hope."

"You put him away?"

"I caught him after he was convicted in a federal court and didn't turn up to serve his sentence."

"Ended his party."

"I found him in a Wal-Mart parking lot. It wasn't much of a party."

O'Hara held up his beer glass to the dim light. "Those aren't my fingerprints," he said, frowning, then set the glass back down on the dark wood table. "How's your Special Forces guy?"

"I have no idea. And he's not 'my' Special Forces guy." Juliet paid for their drinks and got to her feet. "You know how to reach me?"

"You gave me your cell-phone number, apartment phone, apartment address, office phone, page number, personal e-mail, office e-mail —"

"I didn't give you my apartment address."

"Oops. Forgot that one didn't come from you." He didn't seem particularly worried or apologetic.

"If you hear anything, let me know. Do not underestimate this guy. Even if he is a free man, Bobby Tatro is one very bad actor. If you run into him, don't approach him. Don't even think my name."

George's expressive eyes — a warm, deep brown — showed concern mixed with outright fear, but not for himself, Juliet realized. For her. But he simply said goodnight and thanked her for the beer, ordering another as she made her way through the crowd and back outside. She took the subway back to her borrowed apartment on the Upper West Side, making a point to smile at Juan, the new doorman — Ethan's success at sneaking into the building had been the last straw for the old one.

On the elevator, she spoke briefly to a middle-aged couple who seemed self-conscious around her. It took her a few seconds to realize it was probably her badge; she doubted they ran into many federal agents. They were pleasant, artsy types who lived on a higher floor in a bigger, fancier apartment than hers.

Freda, her theater friend, would be back in just a matter of weeks, but Juliet hadn't done a thing to find a new apartment. Even a less desirable street on the Upper West Side would be tough on her salary, assuming she could find something.

She flopped on her futon couch, listening to the familiar, soothing gurgle of her four fish tanks. Why four, she didn't know. She didn't even know why she had one fish tank. And her plants — the place was a jungle. But a lady slipper orchid she'd bought at the New York Orchid Show at the World Trade Center, before 9/11, was in bloom, and that pleased her.

Her cell phone rang. She debated not answering it but rolled off the couch and headed down the hall to her small bedroom. She grabbed her phone off the dresser and took a quick glance at the readout: private. No help there.

She barely got a chance to say hello when she heard a deep, familiar male voice with a west Texas accent. "Hey,

27

Marshal. I didn't wake you, did I?"

"Brooker — Ethan." Had she conjured him up by talking about him, thinking about him twice that day? She shook off the thought. If he was calling her, it wasn't because anything good had happened. "Where are you?"

"On the same island as you."

He was in New York. She sat on the edge of her bed. "At least you sprang for your own room this time." In August, he'd spent two nights on her futon. She'd slept badly both nights.

"I need to see you. Tomorrow morning. Federal Hall at 9:00 a.m. Wait for me at the George Washington statue."

"I'm not waiting for you, period —"

"Don't tell your fellow marshals."

"Marshals are political appointees. One to a district. Technically, my colleagues and me are deputy U.S. marshals." She sighed. "Damn it, Brooker. Why can't we just meet for coffee? What's going on?"

"I'll find you in the morning."

He disconnected.

Juliet threw her phone down on the bed. The bed, the bureau, the refinished ladder-back chair — all Freda's. Juliet had tacked up drawings her nieces and nephews had sent her, photographs of family gatherings

28

she'd missed, a Vermont calendar. Except for her plants and fish, nothing else was hers. When she found a new place, she wasn't relishing having to furnish it. Subletting had seemed like a good idea at the time. Six months on the Upper West Side — why not? Now, her time was up, and she had to find a new place. At best, a pain in the neck. At worst — it made her realize what a tumbleweed she'd become.

She tried not to let Brooker's call get to her. He was dramatic, accustomed to the blackest of black ops and not one, by nature, to reveal too much — especially over the phone.

Would she meet him at Federal Hall?

Of course. There'd never been any doubt. Ethan knew it, and so did she.

Two

Juliet arrived at Federal Hall on Wall Street at nine on the dot and stood next to the impressive statue of George Washington, who'd been sworn in as president there in 1789.

She'd decided not to be early for her clandestine meeting — or late. She was up at her usual time of 5:30 a.m., did her three-mile run, lifted a few free weights in her apartment, stretched, showered and dressed in jeans, running shoes, a stretchy button-down shirt and her black leather jacket — a recent splurge.

She started three hours of firearms training at ten. She meant to have Ethan sent on his way and be back at her desk by then.

The raspberry lip gloss she'd dabbed on before leaving the U.S. Marshals Service Southeastern New York District Office wasn't for his sake. It was a cool, dreary morning, and she didn't want to get chapped lips.

Juliet recognized one of the heavily armed NYPD officers guarding the New York Stock Exchange, a huge American flag draping its familiar colonnade exterior. New York remained at Orange Alert. Cars had been barred from narrow Wall Street since 9/11. Security was as tight there as anywhere on the planet.

She wondered what old George would think if he suddenly came to life. It wasn't even the same building behind him. The original Federal Hall, where the Bill of Rights had been written and the First Congress had met, was torn down; the current one, with its beautiful Greek Revival architecture, was erected in its place in 1842. It was now a National Park Service site.

Brooker turned the corner of Nassau Street, and as she watched him approach the statue, Juliet didn't notice anything different about him since she'd last seen him in late August. Except maybe his concussion from his fall in Ravenkill Creek had healed. The assassin he'd followed to Ravenkill, a picturesque village on the Hudson River an hour north of New York, had beaned him on the head with a rock, nearly killing him.

But that ordeal was over now, and Juliet

had hoped Ethan had gone home to Texas finally, to mourn his wife and come to grips with his guilt and regrets — the unalterable fact that he was still alive and she wasn't.

He walked between two planters — car bomb deterrents — and walked up the two steps to where she stood. He was a few inches taller than she was and broad-shouldered, his dark hair cropped shorter than a month ago. Whether he was on the periphery of the action or right in the middle of it, Ethan Brooker was a catalyst, was the sort of man who made things happen.

"I like the leather," he said.

"Keeps me warm." Juliet noticed that his dark eyes were as superalert as ever. "You're right on time."

The sprinkle of rain had turned into a steady drizzle. Pedestrians by the dozen unfurled black umbrellas. Juliet didn't have one on her. Neither did Ethan. He had on dark charcoal pants, an expensive denim jacket and cowboy boots. His silver belt buckle was right out of the Old West.

She shoved her fists into her jacket pockets. "No Stetson?"

"I didn't want anyone to mistake me for a stockbroker."

As if there were a chance.

His gaze locked on her. "I need your help."

The drizzle glistened on his hair and jacket, but he didn't seem to notice. Juliet licked her lips, tasting the gloss. "I hope you want me to help you move a sofa or something, because if it involves my work —"

"I need a name."

Juliet pulled her hands out of her pockets and realized the steps were shiny with rain, that she and Ethan were the only ones on Wall Street not rushing for cars, cabs, restaurants and offices. "Sure you don't want to go for coffee? We could get out of the rain."

Brooker shook his head. "I have a flight that leaves in ninety minutes."

"Ethan, what the hell —" She contained a sudden bite of impatience. "All right. Go ahead. Give me what you've got. If it makes sense and I can help you, I will."

"I need the name of a man — an American in his mid-thirties. I don't have a good description. Dark, curly hair. Good-looking."

"That doesn't give me much to go on. What else?"

"He's an ex-con."

"Ah. Now we're in my world. But you still have to narrow down the possibilities —"

33

"He's after a blond, female marshal."

Juliet looked at her hands, saw that they were slick now with the rain. "There are other blond, female marshals."

"I need a name, Juliet."

She leveled her gaze on him. "Why?"

He shook his head. "I can't say. If you take this up the food chain, I still won't be able to say. But I'll get my name, one way or the other."

A year ago, Ethan Brooker was a respected, decorated career Special Forces officer. Then his wife, an army captain, was murdered in Amsterdam. When the official investigation stalled — Ethan went after answers on his own. His search took him to Night's Landing, Tennessee, where he posed as a property manager for the Dunnemores, a prominent southern family whose friend and neighbor was John Wesley Poe, the newly elected U.S. president.

Ethan ended up helping to expose Nick Janssen, who'd schemed to capitalize on his connection to both the Dunnemores and President Poe and extort a presidential pardon for himself. Months earlier, Janssen had skipped the country to avoid federal tax fraud charges — but he wasn't a simple tax evader. By the time his plot backfired, the world knew he was an international criminal with an extensive network of illegal arms traders, drug dealers, murderers and extortionists.

Janssen had deliberately ordered the murder of U.S. Army Captain Charlene Brooker, whose questions the previous fall had come too close to him and, ultimately, led to her death.

But it wasn't until August that Nick Janssen, with Ethan hot on his tail, finally was taken into custody in the Netherlands. He was still in a Dutch prison, fighting extradition to the U.S. to face a jury for his crimes. In a last-ditch attempt to control his own fate, he'd hired an assassin — Ethan had been on her target list. But Libby Smith, too, was in prison, not far, Juliet thought, from where she, Ethan and George Washington stood.

"Ethan," she said, pausing for a breath. "I can't let you suck me into another of your semi-legitimate enterprises."

"This one's legit."

"How? Who are you working for —"

"I need the name, Juliet. Everything you have on this guy."

She squinted up at the gray sky amid the skyscrapers, a fat raindrop splatting hard on her forehead. Wiping it off, she looked down at the pedestrians enduring the tight Wall Street security with a nonchalance that was both inspiring and sad. There'd be no going back to pre-9/11 days.

And no going back, she thought, to the days before she'd met Ethan Brooker over two of Janssen's dead henchmen, one of whom had pulled the trigger on the gun that had killed Ethan's wife.

Char Brooker had died just a year ago. Ethan hadn't even remotely begun to live a normal life again.

"Bobby Tatro," Juliet said. "That's the name you want."

"Who is he?"

"An ex-con who doesn't like me. He got out of federal prison in late August, about the time you were here."

"Have you heard from him?"

She shook her head, feeling the rain dripping from the ends of her short curls now. Although her hair wasn't saturated, it was getting there. "Not since he went to prison. I picked him up in Syracuse four years ago. He failed to deliver himself to serve his sentence — he was on the lam for about three months."

"How'd you find him?"

She ran a toe over a tiny pool of freshly fallen rain and didn't look at Brooker. "I

36

was in the right place at the right time. A Wal-Mart parking lot, as it turns out." She raised her gaze to the man next to her, realized she didn't know him at all — and she shouldn't fool herself into thinking she did. "You have access to his file, don't you?"

He nodded. "I can get his file."

"Everything I have is there —"

"No, it isn't."

"He was born and raised in Syracuse. His mother's a domestic, his father's a chronically unemployed alcoholic. He started getting into trouble as a teenager, but he managed to do two semesters of community college before dropping out." Juliet shrugged. "That's all in his file."

"What were you doing at Wal-Mart?"

"Buying potting soil."

"Right."

She heard the skepticism in his tone, remembered that same kind of skepticism in her law enforcement colleagues at the time.

She felt the burn of the three cups of coffee she'd had since five-thirty. She'd pushed herself on her run, did her weights too fast, rushed her stretches. Muscles, stomach, brain cells. Everything about her seemed charged up. "The means I used to find Tatro are irrelevant."

"I'll bet not to him. He went to prison because you found him."

"He went to prison because he was convicted by a jury."

"But he was mad at you, wasn't he?"

"Yes." Juliet let herself remember Tatro sneering at her, spitting at her, when she'd arrested him. "He threatened to come after me when he got out. His exact words were, 'Your pretty blond ass is mine, Marshal. You can count on it.'"

"Anyone watching him since he got out?"

"Bobby Tatro served his time. He's a free man."

"Then you have no idea where he is?"

She sighed, hesitating.

"Juliet —"

"I heard a rumor that he's in South America and may be mixed up with vigilantes. He didn't strike me as the kind of guy who'd want to save the world when he was a free man, but you never know."

Ethan's expression remained neutral.

"You really should just forget whatever you're into that involves Bobby Tatro and take me for coffee," she said.

He smiled suddenly. "How many cups have you had already today?"

She didn't tell him. "Ethan, you shouldn't underestimate Tatro's capacity for violence."

The smile evaporated, and his dark eyes grew distant. "I never underestimate anyone's capacity for violence." He looked up at the massive statue of George Washington. "He's your guy, isn't he? He formed the Marshals Service."

Juliet nodded impatiently. "We're the oldest law enforcement agency in the country. Ethan, why did Bobby Tatro pop up on your radar screen? It's too damn coincidental —"

"How *did* you know he'd be at the Wal-Mart that day?"

"I'm clairvoyant," she snapped.

"Isn't threatening a federal agent —"

"It was your basic emotional threat against the law enforcement officer who caught him. He knew he couldn't stay on the farm forever. The Marshals Service catches thousands of fugitives every year. That time, it was Bobby Tatro's turn."

Ethan caught his fingers around hers, then dropped her hand and touched her hair, his fingertips coming away wet from the steady drizzle. "One day we'll have that cup of coffee, Deputy Longstreet. Not on Wall Street in a cold rain. At a sun-kissed café, with roses and bougainvillea."

"Bougainvillea doesn't grow in New York."

His smile eased into a laugh. "Exactly my point."

"And sun-kissed." There was a disturbing undertone to his laugh — she couldn't quite describe it — that Juliet tried to pretend she didn't hear. "What kind of word is *sun-kissed* for a special-ops type to use?"

"I think 'sun-kissed' every time I see your hair."

"Brooker, you are so full of shit."

He laughed again, and it was there again, a soul-deep regret, a sadness that reached into all the dark places of the heart a man like him preferred not to go.

"Good luck, Ethan."

He didn't respond, and when he turned and started down the steps, back out toward Nassau Street, Juliet knew.

Whatever he was doing — wherever he was going — he wasn't at all convinced he'd get out of it alive.

Ethan took a cab to LaGuardia.

He'd left Juliet standing in front of George Washington, as still and unreadable as a statue herself. She was hardheaded and good at her job, and she could

40

probably mop the floor with him, but his mention of Bobby Tatro, their clandestine meeting . . . Ethan had seen the dread creep into her eyes, overwhelming her questions about what he was up to, her doubts about why she'd agreed to see him in the first place.

If she'd had to do it all over again, Juliet Longstreet probably would have just let Conroy Fontaine shoot him that day in Tennessee back in early May.

Fontaine had convinced himself he was doing Nick Janssen a favor by meddling in his attempt to get himself a presidential pardon.

In accepting the voluntary mission he was now in the process of executing, Ethan had no illusions he was doing anyone a favor.

Except, maybe, Ham Carhill, whose ass Ethan was about to save.

But Juliet had saved Ethan's life that first day they'd known each other, and he'd saved hers — although she'd never admit it — when he'd found her bound, gagged and left to die in a cave above the Cumberland River.

With Conroy Fontaine dying of a snake bite and the law moving in, Ethan had taken off after Nick Janssen, still a free man. He'd chased Janssen all summer. And when he found himself in New York again in August, he landed up on Juliet Longstreet's doorstep.

A dumb move.

And curious, he thought, that his mission to rescue someone he knew — a wealthy, twenty-five-year-old Texan — involved someone Deputy Longstreet knew, an ex-con after revenge.

President Poe himself had asked Ethan to volunteer for the rescue mission. American and Colombian mercenaries had kidnapped an American contractor, and Ethan was one of the few people who could identify him.

Before he even knew the name of the man he'd be rescuing, Ethan had told the president he'd do the mission.

Hamilton Johnson Carhill.

Of all the names that had flashed in Ethan's mind, Ham Carhill wasn't one of them. The Carhills were the Brookers' west Texas neighbors. Billionaires with a passion for privacy. Ham was his own brand of peculiar. He had a genius IQ and the common sense of a chickadee, and one or both, apparently, had gotten him into serious trouble this time.

The last Ethan had heard, Ham was off

to South America in search of precious and semiprecious gems, exotic birds and adventures. He had a Ph.D. from Stanford in some kind of science but had never held a real job. He'd attended Char's funeral a year ago, his usual gawky, awkward self, lacking confidence, humble to the point of being irritating.

That few people outside his family and close friends had much idea what Ham looked like these days didn't come as a big surprise to Ethan. The Carhills shunned publicity, fearing the exploitations of tabloids and con men more than kidnappers. And Ham was self-conscious about his appearance, always aware that he didn't live up to Faye and Johnson Carhill's expectations of what their only son and heir should look like.

Ethan had spent the past week in Colombia trying to pick up Ham's trail.

The tip came from Washington, a call out of the blue — an American ex-con who had it in for a blond, female marshal was holding Ham somewhere in the Andes.

It wasn't what Ethan had expected. Not even close.

Although there were other blond, female marshals, he bet that this one was Juliet.

He'd flown to New York yesterday, and

now he had confirmation — as much as he needed.

Bobby Tatro, Juliet Longstreet.

Coincidences sometimes occurred at random, but Ethan didn't entertain for even half a second that this was one of them. He and Juliet both had had their names in the papers in recent weeks and months, attached not just to thugs, assassins and an international criminal mastermind like Nick Janssen, but to President Poe.

Ethan had a feeling his straightforward rescue mission had turned into something far more complicated and far more dangerous. He just couldn't pin down what. And it didn't matter — Ham still needed rescuing.

When his cab dumped him off, he plodded through security and made his flight to Washington, D.C., with bare minutes to spare. It was an uneventful flight, allowing his questions to crystallize.

When he arrived at Reagan National Airport, he took a cab out to Georgetown. For the past year, he hadn't had a place of his own. The closest he'd come were the weeks he'd spent in the spring playing gardener for the Dunnemores in Tennessee.

Mia O'Farrell lived in a narrow, historic brick town house on a quaint shaded street within a couple of blocks off M Street, Georgetown's main drag. Ethan appreciated the shade, because it was hot and humid in D.C. The recent rains had moved north to New York.

Dr. O'Farrell wasn't home from the White House yet.

Ethan walked down to M Street and got an iced coffee to go at a Starbucks, picturing himself as a Washington type. Some of his West Point classmates were Pentagon desk jockeys. He'd never been interested. Now? Forget it. He was damaged goods. That President Poe had asked him to volunteer for the Ham Carhill rescue mission only muddled Ethan's status even further. It sure as hell didn't help.

Mia O'Farrell had been at the meeting with Poe two weeks ago. She'd done most of the talking, and although it was all somewhat unorthodox at first, everything had gone more or less by the book since then. Ethan had picked two veteran Special Forces sergeants — friends of his — to risk their lives with him. They could have said no, but they hadn't. They were waiting for him in Bogotá. Whoever was supposed to know about the operation within the Colombian government had given their blessings. That wasn't Ethan's department.

Neither was flying to New York to interrogate a deputy U.S. marshal, but he didn't like the feeling that there was a subtext to this operation that he wasn't privy to.

He window-shopped on M Street, pretending he was an ordinary dad waiting for his kids to get home from soccer practice, sipping his coffee as he checked out restaurants and upscale shops — a black leather jacket on a mannequin in a store window display made him think of Juliet standing in the rain in New York.

When he returned to O'Farrell's street, she was on her front stoop, digging her keys out of an enormous, scuffed, soft black leather satchel, her long, straight dark auburn hair hanging over her face. Ethan said hello, startling the hell out of her. She jumped back and all but screamed.

She was very smart, but tightly wound. He put up his palms in front of him and smiled. "Whoa, easy. It's just me."

"Oh. Major Brooker." She seemed slightly annoyed, snatching her keys out of her bag, slinging the bag over one small shoulder as she singled out one key. She had on a trim gray suit, but her silky white blouse was scrunched over to one side, and her brooch — a white lily — had turned upside down and was about to fall off.

"You're going to stick yourself," Ethan said.

"What?"

"With your brooch. The pin's come undone or something."

She glanced down, quickly pulling the brooch off her jacket. He thought she did stick herself, but she'd never tell him. Mia O'Farrell, Ph.D., was all about control. She fastened her green eyes on him, her brow furrowed as she studied him. "You shouldn't be here. What do you want?"

"Let's go inside —"

"No way, Major Brooker. Absolutely no way." She was calm but very firm.

"Okay. Let's take a walk —"

She shook her head. "No. Right here, right now. What do you want?"

"You know, since I'm doing you a favor and risking my life and the lives of my friends in the process, you think you'd be nicer."

She didn't budge. "You're not doing me a favor. You're answering the call of duty."

Ethan almost burst out laughing, but saw she was deadly serious and kept his amusement to himself. What did she know about duty? She was a special assistant to the president on matters of national security.

47

All of her experience was academic. Poe had plucked her out of a Washington think tank. She wasn't any older than Ethan was, probably younger.

How in hell had Ham gotten himself mixed up with her?

Ethan grimaced. Never mind Ham. How had he gotten *himself* mixed up with Mia O'Farrell? One day he was chasing an assassin, falling into rivers, talking the marshals out of arresting him. The next day — well, a week later — he was shuttled off to listen to Dr. O'Farrell suggest a fresh new way to get himself killed.

"How did you know I could ID Ham Carhill?" he asked her.

She paled, then glanced around as if someone might be listening in the bushes. "Please. Not here."

"Now you see why I wanted to go inside —"

"Your family and the Carhills are neighbors in Texas." She spoke briskly, keeping her voice low and obviously thinking that answered his question.

"We're hardly in spitting distance of each other. There are a lot of miles between us. The Carhills are ultraprivate." Ethan paused, watching her for a reaction, but there was none. "Someone tipped you off. Who?"

48

"Irrelevant. You have your orders —"

"It's a voluntary mission."

"It doesn't have to be." She didn't go on, but he could see she wanted to — she wanted to remind him that President Poe was his commander in chief, and although this whole crazy operation had ended up within the chain of command, she had Poe's ear, the president's trust. That she, in other words, was calling the shots. "Don't you leave for Colombia again tonight?"

She hadn't wanted him to leave Bogotá. She'd passed him the information on the American ex-con with a vendetta against a blond, female marshal. It was all she had. No name, no location. O'Farrell agreed that the marshal in question was probably Juliet Longstreet, but saw no reason to alert her — no reason for Ethan to be the one to question her about the ex-con. Ethan disagreed and flew to New York without O'Farrell's blessing.

"When I was in Colombia last week," he said, "I heard talk about psycho mercenaries operating there, guys who tout themselves as being on the side of so-called truth and justice but prefer to be unencumbered by the rules themselves. They don't answer to a chain of command."

She sighed. "Yes. I know the type."

"I ran across a nasty little vigilante network in Afghanistan a few years ago. They'd set up their own interrogation room and prison on the outskirts of Kabul, claimed they were working for the Pentagon — it was all bullshit. They were a rogue outfit, running the war on terror the way they thought it should be run."

Mia was trying to pin her brooch back on her jacket, an awkward process with her keys in one hand. Without looking at him, she said, "I don't see what these mercenaries have to do with your mission. Or me."

"They don't trust the federal government. As far as they're concerned, they're true patriots, but they don't recognize most federal authority."

"What difference does that make? If they violate the law, they're subject to arrest, just like anyone else. Their beliefs are irrelevant." She snapped the brooch into place and looked back up at him, her cheeks rosy. "You should take yourself out for a good dinner. Don't you have any friends in Washington?"

His last meal. He almost smiled, but any humor disappeared, and what he saw in front of him was an intelligent, capable woman who was potentially — probably — in over her head. Where was she getting her information? And what would she do when she suddenly realized she was underwater? Who would she drag under with her?

"Dr. O'Farrell," Ethan said as earnestly as he could, "if you let one of these guys suck you in —"

"I'm in a hurry, Major. I have a meeting at the White House in forty-five minutes, and I need to change my clothes and make a few calls. I didn't expect to see you again before your mission was completed." Her green eyes softened, allowing a rare, unguarded peek into what wasn't, Ethan thought, such a cold heart. "Please, Major Brooker. Ethan. Take care of yourself."

But he recognized her words for what they were — a firm good-night. He was dismissed.

She waited, eyes still on him, until he acknowledged defeat and wished her a good evening.

He walked back down to M Street, the infamous D.C. heat and humidity bearing down on him. He smelled dog crap and car exhaust. He noticed a dead geranium in what had earlier struck him as an attractive flowerpot on a restaurant doorstep.

Preteen boys piled out of an SUV, laughing, ragging on one another. Ethan felt like grabbing them by the ear and letting them in on the real world, telling them to be grateful for their lives of safety and privilege.

But what did he know about these kids? Who was he to judge them, or even Mia O'Farrell?

He was all bluster. He knew — O'Farrell knew — he wasn't about to leave Ham in the Andes with whoever had him, whoever was using him . . . whoever was using Mia O'Farrell.

Ethan paused on the busy street. He had a job to do. He might as well get on with it.

He decided to heed O'Farrell's advice and take himself out for a good dinner before his flight. He'd go alone — the friends he had in D.C. didn't need to see him right now. If some vigilante mercenary was slipping O'Farrell information, playing her for reasons of his own, her ass would get burned. And maybe not just figuratively. The vigilantes Ethan had run into in Afghanistan were violent fanatics with their own agenda.

But whatever Mia O'Farrell had stumbled into wasn't his problem. His job was to get Ham Carhill out of Colombia alive and reasonably unbloodied.

Three

⋘ ⟨⟩⟨⟩ ⋙

Ham Carhill tried not to cough. When he was busy hacking up a lung, he couldn't hear what was going on around him. And, right now, it seemed to him nothing was going on.

Absolutely nothing.

He couldn't hear any of the voices he'd come to know during his captivity, men's voices, speaking Spanish and English or a mix of the two languages. Ham spoke fluent Spanish — the creeps who'd snatched him in Bogotá knew that from the start. It was like they had a nice little dossier on him. *Hamilton Johnson Carhill, only son of billionaires Faye and Johnson Carhill of Nowhere, Texas, who would pay to keep the indignity of his kidnapping from hitting the public airwaves even faster than they'd pay to free him.*

His parents had opposed his trips to South America, but assumed he was hiking in Patagonia or lying on the beach in Rio. They hoped he'd bulk up on his adventures, get a tan and return home ready to join the Carhill empire.

A cockroach crawled up his shin, but Ham didn't move to flick it off.

He was on a bare, flea-infested mattress on a cot in a cinder-block hut somewhere in the Andes. The darkness in the single room was nearly complete. He only knew it was a cockroach on his leg because it wouldn't be anything else. The place was full of them — huge, ugly things that scurried and raided in the dark. He often wondered how such a country, with its startling contrasts of stunning landscapes and stark poverty, of kind and friendly people and incessant violence, could produce the most beautiful emeralds in the world. Precious gems — in particular, emeralds — had become his passion and, in a way, his undoing.

Ham listened, squeezing his eyes shut as if it'd help sharpen his hearing, and for a moment thought he might have gone deaf.

But he was alone in the hut, perhaps alone in the camp.

The handsome, dark-eyed American and the Colombians — they were gone, all of them.

Had they left him here to *die*?

Sitting up, Ham fell into a spasm of

coughing, holding his ribs, thinking they might start breaking off into pieces and stab his lungs. The creeps had fed him pinto beans and more pinto beans, a little fatback once a day, and once — an immeasurable treat — a can of beanie weenies.

His hair hung down his back, stringy and unwashed. He had a sketchy, nasty beard. He figured he must have lice. His bowels were a mess, but he didn't think he had any parasites or infections.

Maybe his captors thought he was such a coward he'd just sit there, whether they were there to guard him or not. When they grabbed him, stuffing him in a jeep, he'd passed out — he had no idea where they'd taken him, except that it was a remote area in the mountains. The altitude made breathing only that much more difficult.

I'll die here like a cockroach.

He felt a draft, smelled the outside air and realized the door was open. He staggered toward the fresh air. He kept expecting his eyes to adjust to the dark, but they didn't. Christ — was he blind? But the nights were often pitch black, only he'd never been allowed to walk around, even with a guard.

Something moved. He saw a shadow, heard a swish — fabric on fabric?

"Shh." A gloved hand clamped down on his wrist. "We're United States soldiers, Mr. Carhill. We're here to rescue you."

"Ethan?"

Ham didn't know if he spoke out loud. His voice was scratchy. He was so damn weak — was he imagining his own rescue?

A flash, a shot.

The camp wasn't entirely abandoned.

All hell broke loose, and Ham scrambled in the darkness for his boots, his pants, refusing to be taken half naked — and desperate, he thought. He didn't want to look so damn desperate.

He tucked a small plastic bag inside his pants. The bag contained fifteen perfect, beautiful cut and polished emeralds that would bring a good price on any market, legitimate or otherwise.

Did Ethan know about the emeralds? Unlikely, Ham thought. He'd found them late that afternoon, when his captors were in a panic about something — bad news, obviously. Colombia was world-renowned for its emeralds. They were popular with smugglers. But Ham didn't believe these were intended for smugglers — they were the ransom payment for him.

He'd switched them for small, worthless stones.

"Let's go," Ethan said.

Ham nodded, but he was hyperventilating, feeling faint. Ethan hoisted him over one powerful shoulder. Ham felt himself go limp, tranquil in the knowledge that his friend, neighbor and idol — Ethan the Magnificent, he'd called him as a boy — had come to save him.

Four

~:ꙮ:~

Juliet tapped the calendar on her computer monitor with her pencil eraser and counted one, two, three, four, five — six days since Ethan had left her in the rain at Federal Hall. And not a word since. She didn't know whether to be worried, annoyed or relieved. That was one of the problems he presented. Her feelings toward him were complicated.

But she didn't want him to be dead. She knew *that* much.

She shook off such a thought, refusing to give it any traction. If something had happened to Ethan, she'd know. If she didn't feel it in her gut, someone privy to such information would get word to her. A matter of courtesy.

Mike Rivera stopped on his way past her desk. He was one of two chief deputies in the office, a bulldog of a man and the fifty-two-year-old father of five daughters. "You're going to stab a hole in your monitor with that pencil."

58

Juliet didn't want to mention Brooker. One, she hadn't told Rivera that she and Ethan had met on the steps of Federal Hall to discuss an ex-con who'd once threatened to kill her. Two, Rivera basically thought her new Special Forces friend was a shit magnet. The chief wasn't one to mince words. And he didn't believe Juliet when she protested that Ethan wasn't, really, a friend. The man had thrown caution — his career, his life — to the damn wind since his wife's death. Rivera and a few others who shared his opinion didn't question that Ethan was a good guy, a combat officer whose commitment and sacrifice they respected. They just questioned the tendency for bad things to happen when he showed up.

And they questioned his interest in Juliet, although they'd never admit as much. She was a federal agent who had a degree in plant science. It wasn't until after college that she'd decided on a career in law enforcement. Her father and brothers had thought it'd be a passing fancy — that she'd flunk out of training. They didn't want to see her fail so much as end up doing what they were convinced she was meant to do. In general, men tended to treat her like a sister, maybe because she had five older brothers and was good at acting like a sister.

Rivera pointed a thick finger at her coffee mug. "How many cups of coffee is that so far today?"

It was two o'clock in the afternoon. "I have no idea. I haven't kept count."

"It's at least your fifth."

"Chief, come on. You're not spending your time keeping track of how much coffee I'm drinking, are you?"

"It's too damn much. You're going to be in the middle of a takedown one of these days and have to pee. That happened with my first partner —"

"It's not going to happen to me."

He sniffed, making a face. "How old is that stuff?"

"I don't know. I finished off the pot." She was notorious for drinking coffee any way she could get it, but she preferred it black, hot and fresh. "I'm not that fussy. The only kind of coffee I won't drink is flavored. Hazelnut, vanilla." She gave a mock shudder. "Raspberry."

"My wife loves hazelnut. She says it's like having a milkshake."

"When I want a milkshake, I'll have a milkshake."

"You ever get tested for ADHD?" he

asked. "Attention deficit hyperactive disorder."

She creaked back in her chair. "No, Mike. I've never been tested."

"My youngest is ADHD. Smart as a whip, funny as hell. She's on the go all the time. I can't keep up with her. I don't know if it's true, but I read somewhere that coffee doesn't affect people with ADHD the same way it does other people. Supposedly it calms them instead of winds them up."

"Do I look calm?"

He grinned at her. "Imagine if you didn't have all that caffeine in you. You'd be shooting up the place."

Fortunately, he left it at that and retreated to his office without launching into a lecture on post-traumatic stress disorder. Better, Juliet thought, to have Rivera watching her for signs of ADHD than PTSD. After two high-stress and highly publicized events this past year — both, not coincidentally, involving a certain Special Forces officer — Rivera had earmarked her as a prime candidate for PTSD. All she had to do was mention a nightmare, and he was on her. PTSD was a serious concern, and a certain amount of vigilance was called for, given what she'd

61

been through the past five months, starting in May with the Central Park sniper-style shooting of Rob Dunnemore, a fellow deputy with whom Juliet had had a brief, romantic relationship, and Nate Winter, a senior deputy and her mentor. Rob was seriously injured, Nate back on his feet that same day. The shooting was the first inclination the USMS had of the very complicated plot to extort a presidential pardon on behalf of Nicholas Janssen. Rivera insisted it alone was reason for Juliet to be on alert of PTSD symptoms, never mind the rest of what had transpired that week. She still had the scars from a killer road rash she'd received after Janssen's goons had grabbed her and she'd leaped out of their moving car. Then it was on to Tennessee and meeting Ethan over the bodies of the same two goons, distracting their killer — crazy Conroy Fontaine — before he could shoot Ethan, too. Fontaine had proceeded to drag her to a dark, dank cave, tie her up, gag her and leave her there with the snakes.

If she'd had to, Juliet would have hurled herself into the river below the cave to escape. Even bound and gagged, she'd have managed to swim. But Ethan had found her and convinced himself he'd saved her life. Conroy Fontaine was dying of a snakebite by the time he was taken into custody. Meanwhile, Ethan took off to find Nick Janssen, who'd placed the order to have Ethan's wife murdered the previous fall.

More grounds, in Rivera's view, for him to watch Juliet for PTSD.

Then came August and the assassin. Juliet had reminded her boss more than once that she'd never been in serious danger, but he'd just give her a skeptical look. After Ethan had chased Janssen over the summer, putting pressure on him, a Diplomatic Security agent — Maggie Spencer — got a tip that led to Janssen's arrest. Even in a Dutch prison, he was dangerous. His hired assassin started working her way down a list of targets he'd given her — with a few of her own thrown in. Maggie Spencer and Rob Dunnemore finally caught up with her in a pretty village on the Hudson River. But Ethan — and Juliet — had been on the scene.

Rivera had warned her that Ethan was a prime candidate for PTSD himself. No doubt. How many people could tolerate the stresses he'd endured? Combat, black ops, the grief and guilt of his wife's murder — and that was all before Juliet had met him in May. But, as she'd reminded Rivera

63

— and herself — as a Special Forces officer, Ethan was uniquely trained, and perhaps naturally mentally and physically suited to endure extreme stress.

Juliet pulled herself out of her thoughts and took a swallow of coffee, but it had gone cold.

Tony Cipriani, her partner, ambled over to her desk. In his late thirties with a wife in the NYPD and two small boys, he was a wiry, mostly bald, ultrafit guy and one of the more likable federal agents Juliet had encountered. They'd been working together for a few weeks, and so far, so good. As a favor, she'd asked him to do some basic research into vigilante mercenaries.

"There were these guys who showed up in Afghanistan," Cipriani said in a low voice. "Americans. One of them was an insurance salesman, for the love of God. They decided the U.S. military was being too namby-pamby with interrogations and flew to Kabul to set up their own jailhouse. The military shut them down."

"I remember reading something about it in the papers."

"Press was all over the story. The military turned two of these wingnuts over to Afghan authorities but there wasn't enough evidence to hold them. The rest disappeared."

"Do we have any names?" Juliet asked.

"No. I'm still working on it."

"Any hint they put up shop in South America?"

Tony shook his head. "That's all I've got."

Juliet wondered if Ethan, as an army officer, had been deployed to Afghanistan at the time, but warned herself not to go off on a tangent. *Follow the facts.* She sighed. "Thanks, Cip."

"Anytime. When you want to tell me what this is all about, you know where to find me."

Juliet understood the subtext. If she wanted him to go further, they'd have to have a talk — he'd want to know exactly why she was interested in vigilantes. With six days and counting since Ethan had turned up asking about Bobby Tatro — and almost a month since Tatro was released from prison — and no sign of him, she doubted that a heart-to-heart with Cipriani would be necessary. In two days, it'd be October. A whole new month. Maybe she'd heard the last of Tatro, vigilantes and Ethan's secret mission.

After a morning picking pumpkins and chasing a few stray chickens back into their pen in the barn — a humane pen — Wendy Longstreet treated herself to a glass of fresh-pressed apple cider on the steps of the side porch. Spaceshot was flopped on his back in the grass. No one was around. Her grandparents, her uncle Jeff and her uncle Will were all off at job sites. Even her uncle Sam, who was usually around working on the machinery and tending to the barn and greenhouses, had driven to town for parts. Wendy was to deal with any passersby who stopped to buy a pumpkin or who wanted to pick apples. It was the end of September, and the leaf-peepers were out in full force.

A truck pulling a small camping trailer turned into the driveway. The truck had an Arizona plate, which Wendy noticed right away because it was unusual to see one in Vermont. She got up, leaving her cider glass on the steps.

The driver got out, a tall, rangy man with a shaved head. He had on a denim jacket, jeans and running shoes, and he waved to her. "Afternoon."

Spaceshot stirred but didn't get up. With all the coming and going at Longstreet Landscaping, he didn't trouble himself to investigate every arrival. Wendy smiled at the man. "Can I help you?"

"I'm new in town. Name's Matt Kelleher. I heard that you all were looking for temporary hires. Anyone around I can talk to?"

Wendy didn't want to tell him no. That was one of the rules her father had drilled into her — never tell a stranger she was alone. "Everyone's busy right now, Mr. Kelleher."

"That's okay. I don't mind waiting." He smiled, as if he knew she was nervous and wanted to help her to relax. "I'll just sit in my truck." He nodded at Spaceshot. "That's some lazy dog, huh?"

"He's old," Wendy said, smiling tentatively back at him. With his shaved head, she found his age hard to guess — forty, maybe? She had no idea. He had lines at the corners of his eyes but none of the puffy bags older men often had, and while he wasn't handsome, he wasn't horrible-looking, either. His nose was kind of big, and his chin was pointy. He looked okay when he smiled.

"You work here?" he asked her.

She nodded. "But I'm family — Wendy Longstreet."

He squinted at her against the bright autumn sun. "Shouldn't you be in school?"

"I graduated in June."

"Not going to college?"

"No, I am. I'm applying early decision to several schools." She didn't want to get into the homeschooling and finishing her requirements for graduation a year early details. "I was going to work on my essays this afternoon."

"Don't let me keep you. What do you want to major in?"

She lowered her eyes, as if he might not see her hesitation that way. "I'm applying as a premed student."

"No kidding? You want to be a doctor?"

She shrugged. "Sure."

"That's a tough row to hoe. I didn't go to college. I got married right out of high school —" He stopped himself, looking out at the hills, the autumn leaves turning fast now. "My wife died in June. Cancer. Hell of a way to go."

"I'm sorry," Wendy said, meaning it. He seemed so sad.

"Well, we had a good twenty years together. I try to remember that. We always talked about buying a camper, seeing the country — I've been tending her the past two years, and before she died, she made me promise to get out and do it, not to wait. So, I bought myself this old rig here and headed east." He seemed pensive, and

Wendy thought she saw tears in his eyes. "I learned the hard way life's too short."

"You're from Arizona?"

"Phoenix. I've lived there my whole life." He smiled at her again. "You probably should go on and get to those college applications. I'm just looking to work a few weeks, until the snow flies. Then I'll be on my way."

"I just poured myself a glass of cider. Would you like some?"

Some of the sadness went out of his face. "Why, thank you, Miss Longstreet. I'd like that."

"You can call me Wendy."

"And you can call me Matt. It's a pleasure meeting you."

But before she could run into the kitchen, her father pulled into the driveway in his state police cruiser. Matt Kelleher glanced over at her. Wendy sighed. "It's my dad. He's checking on me."

"Well." Matt grinned suddenly and winked at her. "I wouldn't procrastinate on those college applications if my dad was a state trooper."

Wendy laughed, but she saw her father's frown when he got out of the car in his trooper's uniform. She went over to him, introducing Matt, explaining that he was from Arizona and his wife had died and he was looking for a job. And although she'd done everything right and Matt was totally *fine*, she knew her father wasn't going to get back in his cruiser and leave her there with him. He stayed until her uncle Sam arrived. But it was only ten minutes, so at least it didn't seem like that big a deal to Matt and she didn't come across as a twelve-year-old to him.

Before he left, her father pulled her aside. "A friend of mine had two tickets to the play in town tonight that he couldn't use. I thought you might like to go."

The local theater was performing *As You Like It*, and Wendy had been dying to go. She couldn't believe her father was offering to take her. "But you hate the theater —"

"No, I hate *musicals*. That last play you dragged me to was a musical." He gave her a dry smile. "I can handle Shakespeare."

"I'd love to go. Thanks, Dad."

He seemed almost relieved, and Wendy felt a twinge of guilt at how hard she could be on him sometimes. He was making an effort to understand her. He got back in his cruiser, promising to take her to dinner before the play.

Later that afternoon, her grandparents and uncles all decided to hire Matt, and

Sam offered to let him hook his trailer up at the cabin off the dirt road by the lake. Matt snapped up the offer. Wendy joined her uncle, walking over to the cabin and getting it ready while Matt drove there, his camper grinding on rocks in the steep driveway. But he made it up the road, and he seemed grateful to have a place to park himself for the next few weeks.

He pulled Wendy aside before she left. "Didn't get any work done on those college essays, did you?"

She shook her head. "I'll work on them tomorrow."

"Ah, yes. There's always tomorrow. Sure you want to be a doctor?"

"Definitely."

"Then I guess writing those essays should be easy."

She didn't respond, just pointed to the door of the small cabin. "I put a jug of cider in the refrigerator. You can put it in your camper fridge if you want. It's not pasteurized, but none of the apples were drops."

"I'm not an expert on apple cider. Thank you, Wendy. I appreciate your help today."

When she got back to the house, she got ready for dinner and the play, and, for the first time since her mother had left for Nova Scotia, she didn't feel unwanted and out of place.

The first of October had arrived in Washington, D.C., with a wave of oppressive heat and humidity that took even seasoned Beltway types by surprise.

Mia O'Farrell tried not to look as if she wanted to run back into the air-conditioned White House. She was Boston Irish. She melted in the heat.

Her boss, John Wesley Poe, the president of the United States, didn't even seem to notice the temperature, never mind feel it. He was, Mia thought, a handsome man. She doubted she was the only one who sometimes forgot just how handsome he was, possibly because he was also so smart and charming — and powerful. It was his surroundings more than the man himself that reminded her of just how powerful he was.

She took a breath, feeling her blouse sticking to her back. But it wasn't just the heat that had her sweating.

She had to tell him about Ethan Brooker.

She was slim, green-eyed and smart. It would be false humility to pretend she didn't know she was smart. She'd attended Harvard on a full scholarship and graduated magna cum laude. Her father, a house painter, had tried to get all the Sherwin-Williams Dover White out from under his fingernails before attending her graduation ceremony. Her mother, a housewife who did her ironing to soap operas, had cried.

Mia had earned her master's and doctorate at Columbia, and when she was hired to work at a prestigious Washington think tank, she thought she'd found her home.

Then the White House had called.

And now, six months later, she was scrambling to dig herself out of the biggest mess of her life.

"The mission was a success," she told President Poe.

Brooker and his team had rescued Ham Carhill and spirited him to the American embassy in Bogotá, where, emaciated and terrified, he nonetheless provided the details to a plot that involved the kidnapping and murder of a dozen innocent Americans working in Colombia, and even more innocent Colombians. Forewarned, authorities were able to avert further disaster.

Mia still didn't know if Ham's kidnappers had realized just who they had detained. A rich Texas adventurer, yes, but a Carhill? A brilliant man who'd been passing on valuable information to the U.S. government for much of the summer? Ham Carhill had an uncanny ability for ferreting out names, addresses, accounts and plots. He could see patterns and connections others missed.

Mia figured his kidnappers hadn't a clue that he was a national security asset — thank God.

Yet in the nineteen days of his captivity, they'd made no ransom demand for his release — at least Mia wasn't aware of any. They could have been taking their time to make their next move, but the absence of a ransom demand was just one of the things about the entire situation that didn't add up.

Nor was Mia certain she entirely understood Poe's close interest in Ham Carhill's predicament. She'd begun to suspect the president's commitment to the rescue mission had more to do with Ethan Brooker than with anything or anyone else.

"Mr. Carhill?" the president asked.

"He's safe, sir."

"Major Brooker and his team?"

"Everyone's okay. There were no deaths or serious injuries to any of our people."

"That's good."

Poe studied her a moment, seeming to

measure her mood. In his late fifties, he was a self-made millionaire and the former governor of Tennessee, but he never forgot his humble origins on the Cumberland River, found as an infant on the doorstep of the family home of two sisters. Violet and Leola Poe had never married, never lived anywhere but Night's Landing. They took him in and raised him as their own. With his polite manner and soft middle Tennessee accent, his tenacity and toughness often went unnoticed at first.

"Why don't you look relieved, Dr. Farrell?" the president asked her quietly.

Mia looked out at the green, perfect lawn and fought an urge to run. She didn't belong here. She was too naive. She didn't have any political aptitude — she tried to be, even when she was keeping secrets, a straight shooter.

"There's been a wrinkle, Mr. President." She shifted her gaze back to the powerful man who'd placed his trust in her. People said her eyes were unflinching, even at the worst of times. She was thirty-two, but felt older. *Seemed* older. She didn't even try to smile. "A small one."

President Poe put a gentle hand on her shoulder. "In this job, Mia, there are no small wrinkles. Tell me."

Five

~:ⓖⓔ:~

Ethan tossed his cigarette on the sidewalk across from Juliet's building and ground it out under the toe of his boot, the last of the pack he'd allotted himself for the duration of the Colombian mission.

He'd flown from Bogotá to Miami to D.C. to New York in the past twenty-four hours, and he looked the part. He hadn't shaved, showered or slept. He and his team had plucked Ham Carhill out of the mess he was in two days after Ethan had met Juliet at Federal Hall. Ham had been free for almost a week. He'd given Mia O'Farrell and her people whatever information they needed and was whisked away, supposedly safe and sound, recuperating from his ordeal with his family in west Texas.

No one seemed that interested in tracking down the people who'd kidnapped him.

Two guys were at the camp when Ethan and his team had arrived. Low-level thugs.

76

One fought and was killed, the other ran off into the mountains. It wasn't within Ethan's mission objectives to go after him. Ham's safety — the information he had — was paramount.

But no Bobby Tatro.

After delivering Ham to the American embassy in Bogotá, Ethan took off on his own. For three days, he tried to pick up Tatro's trail. He only ran into rumors, more questions, and far too many people who wouldn't talk at all.

Juan, the new doorman, had told Ethan that Juliet was at work. To be expected, he supposed, but Juan could have been nicer. Ethan had cheekily walked across the street and lit his last cigarette, but the doorman didn't seem to give a damn. A useless protest. On the other hand, he had to allow that he looked more like one of the USMS's most wanted than the friend of a marshal.

A small, dark-haired girl in a sweatshirt with a peregrine falcon across the front stumbled out of a cab with a huge tote bag and an overstuffed backpack. Ethan almost trotted across the street to give her a hand, but the doorman — friendly Juan — ran out to help. She couldn't have been more than sixteen or seventeen.

She and Juan, carrying both the tote bag and backpack, disappeared through the glass doors.

Ethan flagged the girl's departing cab. Although it was not even two o'clock, he had an evening flight to D.C. for an early morning meeting with Dr. Mia — and a lot to do between now and then. He'd have to lure Juliet away from her marshal's desk or take the bit in his teeth and try to see her there.

The clock was ticking. They needed to talk.

Wendy decided she loved her aunt's doorman and her building and *everything* about New York. She had just introduced herself as Wendy Longstreet, Juliet's niece. "I know Juliet's at work," she told Juan. When she'd recognized his accent, she tried speaking Spanish to him, but he was so much faster and more fluent — once they got past her name and what a pretty day it was, she was mostly lost and had reverted back to English. "I was hoping I could leave my bags here and come back later."

"She's expecting you?"

Well, no. "I'll call her —"

"You can call her now. If she gives me

78

the okay, I can let you into her apartment."

"That's not necessary." Wendy had counted on her aunt not being around, since there was still plenty of time for her dad to drive down from Vermont to collect her. He wouldn't approve of her trip to New York, even less the way she'd gone about it. She smiled at the doorman, in case she'd been too brusque. "I've got a few things I want to do in the city this afternoon."

She thought she sounded mature and reasonable, but Juan looked suspicious, or perhaps just more official. He was about five-six, probably in his midthirties. His hair was very black and straight, and he had bulging muscles, like a weight lifter's. Wendy felt slight next to him. She'd pulled her hair back into a ponytail.

"I can hold your bags for you here, but I'll have to check them out," Juan said.

"Oh, sure. *No problemo.*" Gad, she thought. *That* was stupid. She felt herself blushing. "I'm sorry —"

He laughed and said something in Spanish that she didn't catch, then motioned for her to open her bags. She knelt on the cool, golden marblelike floor and unzipped the various compartments on her backpack. The lobby wasn't very big. It had a glittering chandelier and mirrors, and there were curving stairs with a beautiful wood banister and a brass elevator on the back wall. Wendy had desperately wanted to see it before her aunt had to move out.

Juan dutifully peeked at everything in her backpack but didn't seem concerned about what he might find.

A thin, beautiful woman in black jogging pants came off the elevator, two small dogs yipping at her side. Wendy didn't recognize the breed. Maltese, maybe? "I'm expecting a FedEx delivery this afternoon," she said breezily. "Keep an eye out for it, won't you, Juan? You're a doll. Thanks!"

She was through the door and down the steps with her little dogs before Juan could answer. Four more tenants had strolled into the building, each with a greeting and a reminder for Juan to tend to something.

"I don't think I could be a doorman," Wendy said with a smile.

"You get used to it."

He looked in her tote bag, filled with snacks — Wendy didn't trust the train to have food she'd eat. She'd hitched a ride to Rutland with a friend and got on the train there instead of in White River, because it was a shorter ride — five hours instead of

80

seven — and would take her along the Hudson River. And also, she thought, because she was less likely to run into a Longstreet.

She hadn't run away. Not at all. She'd left a note for her father telling him what she was doing. But, as Matt Kelleher had reminded her when she'd helped him pick pumpkins, she was almost eighteen. She wasn't twelve, and it was time she stopped being treated like she was.

Juan moved aside her iPod, exposing the library book she was reading. Embarrassed, Wendy bit her lip, hoping she wasn't blushing. She'd figured out an hour into her train ride that it was a young adult novel. *Way* too young for her.

He pointed to a small tin. "What's that?"

"Loose-leaf tea," she said, lying. The tin contained Teddy's ashes. She couldn't bear to bury them yet. She was afraid if she left them behind in Vermont, her father would dump them in the compost pile. He'd liked Teddy, but he wasn't sentimental about a dog's ashes.

"I thought it might be jewelry," Juan said. "Girls your age love sparkly things, don't they?"

"Some do."

"That's a pretty necklace you're wearing."

Wendy self-consciously fingered her small polished rose quartz and silver chain. "I made it myself. It's not worth anything. I don't like fancy gems."

Juan grinned at her. "No diamonds and emeralds for you, Miss Wendy?"

"Not for me, no."

"Your aunt doesn't seem the type, either, but you never know. She could have a soft side that likes a little luxury, huh?" His dark eyes twinkled at his own teasing as he set her tote back next to her backpack. "You have ID? I have to ask."

"Oh — um — yes." As she unbuttoned the small quilted bag she'd made last year from scraps of vintage fabric, she noticed her hands were shaking. She wasn't used to people searching her bags and asking her for ID. She found her driver's license and handed it to the doorman, whose thick hands, she noticed, were very steady. "It's a terrible picture, I know."

"Nobody takes a good picture for their license." He glanced at it, then handed it back. "I'm sorry. It's because I don't know you and you leave your bags here —"

"I understand."

Actually, she didn't. But Juan was being so nice, and obviously the extra security was something he was required to do, so

Wendy decided not to make a big deal of her objections.

He jumped forward, opening the door for someone else coming into the building. "I'll take good care of your bags," he called back to Wendy, then told her in Spanish to have fun in New York.

She scooted past him and another tenant, a middle-aged man this time, then trotted back down the steps. Her legs felt jittery from all the exertion that morning, but she wasn't hurting anymore. Feeling dismissed, she stood in the middle of the sidewalk and squinted up at the blue October sky. No clouds. In Vermont —

You're not in Vermont.

It was only one-thirty. At least four hours before Juliet would get back from work.

The Museum of Natural History was within walking distance of her aunt's building. But Wendy was starving. She wondered if there were any vegetarian restaurants nearby. She could probably find something vegan at any of New York's numerous diners, but her stomach churned at the prospect of eating next to someone gobbling a rare hamburger.

She debated going back to her aunt's building for her iPod. She could listen to music and walk around in Central Park — it was a gorgeous day. But she didn't want to get lost in the park. That sounded dangerous. She decided to get something to eat and check out the museum.

After a couple of blocks, Wendy was so hungry that she ducked into a diner without even thinking about meat-eaters. She sat on a red vinyl stool at the counter. She was sure she could smell raw meat but tried not to think about it and ordered a salad, asking the waitress if she could substitute chickpeas for the cheese. The waitress didn't even bat an eye. It was as if Wendy's request wasn't unusual at all.

New York was *so* great.

A man sat down on the stool next to hers, his elbow brushing her arm as he reached for a plastic menu. He ordered a turkey club.

Gross.

He was very good-looking. He reminded her of Johnny Depp. Not Johnny Depp when he was playing the pirate in *Pirates of the Caribbean*, but the character he played in *Chocolat*, which was her mother's favorite movie. Sexy, earthy. He had dark curly hair and pale gray eyes. Then she noticed a jagged white scar on his jaw and quickly glanced away, wondering if he'd think she'd been staring.

The waitress plopped down a plastic bowl of salad in front of her. It was mostly iceberg lettuce, with a few dry carrot scrapings, half a radish, a green pepper ring, two cucumber slices, a cherry tomato, and chickpeas that were straight out of a can.

A chickpea fell onto the counter and rolled toward the Johnny Depp-looking man. He picked it up as if it was an errant golf ball and grinned at Wendy. "One got away."

"That's okay." She felt awkward but didn't know what else to say.

He popped the chickpea into his mouth. "Chickpeas are an acquired taste, don't you think?"

"Especially plain. They're great in falafel or hummus."

"Ah."

She didn't know if he was teasing her.

"Is that a hawk on your sweatshirt?"

"A peregrine falcon."

He seemed to sense her hesitation. "You're not from New York, are you?"

"Vermont," she mumbled.

"The Green Mountain State. Leaves changing up there?"

She nodded. "Especially in the mountains."

"Must be crawling with — what do you call them? Leaf-peepers, something like that?"

"That's right."

The waitress slid his turkey club over to him. Bacon fat poked out from the edges. Wendy couldn't bear to look at it. Meat had become very unappealing to her.

"You okay?" the man asked.

She took another bite of her salad. "Just not as hungry as I thought."

She paid her bill from cash in her quilted bag and slid off the stool, smiling shyly at the man, who was shoving a triangle of his turkey club into his mouth. He winked at her, and she reminded herself not to judge him just because she'd given up eating animal products.

"See you around, Wendy."

"How — how did you know my name's Wendy?"

He shrugged, swallowing his bite of sandwich. "You just told me."

No, she hadn't. She wasn't *stupid.* She would never tell a perfect stranger her name. Her father had drilled basic safety measures into her from the time she could walk. With a prickly feeling at the back of her neck, she picked up her pace and hurried out of the diner.

Had he overheard her talking to Juan, Juliet's doorman?

That must be it, she thought. This was the closest eatery to her aunt's building, and some of its residents were bound to eat there on a regular basis. She'd been busy with her bags and ID and probably hadn't seen everyone coming and going.

Looking over her shoulder every few seconds, Wendy quickly crossed the street and walked in what she believed was the direction of the Museum of Natural History, hoping she hadn't gotten herself all turned around.

When she recognized the planetarium dome, she felt a rush of relief but didn't slow her pace. She used the Rose Center for Earth and Space entrance and stayed at the fringes of a group of schoolchildren, fourth- and fifth-graders as enthralled by the displays as she was.

After glancing behind her every two seconds for twenty minutes, she decided that the man in the diner hadn't followed her. She bought a ticket for one of the space shows. When she sat in her seat in the beautiful auditorium, she liked New York again and dropped into her fantasy that she lived here and knew her way around.

Wendy convinced herself that the man *had* overheard her talking with the doorman but was already on his way to the diner and didn't recognize her until he was sitting next to her.

No longer feeling so unnerved, Wendy sat back in her seat and focused on the show. She decided she wouldn't tell Juliet about the man in the diner and how he'd known her name. It was just a coincidence, and she didn't want her aunt thinking she couldn't handle herself in the city.

"Is Wendy there?"

Juliet could hear the strain in her brother's voice. She was working at her desk and hadn't expected Joshua to call. "No, why would she be?"

"She took off for New York this morning. She took the train from Rutland —"

"Wendy?"

"Yes, damn it, Wendy," he said with impatience, then reined in his frustration, proceeding more calmly, if a little icily. "She left a note saying she was spending a few days with you. Juliet, if you two planned this little scheme and didn't tell me —"

"I wasn't in on any plan." Juliet suddenly realized what he was saying and felt a crawling sense of dread. "What time did the train get here?"

"Twelve-thirty."

"Good God, Joshua, that was almost three hours ago!"

"I didn't find out she was gone until now. I stopped by the house — she left a note on the kitchen table. Sam's been in and out all day, but he thought she was here. I called her cell phone and left a message. I tried your apartment —" He paused, his emotions surfacing again. "I was hoping you two were off shopping."

"When I was home a few weeks ago, Wendy said she wanted to come visit me, but we didn't set a date. I was open to the idea, but, Joshua, I'd have cleared it with you first."

"I know. We argued about this vegan thing last night. I told her to eat a damn steak and put some color back in her cheeks. She looks so stressed out and unhappy all the time — I don't know what's going on. It wouldn't have mattered what I said. She was in a mood. She's been working on college applications — I offered to help, and she bit my head off."

Juliet could envision the exchange between father and daughter. "Maybe the pressure's getting to her — all these strangers looking at her grades, judging her. I remember hating it. Plus, her mother's not here to give her moral support. She's used to that, even more so since she was homeschooled." Juliet stopped herself. "Never mind. It's none of my business."

"Find her, will you?"

"I'll call you as soon as I know anything."

Juliet hung up and grabbed her jacket, quickly telling Tony Cipriani what was going on. He immediately offered to go with her, but she shook her head. They both were tackling paperwork of the dullest kind. She didn't blame him for looking for an excuse to get out of there, but her partner didn't need to be tracking down her errant niece with her.

She took the elevator down to the lobby of the nondescript federal building hoping she wouldn't have to fight traffic to get uptown. Out on the street, Ethan Brooker was just getting out of a cab.

Juliet thought she must have conjured him up and was losing her damn mind. She charged out to the street.

He was real. She hadn't made him up or mistaken someone else for him.

"Good," he said. "You're here. Saves me

from having to lure you out here."

He had on a battered brown leather jacket, a denim shirt, jeans and cowboy boots, and he hadn't shaved in several days. His eyes were harder, blacker, more piercing even than Juliet remembered. They looked as if they could set fire to the building.

"Man, Brooker," Juliet said. "Wherever they sent you, it wasn't a Club Med."

"Where are you going in such a hurry?"

She gave him the basics, and his reaction — as if he, too, was worried that someone had harmed Wendy, or, God forbid, thought she was Juliet — scared the hell out of her. "You've seen her? My niece?"

"I saw a teenage girl get out of a cab and drag a backpack and tote bag up the steps to your building. Small, long dark hair?"

"That's her. When —"

"Over an hour ago. I've been sitting in traffic."

Juliet frowned, trying to think. "We have a new doorman." She didn't tell Ethan that letting him sneak up to her apartment in late August was the reason the old doorman was gone. "He should have called me —"

"Water over the dam. Let's go."

She didn't budge. "Wait a minute. You

91

were at my building — and now you're here?"

"We need to talk." His tone held no hint that he was thinking about roses and sun-kissed cafés. "I didn't get your guy."

Bobby Tatro. Juliet didn't want him in her thoughts at the same time as her niece. "I supposed I'd have heard if you had. All right. Come with me. We'll take my truck. We can talk on the way."

Joshua Longstreet headed outside, Wendy's note still on the long, scarred pine table where she'd left it. Only by chance was he the first to see it. Everyone else was at landscaping jobs.

The late afternoon air was chilly, the sun low in the sky.

He debated getting into his truck and heading to New York himself. But what good would he do at this point? If Wendy had changed her mind and was on her way back to Vermont, he wanted to be here when she arrived, if only to — What? How did he punish a seventeen-year-old girl who barely acknowledged him as her father?

Matt Kelleher was stacking pumpkins on a wooden trailer that Joshua had pulled out to the edge of the driveway yesterday.

Wendy had intended to decorate it with dried cornstalks. Her grandparents had said she could keep the money from whatever pumpkins she sold. But Joshua had said the wrong thing, a lame joke about whether the pumpkins felt pain when they were carved, and they'd argued, and apparently they hadn't patched things up as well as he thought they had, because first thing this morning, she'd lit out for New York.

"Thought I'd finish up these pumpkins," Kelleher said, lifting a big one onto the trailer. "I didn't see you get here. I was up at my trailer."

"Did you happen to see my daughter this morning?"

"Wendy? No, not this morning. I haven't seen her all day, in fact. I assumed she was with her grandparents." His brow furrowed with concern. "Why? Has something happened?"

"She sneaked off to visit my sister in New York."

"Oh, I get it. That's not good. She mentioned wanting to see her aunt's apartment — I guess she's moving?"

Joshua nodded. "It's a long story."

Kelleher set the pumpkin on the trailer. "Wendy seems like a good kid. Levelheaded for seventeen. You worried about her?"

"My sister — Juliet — had no idea Wendy was coming." Joshua didn't know why he was telling this man his troubles. "Need a hand with the pumpkins?"

"No, there aren't many left. I like the work."

It'd only been a couple of days, but so far, Joshua hadn't heard any negative reports from his family about Kelleher — they all seemed to like him.

Sam's truck pulled into the driveway. Joshua filled him in on what was going on with Wendy. Sam's kids weren't angels, but they'd never gone traipsing off to New York without permission. They went to public school. They played soccer and field hockey, and they hated carob.

Normal kids, Joshua thought, hated carob.

His daughter loved it.

But he was damn near in tears when he climbed back into his cruiser and headed for town. He glanced at himself in his rear-view mirror. He had a hint of gray in his darkish blond hair, and he looked tired and cynical, even for forty. He'd been divorced for a decade and hadn't remarried. There was no woman currently in his life.

And his only daughter hated him.

It wasn't a pleasant thought, and Joshua

had no idea what to do about it.

He pounced on his cell phone when it rang.

"She's fine," Juliet said. "She was just back from the Museum of Natural History when I got here."

"Put her on."

"We're still in the lobby. Let me get her up to my apartment. Then I'll have her call you."

Joshua gripped the phone. "Juliet —"

"Trust me, Joshua, okay?"

And he heard his daughter say cheerfully, as if she hadn't done a damn thing wrong, "I'm fine, Dad. Really!"

Relief and anger flooded over him, and he knew his sister was right; if he talked to Wendy now, in his current state, he'd just make matters worse. "All right," he told Juliet. "I'm on my way home. Have her call me there."

It was almost dark when he reached White River Junction. The temperature had fallen. He parked in the short driveway of the Victorian he'd bought after his divorce and had slowly renovated over the years. His downstairs tenant, Barry Small, a member of the Greatest Generation, was up on a stepladder, stringing pumpkin-shaped lights across the porch in his shorts.

Joshua got out of his truck. "You're going to freeze your nuts off."

"Good. At least I'll know they're still there. Grab the other end of these lights, will you? I picked them up at Wal-Mart on sale."

"Pumpkin lights?"

"For the trick-or-treaters."

Joshua didn't point out Halloween wasn't for nearly a month.

Barry stretched a bony arm, hooking a length of wire over a thick staple. "You can never have enough light up here this time of year. Another few weeks and it'll be darker than the pits of hell at three-thirty in the afternoon."

He wasn't exaggerating by much. Except for his years in the army during World War Two, Barry had lived in Vermont his entire life, but he hated the long, dark winters. From October through the middle of May, he'd bitch to Joshua and threaten to move to Key West. He was a widower with four adult kids, none of whom lived in Vermont.

"How's Wendy the Vegan?"

"She's with her New York aunt," he said, outlining his daughter's adventures for the day.

Barry glanced down from his stepladder,

his lined face picking up the orange glow of one of his plastic pumpkins. "You sound irritated, Trooper Longstreet. Cut the girl some slack. She took a train to New York. It's not the moon. You're just ticked off because she likes everyone else better than she does you."

"Thanks, Barry."

The old man shrugged. "Comes with the territory."

Joshua walked behind him and caught the other end of the lights. "I think you're going to need another strand. You're about three feet short of the other end of the porch."

"This is it. It'll have to do. I'm only spending so much on pumpkin lights."

It wouldn't do. It'd look bizarre, but Joshua didn't care.

Here he was on a cool autumn night, stringing up pumpkin lights with his eighty-year-old tenant and neighbor.

"I have no life, Barry."

The old man put one hand on Joshua's shoulder, balancing himself as he climbed down off his stepladder. "This is what I've been trying to tell you for how long? I made up a pitcher of margaritas. We can pretend we're in Acapulco."

Joshua eyed the old man's lights. Pitiful. "Got salt for the margaritas?"

"And little umbrellas."

Before he realized it, Joshua cracked a smile.

Barry gave him a victorious slap on the shoulder, and they headed inside.

Six

Ethan could tell that the bartender didn't like him. He had trim gray hair and looked as if bartending was his vocation, not the backup plan, and he'd had his eye on Ethan since he took a high stool at the bar and ordered a Belgian beer on tap. The restaurant was on Amsterdam Avenue, on a corner, with a lot of windows and a neighborhood feel. He had more to tell Juliet. They hadn't talked much on the tense ride uptown. She'd ordered him to meet her there after she got her wandering niece settled. Ethan almost told the bartender that he was there at the request of a deputy U.S. marshal, but doubted the man liked federal agents any better than whatever he thought Ethan was.

"Not from around here?"

"No, sir. Texas."

"There's no smoking in here. It's the law."

"I quit smoking."

The guy rolled his eyes. "When?"

99

Ethan glanced at his watch. "About six hours ago."

Muttering about how much he hated wiseacres, the bartender set a frosty glass in front of Ethan and moved to the opposite end of the bar to wait on another customer, presumably one who didn't smell like cigarettes.

Ethan had finished his beer and was resisting ordering another one when Juliet pushed past a trio of women examining the menu posted in the entry and sat next to him. "Saving me a seat?"

"It was easy. Nobody wants to sit next to me."

"I wonder why."

The restaurant was warm and pleasant, the plates passing by on waiters' trays piled high with comfort food. Mac and cheese, meat loaf, mashed potatoes. Ethan supposed he should have been hungry, but he wasn't.

"How's your niece?" he asked.

They'd found her skipping on the steps of Juliet's building. When she saw her aunt, she got a little weepy, which made Ethan more compliant when Juliet, tight-lipped, said to give her an hour.

"She's camped out in front of the television watching an episode of *The Vicar of Dibley.*" At his puzzled look, Juliet added,

"British comedy. Wendy gave me the DVD set for Christmas."

"Just as well you didn't invite me up."

"Have you eaten?"

"I had a beer."

"I had Thai food with Wendy before I left. She's a vegan."

"Orthodox vegetarian, right? No animal products at all."

"Correct. She thinks she might eat eggs. She's only been at it a few weeks. Her dog died —" Juliet caught herself. "Never mind."

She ordered sparkling water with lime. Ethan resisted ordering another beer. The bartender obviously didn't recognize her nor seemed to notice that she was armed, which probably meant she wasn't one of the locals who frequented the place. She could have picked the joint for that reason, but Ethan suspected Deputy Longstreet wasn't a regular anywhere in her neighborhood.

When her water arrived, she stared at it a moment. Her cheeks were flushed. With her fair skin, she flushed easily. The warm restaurant, the upset with her niece. Him. She had reasons to get a little pink in the cheeks.

"I'm glad you weren't killed," she said, still not looking at him.

"I never said that what I was doing was dangerous."

She drank some of her water. "Did our mutual friend do anything illegal?" *Friend* didn't exactly describe Bobby Tatro.

Ethan didn't answer her. He didn't want to lie, and he didn't want to tell the truth.

"I want to know what's going on," Juliet said. "I'm not playing your game anymore."

Ethan smelled the cigarette smoke on himself and decided he at least could have shaved before he'd beelined for the marshals. For Juliet.

Something was freaking wrong with him.

"Tatro and a handful of other bad operators grabbed a guy I could identify. I can't go into who he is. It didn't happen in this country." Ethan spoke quietly, but he wasn't concerned about anyone overhearing him. Who'd know what in hell he was talking about? They'd think he was describing a movie script or something. "Tatro cleared out before my team arrived. We never saw him."

"Convenient. He was tipped off?"

"We weren't there for answers. We were there to get our man."

He noticed her throat as she sipped more of her water, the frost on the glass melting onto her fingers. She had slender fingers with blunt nails — some nicked — no doubt from the physical, hectic life she led, the work she did. When she looked at him, her blue eyes were wide and clear. "It's odd, don't you think, that Tatro chose a 'guy' you could identify?" She set the glass down hard but with control. "That's a hell of a coincidence, Major."

"I agree." Brooker's head hurt. He needed a shower, sleep. A pity the niece had turned up . . . He shut off that thought fast. "My guy's safe. Your guy's still on the loose."

"If Tatro's responsible for a kidnapping —"

"What kidnapping?"

Juliet glowered at him. "You just said he grabbed a guy you could identify. That sounds like kidnapping to me. I could take you in and get answers that way. Rivera would love it. He hasn't liked you much since you took off on us in Tennessee."

"I came back."

"That's not the point."

"I have a lot of questions of my own," Ethan said in a steady voice, knowing he could only tell her certain things. "If Bobby Tatro blames you for putting me on to him —"

"I can handle whatever Tatro throws my way. Including himself."

The bartender skewered them with a suspicious, unfriendly glare. Ethan figured he and Juliet looked intense, wired tight and far from upscale. Perhaps they even looked a bit dangerous.

"Is he still out of the country?" she asked.

"I don't know."

"What about the hostage you rescued? Does he know?"

"There's your assumptions again. 'Hostage.' I never said my guy was held hostage."

"Okay, we won't go there. I told you I'd heard that Tatro got mixed up with vigilante mercenaries. That true?"

He shook his head. "Another place I can't go."

That obviously didn't sit well with her. "No promises I'll be keeping any of what you tell me to myself this time."

"There were no promises last time."

"What else, Ethan? You aren't here unshaved and unwashed to tell me that Bobby Tatro might be mad at me. He's been mad at me for four years."

"It's not important," Ethan said, suddenly regretting the whole trip. "Forget it.

Go eat vegan food with your niece."

"Ethan —"

"I shouldn't have come here. Just watch your back for Tatro."

Juliet sat back, studying him. "You didn't need to come to New York to tell me that. Where do you go from here? Back home to Texas to play rich rancher?"

"I'm a soldier. My father and brother are the ranchers."

"Bet you're in the will."

"I've never asked."

Ethan eased off the stool and pulled out his wallet, laying a few bills on the counter to cover the beer and the water. He left a reasonable tip. If he lived in the neighborhood, he'd want a suspicious bartender.

Juliet touched his upper arm, but he couldn't feel her fingertips through the leather of his jacket and found himself wishing he could. Her eyes had softened. Not much, but enough for now. "Get some rest, Ethan. Don't worry about me."

"I'm sorry we couldn't grab Tatro. It wasn't that other priorities prevented it. He just wasn't there."

"I want to be able to reach you."

He plucked a pen from a cup on the counter, jotted his cell-phone number on a

105

paper cocktail napkin and handed it to her. "Call anytime. Day or night."

The napkin disappeared into her jacket pocket. "I'd invite you up for leftover vegan Thai food —"

"Nice try, Longstreet. You're on your own with the weepy niece."

"She's a great kid."

"Looks it."

"Your bosses — will they object to what little you've told me?"

He grinned at her. "I've never been much of an ass-kisser."

"Much?"

"See you around, Deputy." He resisted an urge to kiss her and totally spoil her chances of becoming a regular at the cute neighborhood restaurant. But as she started out the glass door, Ethan grabbed her arm, tucking an envelope into her pocket. "Don't open it in front of your niece."

"What?"

"Or here."

She thumped his chest. "Be where I can find you."

He waited until he saw her walk past the restaurant windows on the corner, toward her apartment, before he headed outside.

Bobby Tatro had been a busy boy in the

past few weeks. He'd gone from federal prison to snatching an American contractor — an unlikely covert agent — in Colombia. Tatro had left a photograph of Juliet behind in the bleak Colombian shack where he'd held Ham Carhill. Ethan had spotted the picture and grabbed it, as if it were a warning of some kind — an omen.

When Juliet opened the envelope and saw the photo, she'd understand why he hadn't taken the time for a decent shower and shave, never mind to decompress from his mission, before getting on a plane to New York and finding her.

The night air had turned downright cold, and the city lights obliterated any sign of the stars and moon. As Ethan stepped off the curb to hail a cab, he tried to remember when he'd last seen the big west Texas sky. A long time ago.

You should go home.

Instead, he was taking an evening shuttle to Washington, D.C.

It took Ethan several tries before he could get a cab. Halfway to LaGuardia, his cell phone rang.

"You didn't add the horns and the blood-dripping eyes yourself, did you, Brooker?" Juliet asked dryly.

She'd opened the envelope. She'd seen

the photo, a digital shot of herself coming out of her apartment building. Bobby Tatro added his own sick, childish artwork.

"No, ma'am."

"I didn't think so. Tatro. You want to tell me how a picture of me came into his possession?"

"If I knew, I'd tell you."

"I'm not so sure about that."

She hung up, and Ethan wished he could press some kind of rewind button that would take him back in time. He could arrive at Tatro's camp an hour earlier and capture him, shove his grotesque photo of Juliet down his throat — demand answers. Where did he get the photo? Had he taken the picture himself? If so, when — how? If not, who had?

He'd find out why Tatro was bugging out of his camp and leaving his hostage behind — he'd find out who'd tipped Mia O'Farrell off that Ham was being held by a blond female marshal.

Then, Ethan thought, he wouldn't have the painful feeling in his gut that he did right now, that he'd missed something — just as he'd missed something, everything, with Char when she'd told him she was going to Amsterdam on "holiday."

A few days later, his wife had turned up in a Dutch morgue.

Ethan hadn't had a painful feeling in his gut then. He'd been totally oblivious that Char was on the trail of a dangerous and violent international fugitive, a man who'd ordered her murder. If anything, news of her Dutch vacation had been a relief. She was having a good time without him. They'd had separate careers, separate lives, for so long. In the two years before her death, they'd been together all of twenty-one days.

Guilt, he thought. That was why he was overreacting to the cracked and dog-eared picture of Juliet Longstreet he'd found in Bobby Tatro's cinder-block Colombian hut.

When he arrived at LaGuardia, Ethan had just enough time to get through security and on to his flight to Washington. He had clothes waiting for him at his hotel.

He'd left no detail to chance — except the whereabouts of Bobby Tatro.

Mia O'Farrell collapsed onto her four-poster bed without so much as kicking off her shoes. She stared, unblinking, at the plaster ceiling, wishing for nothing more complicated than a hot bath and a tall glass of cold milk. But she didn't have the energy to move. It was after ten, the end of a very long, upsetting day — no matter how many times she reminded herself that Hamilton Carhill was home in Texas, recuperating from his ordeal after providing actionable intelligence that had saved innocent lives. His secrets were safe. *He* was safe.

That she'd taken risks to make it happen — that she didn't have all the answers she wanted — was a problem. But initially, when word had first reached her that Ham had been kidnapped, she hadn't believed he'd get out of Colombia alive. He was being held by brutal criminals on a remote Andean mountainside, and no one even knew what in blazes he looked like.

Mia lifted her head onto a pillow, to keep the stomach acid from crawling up her throat. She'd fought indigestion since she woke that day. Smarter, she thought, to wait and have her milk *after* her bath. Having it beforehand would only make her stomach worse.

Her ceiling fan whirred steadily in the quiet night. She wasn't a hardened Special Forces officer like Brooker or an eccentric genius like Carhill. She wasn't experienced in power plays and political machinations like President Poe. She was just a smart kid from South Boston.

"Not so smart."

She didn't like the note of self-pity in her tone. But if she was so damn smart, why was she lying in bed at ten o'clock with indigestion? Why hadn't she realized she was being played?

Carhill hadn't provided many details of his kidnapping and incarceration. He'd said he was too traumatized and needed time. His kidnapping struck Mia and the experts — the very few who knew about it — as a reasonably well but not exactingly planned mission. A forty-eight-hour plan versus a one-month-in-the-making plan.

Her assumption had been that profit was the motive. Greed, not power and secrets. Except Mia wasn't so sure about that anymore, either.

A profit motive she could understand. As a Texas Carhill, Ham had to have been a prime target for kidnappers-for-ransom in the wild circles in which he operated. He didn't advertise his background, but if someone shady — someone like Bobby Tatro — did happen to find out about Carhill's extreme wealth, then it made sense; snatch him, demand a ransom, get paid a fortune and either let him go or kill him. It was straightforward.

But Tatro, only recently out of federal prison, hadn't had much time to pull off such a complex mission. Someone else must have pointed him to Ham Carhill, helped him put together his team, lured him with the promise of a big payday — except there hadn't been a ransom. Again, Mia stumbled on that one.

Therein lay the little wrinkle she'd discussed with the president. Bobby Tatro couldn't have masterminded the kidnapping on his own.

She hadn't mentioned to John Wesley Poe her fear — her near certainty — that she'd been played by some vigilante psycho.

In some ways, Mia thought, it would have been simpler if they'd all been killed. Tatro and his men. Even Brooker, Carhill. Just close the book on the mission and walk away. No one would expect answers with so many key players dead. But she squeezed her eyes shut, appalled at her thinking. She could never allow herself to become that cold and analytical. That self-serving. *Never, never, never.*

Hot tears dripped down her temples onto her pillow.

You're only as good as your last mistake.

She opened her eyes and rolled onto her side. She'd lived in her apartment for more than two years, but it still didn't feel like home. It was charming, with traditional furnishings, fireplaces in the bedroom and living room, wainscoting in the kitchen, a chandelier in the dining room. It had its own courtyard, lush with ivy and always cheerful, somehow, with its splash of morning sun. She could walk to the shops on M Street and the fancier houses — the places she couldn't afford — with their carefully designed window treatments that looked so welcoming and yet, artfully but deliberately, obstructed prying eyes.

Mia Frances O'Farrell wasn't someone who made mistakes. She'd always earned good grades, from kindergarten through graduate school. She'd risen fast in the competitive, high-stakes world of national security, where mistakes didn't get you a failing grade — they got people killed.

The safe return of Ham Carhill had been the clear-cut objective of the mission.

It had been a *success.* Not a mistake, not a failure, she reminded herself.

The telephone rang, startling her. She reached for the extension on her bedside

113

table without sitting up, her stomach churning.

"I'll expose you for the traitor and fraud you are."

Mia bolted upright, bile rising in her throat. She thought she recognized the voice on the other end but couldn't be sure, didn't dare commit herself. "Who is this?"

"If you're the wolf guarding the henhouse, I'll find out. Mark my words."

"Excuse me —"

"You have very little time to make things right."

Click.

Mia dropped the phone onto the floor and half fell, half rolled, off the bed and ran into the bathroom, dry heaving as she leaned over the toilet. Nothing came up. Finally, she placed her forearm on the cool tile wall and leaned her forehead against it, trying to clear her mind, soothe her thoughts.

She had enemies. More than one no doubt thought her a fraud and even a traitor. But a wolf guarding the henhouse? *Her?*

She returned to the bedroom, kicking off her heels and kneeling on the fuzzy rug on her narrow-board floor, feeling under her bed for the phone.

Her caller ID registered only Private Name, Private Number.

She climbed back onto her bed, sitting cross-legged in the middle of her pale blue chenille coverlet, no thought now of a hot bath and cold milk.

Major Brooker should have arrived in Washington by this time for their morning meeting. But he had no reason to make such a call. Technically, he'd volunteered for the Carhill rescue mission. He'd been *asked* to volunteer, but he could have refused. President Poe had involved himself — Mia suspected he had his own agenda with Brooker.

Poe hadn't asked her how she'd figured out that the Brookers and the Carhills were neighbors and that Ethan would recognize Ham, which made him perfect for the rescue job. The president had stayed away from details. Something about the army major, who'd had an awful year by anyone's standards, seemed to have resonated with Poe — he was totally untroubled by any of Ethan's exploits since his wife's death.

Subtext. Connections. Mia had pushed them aside and focused on getting Ham Carhill to safety — nothing else.

"You want your guy. You need to send Ethan Brooker. . . ."

A voice on the other end of a telephone. A confidence. A hope, she had thought, pushing back the memory of just how easily she'd succumbed to that hope.

Every time, it was the same. Male, sincere, urgent and anonymous.

"Your guy's being held by some ex-con who has a thing for a blond, female marshal."

The same voice. The same sincerity and urgency.

The man on the other end had first called her over the summer, providing her with information that had led to the arrest in Miami of illegal arms-traffickers with Colombian ties. Then he'd put her in touch with Ham Carhill as a potential informant. But Ham had proved to be so much more, a true genius at clandestine work.

In retrospect, Mia knew she should have flown to Bogotá herself and met Ham in person, or had him fly to Washington. Smarter yet, she should have asked for help from people better suited to handle operatives.

But she'd continued to take the anonymous calls, and now she had to pay whatever the consequences might be.

She crawled stiffly out of bed and turned

on the tub in the small, adorable bathroom, scooping out lavender salts and sprinkling them under the hot running water. She'd postpone her meeting with Ethan in the morning and see if she could find out more about what really happened down in Colombia.

In the meantime, she'd have her bath, after all.

Wendy seemed to put all her concentration into choosing a Lake Champlain Chocolates truffle from the box she'd brought with her, stuffed at the bottom of her tote bag, but Juliet knew her feelings were hurt. Her niece was sitting cross-legged on the rug in front of the futon couch, the television off, the street sounds — traffic, the occasional siren — the only real distraction.

"I'm saving the coffee-flavored ones for you, Aunt Juliet." Wendy managed a half-hearted smile. "Dad says you drink more coffee than all your brothers combined."

"It wouldn't surprise me if I did. I need to cut back."

She picked a truffle and handed the box up to Juliet. "Your turn. I've got a raspberry one. You can tell by the marks on the tops."

"I'll take my chances."

"You just reminded me — I didn't check the ingredients. Actually, I'm scared to. I mean, if truffles aren't vegan, what do I do then?"

Juliet smiled. "We all have our sins." But she grew more serious. "Wendy —"

"It's okay. I should have called. I was so into the idea of going to New York on my own —" She bit just the top off the small truffle, savoring it as she leaned back against the futon. "I should have gone to college this year instead of waiting. I want to be more independent than Dad or Grandma and Grandpa are willing to let me be. I decided — I don't know, I just decided to do it. Be independent. Not ask permission."

"That'll be easier for them to swallow when you're eighteen," Juliet said, plucking what she thought was a vanilla malt truffle from the tempting lineup in the box. "Six months to go. Right now, you're still a minor."

She sighed, taking another tiny bite of her truffle. "I know. It stinks."

"But I promise, Wendy. I'll get you down here for a few days before I have to vacate the premises. We'll go to museums, visit the park. I'm looking forward to it. It's just that right now, I've got some loose ends I need to tie up."

"Do they have to do with what was in that envelope?"

Juliet hadn't shown Wendy the photograph of her on the steps of her building, on her way to work on a relatively recent morning — she was in the jeans she'd bought in late August, the same day as her leather jacket. The blood-dripping eyes and horns made her skin crawl. But the idea that Bobby Tatro had taken a picture of her at her home without her even being aware of it had her wanting, at the very least, to get her niece safely back home. He'd crossed the line.

"Yes," she said, "they do."

"Marshal business?"

Juliet nodded. "There's a chance a fugitive I took into custody wants revenge now that he's out of prison."

"Has he threatened you?"

"Not directly, no."

Wendy bent her head back so that it was resting on the cushion next to where Juliet was sitting. "I'm glad you like your job, Aunt Juliet, because I sure don't want to be in law enforcement. I don't want to be a landscaper, either, although I think I like it better than all that cop stuff."

"You want to go to med school, right?"

She sat up straight, finishing off her truffle. "If I ever write the stupid essays for my applications."

"You've got time," Juliet said. "Take a break."

She shook her head. "Mom wants me to apply early decision. I need to get them done. I should have stayed home this weekend and worked on them, so I guess it's just as well —" She broke off, heaving another sigh. "I'll take the train back in the morning."

Juliet touched her niece's shoulder, stiff with tension and hurt feelings. "Your dad said he'd drive down and meet you in Katonah tomorrow. That's a cute village in Westchester. You can take Metro North, a commuter line — it'll be an adventure."

She shrugged. "Yeah. Sure."

"It's a three-and-a-half-hour drive back to Vermont from Katonah. Maybe you and your dad can sort out a few things —"

"Like what? He thinks I came here without telling him, when I left a note."

"You didn't ask his permission."

Wendy rolled her eyes. "I never asked him his permission when I went on trips with my mom."

Juliet was sure Wendy knew that traipsing

off to New York on her own was different — she was just being stubborn. A Longstreet trait. On the other hand, as the youngest of the six Longstreet kids and the only female, Juliet could commiserate with Wendy about going up against the prevailing wisdom of the Longstreet side of her family.

Her niece was frowning at her. "Aunt Juliet! Haven't you picked out a truffle yet?"

Juliet grinned. "I did. I just haven't eaten it yet."

Wendy selected another, and they each ate their truffles and talked for an hour, before making up the futon together. Wendy crawled in, pulling the blanket up to her chin, looking so small and young. "Thanks, Aunt Juliet," she said. "I'm sorry if I've been difficult. My dad — I don't mean to cause a hard time for him."

"Don't worry about your dad. Worry about yourself and what you want and making the best decisions you can."

"Coming to New York today probably wasn't a good decision, was it?"

"I don't know, Wendy, you've always been the good kid — maybe it's about time you rebelled a little. We'd all worry if you were too perfect."

Juliet saw the spark in her niece's eyes, and the start of a smile at her comment. Wendy no doubt knew what she'd done was over the top but she had a hunch Wendy wouldn't be taking off again anytime soon. Juliet wished her good-night. But she took the envelope with Tatro's picture of her into her bedroom with her. If Wendy had sneaked off to New York, she wouldn't necessarily be above peeking inside the envelope. Then she'd tell her father, and Juliet would have all her brothers wanting specifics. It was enough for them to know — and Wendy would surely tell them — that she had an ex-con on her case.

Seven

~: ❦ :~

Wendy fought back tears, ignoring the pain in her arms and back from the muscle strain of carrying her overloaded backpack and tote bag. She wished she was as strong as her aunt. But she had to keep going — she couldn't stop now.

She'd jumped off the Metro North train at 125th Street and was walking the block to the subway station. Another passenger had given her directions. She needed to go back to Juliet's apartment. She had no choice — she'd left Teddy's ashes under the futon couch. She hadn't wanted her aunt to see them and had hidden them there, feeling his spirit as she'd slept, dreaming about him running through the apple orchard.

She couldn't believe she was so stupid as to have left his remains behind in New York. If Juliet found the tin, she might think his ashes were dirt or some whole-grain organic flour or *something,* and dump them in the trash.

Wendy couldn't bring herself to call and ask her aunt to mail the ashes to her in Vermont. It was too embarrassing — she didn't want to admit she'd carried her dog's remains all the way to New York — and too risky. Ashes by mail?

When she spotted a subway car at the station, Wendy ran, squeezing her way between the closing doors. She found a seat right away and decided her luck was changing. The man who'd given her directions had told her she could get off at Eight-first Street without having to go all the way down to Grand Central. Once she recovered Teddy's ashes, she could take the subway back to 125th Street and wait for another Metro North train.

But she knew when she didn't show up on time in Katonah, her father would go nuts. She could imagine him calling Juliet and getting the marshals involved. He was always overreacting. It would never occur to him that she might know what she was doing. She vowed to call him as soon as she got aboveground.

The Eighty-first Street station was the Museum of Natural History stop — its walls were decorated with reliefs and mosaics of dinosaurs and whales. On a different day, Wendy thought, she'd have

124

been mesmerized. Today, she charged to the exit like most of the seasoned New Yorkers around her.

When she reached the street, she got out her cell phone and dialed her father's cell phone, getting his voice mail. Thank *God* he didn't answer. "Hi, Dad, it's me, Wendy. I'm going to be late, I think just an hour or so. I'll call you when I know for sure what time I'm getting to Katonah. See you!"

She shut off her cell phone. She didn't want him calling and telling her what to do. She had a plan — she knew what to do. But when she looked up at her surroundings, she didn't recognize where she was and felt a jolt of panic. What if she couldn't even remember Juliet's address? And her arms and legs — they couldn't hold up while she tramped all over, lost, with her heavy backpack and tote bag.

But she turned, saw the museum and relaxed. She'd found her way to her aunt's once. She could do it again. Taking a few seconds to get her bearings, Wendy reminded herself that she was doing the right thing. She'd thought it all through on the train after she'd realized she'd left Teddy's ashes behind. She was convinced he'd died just before her mother left for Nova Scotia because he'd sensed she was renting their house for six months and wanted her to feel free of him.

And her father. Always so practical. "Most dogs don't live to sixteen. He had a good run."

Although she was seventeen and knew sixteen was very old for a golden retriever, Wendy still had wanted Teddy to live forever.

When she reached her aunt's building, Juan, the doorman, ran down the steps and took her bags from her. Wendy smiled, her arms and legs screaming. "Thank you, thank you! I don't think I could make it up the stairs with them. I shouldn't have packed so much."

"I thought you left —"

"I forgot something."

He carried her bags into the lobby and offered to hold them for her, but she didn't want him to see her with a cracker tin and have to explain its contents. She shook her head, thanking him for his offer. "But can you let me into my aunt's apartment? She's at work. I don't want to bug her. I'll only be a minute. If you have the key —"

"No problem."

He went into a small room behind the stairs and returned with a set of keys. "Just

126

bring them back when you're finished."

"I will. Thanks!"

Juan carried her bags back to the elevator and pressed the up button for her.

Once inside the elevator, Wendy leaned against the shiny brass wall and let her backpack and tote bag sink to the floor. She was so spent! She thought she was in good shape, but tramping around New York was killing her.

The fourth-floor hallway was quiet and steamy warm, much warmer than Juliet's apartment. Wendy dragged her bags to her aunt's door and set them in front of it as she tried to figure out which of the two keys to use, in which lock.

This one . . . top lock.

Getting it right the first time, she gave a little cry of victory and pushed open the heavy door.

She heard a noise. Not the elevator — someone in the hallway. Footsteps, breathing. She paid no attention, concentrating on moving her bags inside the door.

She started to reach for her tote bag when a man materialized behind her. "Don't scream, little Wendy. I won't hurt you."

He grabbed her wrist, forcing her to drop the backpack, and she looked up, unable to grasp what was happening.

Dark curls, black running shoes. Good-looking.

The man from the diner.

He had on a zip-front jacket and cargo pants. He didn't look scary, but he *was* scary, and Wendy got out half a blood-curdling yell before he shoved her into the apartment. The door caught on her back-pack as it swung shut, and she went flying, landing on her butt on the hardwood floor, nearly toppling over one of her aunt's fish tanks.

Gulping for air, she screamed for help as loud as she could.

"Well, well," he said. "I wasn't expecting you, Wendy."

She shrank backward toward the fish tank.

Her dad was a state trooper . . . maybe he'd gotten her message and was so furious with her now that he was on his way to New York, and he'd come to the apartment and save her.

"Wendy. That's the name of the girl in *Peter Pan.*" The man who looked like Johnny Depp but wasn't stepped toward her. "I always thought she was a pain in the ass."

Wendy tried to scream again, but no sound would come out.

The intruder was slightly red in the face and out of breath. Had he taken the stairs instead of the elevator? How did he get past Juan in the lobby?

A knife . . . *oh, God!* He had a knife in his hand. How could she have not noticed? She'd been around cops long enough to recognize it as an assault-type knife.

Something was on the blade.

Her stomach twisted. She heard herself whimper.

Blood.

"Don't move. Understand?"

Wendy nodded without making a sound.

With a sudden movement, he shot over to the couch and ripped its futon mattress off the frame. "Your fucking aunt. I knew the minute I laid eyes on her she was corrupt. I fucking hate corrupt cops." He turned around and pointed the knife at Wendy. "She tell you how she found me in that Wal-Mart parking lot, huh?"

Wendy began to piece together the puzzle. This man was the fugitive — the man Juliet had put in prison — and who wanted revenge.

"She thinks I don't know," he said. "*I* know. She cheated. That's how she found me. She fucking turned my own family against me."

Wendy didn't say anything. She saw the cracker tin of Teddy's ashes on the floor, pictured her beautiful old golden retriever running through freshly fallen leaves on a sunny autumn day at home. But he was gone now. Dead. Those were his *ashes* in the tin. His spirit was somewhere else.

Dad's not coming to save me.

No one was.

She'd have to save herself.

Juliet shut the door to Mike Rivera's office and sat on one of the two plastic chairs in front of his superneat desk. "I need to talk to you."

"Damn right, you do." He paused, narrowing his dark eyes on her. "Ethan Brooker — what did he want with you? I had a report he was outside the building yesterday when you went after your niece. I got your message that she's okay, but what's Brooker —"

She smiled at him. "You've been stewing on that one all night, Chief?"

"Longstreet, that mouth of yours —"

"He brought me a present."

She dug the envelope Ethan had given her out of her jacket pocket and handed it across Rivera's desk to him. He opened it, pulled out the picture and sighed. "Not

Brooker's artwork, I take it. He may be a shit magnet, but he's not a whack job. Besides, I think he kind of likes you."

"Ethan says he found the picture during a highly classified rescue mission. Apparently it was left behind by an ex-con named Bobby Tatro." She tried to keep her tone clinical, professional. No emotion. "Tatro was a fugitive I picked up four years ago in Syracuse. He didn't believe I just happened upon him. I didn't — I had a source I didn't want him to know about. He threatened me."

"Threatened you how?"

"He said my pretty blond ass was his when he got out."

"When did he get out?"

"Late August."

"And you're just telling me this now?"

She shrugged. "I guess I am."

"You haven't heard from him —"

"No. I'd have told you."

"Damn right you'd have told me." He sighed, staring again at the offensive picture. "This is in front of your apartment building, isn't it?"

"That's right."

"Your niece?"

"On her way back to Vermont."

He nodded with satisfaction. "Good. All

131

right, fast-forward to Brooker. What's his role in all of this?"

Juliet told Rivera what she knew, which wasn't much.

When she finished, Rivera leaned back, his chair giving an annoying squeak. "Where's Brooker now?"

"He didn't say. I have his cell-phone number —"

"Good. Call him. Get him in here."

"He's solid, Mike."

"Maybe." He glanced down at the picture on his desk, but his face remained expressionless. "I don't like putting Bobby Tatro and Ethan Brooker together and coming up with you as the common denominator."

Juliet got to her feet. "Neither do I."

"And let's get looking for this Tatro character."

Tony Cipriani poked his head in through the door. "Sorry to interrupt. Juliet, I've got a Vermont state trooper on the phone. He says it's important. Something about your niece."

Juliet jumped to her feet, and Rivera waved her toward the outer office. When she picked up the phone at her desk, Joshua, seething, told her about the cheerful, cryptic message his daughter had left on his voice mail. "It's been over an hour. She said she'd be just an hour or so late and there's no sign of her. Juliet —"

"I haven't heard from her."

"*Damn* it."

But she heard the concern in his voice. As out of patience as he was with Wendy, he didn't want anything to happen to her. "Maybe she forgot something at my apartment. I'll run up there and check, okay? You're still in Katonah?"

"I'll stay here until I hear from you."

Juliet tried to grin. "Don't bite the steering wheel in two."

When she hung up, Tony Cipriani and Mike Rivera both were frowning at her. She rubbed the back of her neck, awkward at having family complications interfere with her workday. What was Wendy up to this time? Juliet quickly explained the situation. Cip, for whom teenagers were still a mystery, offered to go with her, but she shook her head. The last thing she wanted was a fellow deputy mixed up in a family matter.

Rivera cut her loose to go find her niece. "The kid probably got a wild hair to see the Temple of Dendur at the Metropolitan," he said. "Teenagers and impulse control, you know?"

133

"I'm beginning to," Juliet said.

"Take the time you need. Escort Miss Wendy back to her father if you have to."

When she arrived at her building, Juliet forced herself not to charge inside like some kind of wild woman. She'd had to fight off her own guilt. She'd believed her niece capable of getting to her father on her own. She'd put her on the train at Grand Central and waved her goodbye. She'd *trusted* Wendy not to get off until Katonah.

Muttering to herself about the difference between independence and responsibility and courtesy, Juliet pushed open the glass door to the lobby, faintly surprised that Juan hadn't beaten her to it.

She slowed her pace once through the door. He didn't seem to be around at all. If Wendy had forgotten something, she'd have had to get the keys from him. "Juan?" Juliet walked back behind the stairs to the tiny room he used as an office and a place to lock up bags, hold packages for people.

She knocked on the door, calling him again. When there was no answer, she tried the knob — the door was unlocked. Maybe he'd just run to the bathroom. He should have locked the office, but Juliet wasn't about to rat him out. She pushed open the door, just to make sure he wasn't in there with headphones on or passed out drunk or ill, although he'd so far proved himself ultra-responsible and in good health.

The door struck something — his foot — and Juliet immediately saw that he was sprawled facedown on the floor. "Juan!" But she took in the blood pooling on the polished floor, the unnatural angle of his neck, and even as she grimaced at the certainty that this friendly man was dead, murdered, she drew her Glock.

Tatro.

In all likelihood, Juan — she didn't even know his last name — was dead because of her.

Knowing she couldn't think about that now, Juliet got her cell phone out of her jacket with her free hand and hit the automatic dial for Tony Cipriani's direct line.

"Cip — it's Juliet. I'm in the lobby of my apartment building. My doorman's had his throat slit." She pushed back her emotion and focused on what she had to do. "It can't have happened that long ago."

"I'm on my way. I'll notify NYPD."

"Rivera —"

"He's standing right here. I'm handing him the phone. I'll use another line."

No matter how long she stayed in law enforcement, Juliet doubted she'd ever get used to what horrors some people inflicted on their fellow human beings for profit, revenge, fun — or the plain old hell of it.

She glanced at the elevator and saw the light above it indicating it was on her floor.

Not moving.

"Wendy. Oh, God."

"Longstreet?" It was Rivera's voice.

"I can't wait for Cip or NYPD, Mike. I think Tatro's in the building. He could be in my apartment. If my niece is up there —"

He didn't hesitate. "Go. Keep the line open."

Juliet dropped the phone into her pocket and left poor Juan where he was. She took the stairs two at a time to the second floor, then ducked through a fire door. No more open, elegant stairs. They were metal now, functional. She moved quickly, quietly, not wanting to draw any attention to herself, have neighbors poking their heads out of their doors or calling down to Juan to find out what was going on.

When she reached her floor, she let the fire door shut soundlessly behind her. The hall was empty. She headed for her apartment, passing the elevator, which was jammed open, keeping it on her floor. The killer's escape route, she thought. He'd take the elevator down to the lobby or the basement or up to the roof, depending on how much time he had — whether the body in the lobby had been discovered and the police were there or on the way.

Bobby Tatro was a loner. He was arrogant, sadistic and self-absorbed. If he was responsible for Juan's murder, Juliet would be surprised if he had an accomplice.

But Tatro couldn't have kidnapped whoever Brooker and his team had rescued on his own. He'd had help.

Juliet's heart jumped when she saw Wendy's backpack wedged in her apartment door, keeping it slightly ajar. She didn't risk telling Rivera, still listening in, and have Tatro or whoever was inside hear her.

The sound of water dripping. . . .

"Open the door, Wendy." It was a man's voice, sickeningly cajoling, "I forgive you. It's okay. I'll take care of you."

Wendy . . . Juliet felt as if her heart had just been ripped out. Her niece was in the apartment, at the mercy of this bastard. Juliet didn't recognize the voice. It could be Tatro — it could be anyone. But she knew she had to tunnel her thoughts, zero in on the situation and her options.

The bedroom, the bedroom closet and the bathroom all had doors. But only the bedroom door locked. That likely put the intruder in the hall, talking to Wendy through the bedroom door, trying to lure her out to him. Tatro would toy with her, have a little sadistic fun for himself, let her believe she was safe from him before he burst in on her.

Juliet stepped over Wendy's backpack, pushing her apartment door open wider, and landed in water.

The fish tanks.

Wendy's tote bag was acting as a dam for a flood of water flowing from her living room and two smashed tanks. Gold and bright blue and purple fish flapped helplessly or lay unmoving on the floor, amid blue gravel and a little ship's wheel she used as a prop.

Orchids and spider plants were upended, loose potting soil soaking up some of the gallons of aquarium water and turning to mud.

"Wendy, Wendy." The intruder was obviously unaware that someone had entered the apartment. "I can't wait forever."

Juliet had no idea if Rivera could hear what was going on — if he knew Juan's killer was in her apartment with her niece and had relayed the information to Cip and NYPD.

Juliet heard sudden pounding on the bedroom door, and, using the noise to cover the sound of her movement, she charged down the hall and pointed her gun at a dark-haired man in cargo pants. His back was to her as he gave the door a hard kick.

Juliet didn't waste any time. "Freeze! Federal marshal! Hands in the air. *Now.* Do it now!"

He went still.

Juliet saw a K-bar in his right hand — the assault-type knife he must have used to kill Juan. "Drop the knife and put your hands up. I'm not saying it again. I'll shoot you where you stand."

The knife clattered to the floor. "I guess you've got me, pretty marshal." He raised both his hands above his head. "For now."

Tatro. Eyes and gun on him, Juliet called through the bedroom door. "Wendy, are you okay?"

"Yes." Her voice sounded strong but very young — and frightened. "I'm by myself."

Juliet didn't let herself feel any relief. "Hands flat against the wall, Tatro. Then your forehead. Touch the wall with your forehead. Do it!"

He glanced back at her with a cocky smile, a dark curl dropping over his right eye. "I know the drill, blondie."

But he complied, spreading his legs without her having to order him to do so. With one hand, Juliet got her cuffs, then approached him, her Glock still trained on him. "Right hand behind your back. Keep your left hand and your forehead against the wall."

"I've got a headache —"

"Do it."

Sighing as if she were imposing on him, he put his right hand behind his back. Juliet placed her right foot next to his right foot. If he tried anything, she'd knee him in the back of the leg, and he'd go down.

She cuffed his wrist and gripped the cool metal with her left hand while holstering her gun with her right. If he moved a muscle, she'd yank upwards on the cuffs until he felt the pain. "Left hand behind your back."

"My head —"

"Now, Tatro."

He gave her his left hand, most of his weight on his forehead now as he leaned into the wall. Juliet cuffed his other wrist, then locked the cuffs with their little key. Taking a breath, she held the chain that linked the two bands, patted him down on the right side. She switched hands and patted down his left side. Except for the K-bar he'd dropped, he was unarmed. She gave the knife a side kick and sent it sliding across the floor away from Tatro. It'd get bagged as evidence later.

"Facedown on the floor," she said. "NYPD's on their way."

Cursing her, Tatro did as Juliet ordered. He was an experienced criminal and would know the conditions under which she was authorized to use deadly force.

"Don't think this ends here," he said into the floor. "Your pretty ass is mine, blondie. Just like I promised. It's only a matter of time."

Juliet ignored him. "Wendy — open the door, honey. Come on out. Slowly. Let me see you."

"It's going to take a minute. I barricaded myself in."

Juliet heard the sound of what had to be the bureau scraping across the wood floor. Then the door opened, and Wendy cowered on the threshold, pale and shaking badly.

Tatro snorted. "Fucking little bitch. Auntie showed up in the nick of time, didn't she? Saved your ass."

"Shut the hell up, Tatro," Juliet said, no

intention of chit-chatting with him. Wendy must have smashed the fish tanks, distracting him long enough for her to take off to the bedroom.

"I caught him by surprise." Wendy's voice was quiet and steady, not with bravado, Juliet thought, but with shock. "The water was like a dam breaking. It nearly knocked us both down. He dropped his knife. I ran into the bedroom. I knew I couldn't get past him to get to the elevator."

Juliet pushed back an image of her niece struggling with Tatro and tried to reassure her. "He can't hurt you now."

Tony Cipriani arrived on the scene first. NYPD officers were right behind him. Juliet leaned down to Tatro on the floor. "You're a sick son of a bitch, Tatro, terrorizing a teenage girl. When did you take my picture? How long were you spying on me?"

"I don't know what you're talking about."

"You come near me or my family again —"

Cip tugged on her arm. "Come on, Longstreet. Let's go."

Juliet about-faced, nodded at her partner, then ran to her niece, Wendy's fingers clawing into her as the girl held on and sobbed.

"The fish." Wendy stiffened, standing up straight, shaking off any display of affection — of weakness. "We have to save them."

Without making contact with any of the law enforcement officers descending on the building, she started scooping up fish. Most were dead already, Juliet saw, but a few had managed to land in small pools of standing water. The rest of the water had soaked into the floorboards, probably drenching the apartment under hers.

Tony winced at Juliet as he watched the girl do her best to save what fish she could. "Longstreet. Jesus —"

"There's still water in two of the tanks," Juliet told Wendy softly. "Put the survivors in there."

"They won't fight with one another?"

"Not those fish." And not in their shocked condition.

Wendy gently lowered survivors into one of the tanks. She was ghostly white and not shaking, not anymore. But Juliet knew that wasn't necessarily a good sign. "I have to save the fish," Wendy mumbled. "I don't want them to die because of me."

Cip scooped up a plump goldfish and dumped it in one of the intact tanks. "Look at him go. He probably thinks he

143

jumped in there by himself."

Juliet turned away, fighting tears she'd never let Cip or any of the law enforcement types around her see. Her niece shouldn't have had to face Bobby Tatro. "I need to call my brother. Wendy's father."

Discreetly toeing a dead fish under the leaves of an upended orchid, Cip nodded. "Yeah. You sure as hell do."

Eight

~: ✺ :~

The Hay-Adams on Washington's Lafayette Square was one of the more prestigious hotels in a city where prestige mattered more than it did virtually anywhere else in the world. For a few thousand dollars, Ethan could have had a suite with a view of the White House, but he'd opted for a smaller suite with a view of St. John's Church, indulgence enough to make him feel alive and no longer under even the oblique direction of Mia O'Farrell.

Obviously O'Farrell hadn't expected the Hay-Adams. Her reaction to his choice of hotel was fun to watch.

Her thin, carefully plucked eyebrows went up almost imperceptibly.

That was it.

"I'm on my own nickel, if you're worried about squandering the people's money."

She sat on a small sofa in the living area of his suite. "You don't care much about squandering your own money, do you?"

"No, ma'am. I've never been much of a penny-pincher."

She sipped a Coke. He'd had to find her a glass and ice. She was pretty and she looked delicate, but Ethan wasn't misled. Dr. O'Farrell wasn't anyone he'd want to cross.

She'd rescheduled their morning meeting until after lunch, compelling him to spring for a second night in D.C., unless he'd wanted to check out and meet her in a public place or go to her office. And he didn't.

"I knew you'd make it out of Colombia alive," she said.

He wondered if she'd ever been out of the country. Paris, maybe. London. Montreal. He let his eyes connect with hers. "Did you?"

Something about his look must have bothered her, because she glanced away and quickly set her Coke on the cocktail table. "Have you told me everything that happened with Tatro and his henchmen?"

Henchmen. Ethan couldn't remember someone ever using that word in a high-level meeting. Any meeting. "Yes, ma'am."

"You can call me Mia." She smiled tentatively. "It's fine."

He didn't respond. After today, he

hoped never to have to see her again. Not that he disliked her or there was anything wrong with her particularly. He just didn't want to stay in the same orbit as the Mia O'Farrells of the world.

"Bobby Tatro was the ringleader?" she asked.

Her language reminded Ethan of old westerns. Yet he didn't know many people more tapped into the real world than Mia was. She wasn't naive — she just seemed that way. A tactic, maybe. A habit. He didn't know if she was an ideologue or a nut or a pragmatist, or simply an intelligent woman navigating her way through a tough town and a hard job, just trying to do the right thing. Ethan didn't know if he could trust her. But none of that mattered anymore. He was done. He was going home, even if he didn't know where that was.

"It was my job to get Ham Carhill safely out of Colombia. Nobody asked me to sort out the players."

O'Farrell frowned so deeply her eyes shut. "There are still a lot of unanswered questions."

"I don't see how that's my problem."

Actually, he did see how it was his problem. After finding the picture of Juliet in Tatro's hut, Ethan had known he wouldn't just be flying home to Texas and leaving all the unanswered questions about Mia O'Farrell and who had her ear behind him.

But he could pretend, at least for now.

She sat back on the elegant sofa, turning her frown on him. "Who do you think you're kidding, Major Brooker? That's why you're here. Because of the unanswered questions."

So much for pretending, he thought. He just shrugged at her without comment.

"How did Bobby Tatro choose Ham Carhill as his victim? How did he find him? How did he pull off such a complicated operation so soon after his release from federal prison? We can start with those questions. You think I have the answers. I don't."

"Who tipped Tatro off we were on our way?" Ethan fired back. "That's another good question."

Mia's frown deepened. "You say that as if you think I did."

"I don't know. Did you?"

"No." She inhaled through her nose. "No, I didn't. Perhaps it was just a coincidence that he wasn't there —"

"It wasn't a coincidence."

148

Ethan glanced around his tastefully decorated suite. He was more suited to a desert foxhole or a HALO jump into the middle of nowhere — swatting mosquitoes in Colombia as he'd done just three days ago. Washington wasn't his world. Neither was his fancy hotel. But he'd showered, shaved, had a good breakfast and lunch. He could check out now and walk away, not sit here and play games with a presidential adviser who wasn't telling him everything she knew about Bobby Tatro, Ham Carhill and what had gone down in Colombia over the past few weeks. Not even close. And whatever she was holding back had her scared.

He hadn't told her about the photograph of Juliet he'd found in Tatro's hut. If he was wrong about Mia O'Farrell and she wasn't just in over her head — if she was a snake — then she didn't need to know any more details than what he'd given her.

"You and Deputy Longstreet have had your names in the papers a couple times this year," Mia said. "It's possible someone saw the stories and made the connection between you and Ham because of them."

"I was more or less a footnote," Ethan said.

"Nevertheless, it wasn't long after your

149

name was in the media this last time, in connection with the assassin in upstate New York in late August, that Ham was kidnapped — a fellow Texan, a neighbor of yours, a very private individual only a handful of people would easily recognize. You 'just happened' to be one of that handful."

Mia finally drank more of her Coke, but she didn't relax. "You're worried about me, Major. What if I should be worried about you? Ham spent most of the past two years in South America. So that brings me back to the same questions. How did Bobby Tatro figure out who he was, where he was? How did he get to Colombia so soon after his release from prison, find men to hire, get the money to pay them?"

Ethan half smiled and said to her, "Tatro might not be your ringleader after all."

She didn't seem to notice he was teasing her.

"What's Ham saying?"

"Very little. He blanked out a lot of the past few weeks."

Ethan doubted that. Once something got in Ham's brain, it stayed there. "That's what he told you?"

"For now. He needs rest. He doesn't have the training or the experience you do." Mia's frown deepened again, as if she were trying to convince herself that Ham Carhill wasn't pulling a fast one on her. "He retained every detail of the information he'd gathered pre-kidnapping. We got it in the nick of time. It saved lives."

This woman operated in the very bowels of government, knew things few others did — and she tried to get it right. Ethan was fairly certain that whatever Mia O'Farrell was hiding, it wasn't because she was venal, or just didn't give a damn about anyone else.

She leveled her very green eyes on him. "*You* saved lives, Major Brooker."

A torturous route she'd had to take to where he'd saved lives. "Have you considered that Ham's kidnapping might have had nothing to do with the work he did for you? The Carhills aren't just rich, you know. They're richer than God."

She reddened slightly. "I realize that. Everything's happened very fast. Ham has been a surprising asset. He has a brilliant mind —"

"His family thinks he's strange."

She nodded, looking at her hands.

"I hope his life and the other lives 'we' saved were worth the risks. If you'd wanted answers to the kidnapping, you could have gotten them. Some, if not all of them. But you wanted Ham. That was the mission." Ethan was just repeating, in essence, what she'd told him. "If my team had been killed, Ham would have been killed."

"It's not what we wanted —"

"It was an acceptable risk. Better Ham dead and quiet than alive and talking to the wrong people, endangering lives."

"Rescuing him *saved* lives. I just told you. Ham gave us information about a plot that would have killed a dozen innocent people — we averted a real disaster."

"Rescued is better than dead. But dead was better than leaving him in the hands of Tatro and his goons. You couldn't take the risk that Tatro wasn't after money — that he or whoever was manipulating him wanted what your guy Ham had tucked in that super-charged brain of his. Contacts, information, connections. It's all what he's good at acquiring. He absorbs and processes things the rest of us never see to begin with. *That's* what you were protecting, Dr. O'Farrell. Not Ham himself, or the lives his information saved."

O'Farrell raised her chin, a coolness coming into her steady gaze. "I didn't call this meeting to explain myself to you, Major Brooker."

Ethan ignored her. "Did Tatro make a ransom demand?"

"No. Not that I know of. Believe it or not, I haven't figured out precisely what he wanted with Ham." She paused a moment, as if waiting for him to argue with her. "It's possible you and your team rescued him before Tatro could decide on his next move."

"Possible," Ethan said, but didn't believe it. He doubted O'Farrell did, either.

She set down her Coke and stood, and when Ethan got to his feet, she tilted her head back, studying him, nothing about her expression softening. "What does Deputy Longstreet know about your mission?"

Not naive at all, Dr. O'Farrell. "She knows I didn't catch Bobby Tatro."

"Do you trust her?"

"As much as I trust anyone."

Mia smiled a little. "You've heard it all and done it all, haven't you, Major? I'm sorry. If I had to do it over again, I can't say I'd ask you to get involved in this situation. Ultimately, we did everything by the book, and I didn't have the final say about your role. But I could have kept you out of it."

"President Poe wanted me in."

The clear green eyes focused on him. "Yes, he did."

She didn't go further — why the president wanted him, why Poe had stuck his nose in the Carhill mess at all. For all Ethan knew, those were more questions for which Mia O'Farrell had no answers.

"Go home, Ethan," she said quietly, lifting her briefcase and holding it next to her. "You've never taken the time to mourn your wife. Take it now and go home."

"Right now, my home's here in this suite."

He could tell she didn't think he was serious.

His cell phone rang, and she jumped a foot in the air, landing sideways on her right ankle. She let out a yelp that sounded like a swearword to Ethan, although he was sure it couldn't have been. *Not the swearing type, Dr. O'Farrell.*

He'd turned off his phone at breakfast and left it off, but had deliberately turned it back on when she'd arrived. There was no number on the readout. "Brooker."

"I was beginning to think you were dead in a ditch." It was Juliet, and she wasn't happy. "Where are you?"

"D.C. You?"

"My apartment. I'm flushing dead fish down the toilet."

"Something's happened —"

Juliet didn't seem to hear him. "Unless you've got the secretary of defense or a four-star general sitting on you, I want you on the next flight to New York."

Mia reported directly to the president. Ethan wondered if she'd do.

But he could hear the tension in Juliet's voice.

"Or," she went on, not breathless but not in the mood to listen, either, "I can get someone to find you and bring you up here."

"I don't need more marshals on my case. Think I killed your fish?"

She let out a breath. "Bobby Tatro had my niece pinned in my bedroom. He killed Juan, our doorman. Tatro was —" She paused a fraction of a second. "He said awful things to Wendy. He enjoys scaring the hell out of people."

"Is she —"

"I got here before he could break into the bedroom. Wendy bashed in a couple of my fish tanks to distract him. Her father's on his way now. He'll take her back to Vermont tonight."

Mia held her briefcase against her chest with both arms. "Major?"

He didn't get a chance to respond before Juliet spoke again. "Next flight to New

155

York, Brooker. I mean it. Be here before nightfall."

After she hung up in his ear, Ethan tossed his phone onto his chair, the elegant surroundings suddenly seeming phony to him, incongruous to the life he led, the man he was.

Mia looked at him with the incisiveness he'd noticed about her during their first meeting in D.C. three weeks ago. John Wesley Poe had been there. The president and O'Farrell had presented the outlines of the mission. Ethan had been aware that Poe's personal involvement was unusual, unexpected, if not improper. Once Ethan accepted the mission, it'd gone through normal channels for clearance and preparation. But he'd accepted before he knew Ham Carhill was the unnamed American contractor in the hands — ostensibly — of American and Colombian mercenaries.

Ham wasn't the driving force behind Ethan's willingness to put his life on the line. Ethan wasn't all that sure what was. He'd been charging into the unknown since Char's death, not giving a damn what happened to himself, just pushing for answers to who'd killed her and why, making sure whoever it was faced justice.

For all he knew, Mia O'Farrell was as

out of control as he'd been for most of the past year. She was just quieter about it, pushing computer buttons and using a pen instead of going after her enemies herself. He wondered what demons she was facing.

"Tatro?" she asked, her voice tight but composed.

In terse language, Ethan repeated what Juliet had told him. Then he picked up his phone and tucked it into the pocket of his jacket, which hung over a chair, and said without looking at Mia, "If there's anything else I should know, now's the time. Anything you haven't told me, I want it."

She was silent, her lower lip pulled in under her top teeth.

He didn't relent. "If you've got something to hide, I'll find out."

"I resent your implication."

"The thing about covering your ass is that once you start, you can't stop. At first you rationalize the lies, the omissions, as the right thing to do. Then the cover-up is the only thing to do. You keep thinking there's an end, but there never is. Exposure's always the next breath away. You start to sweat. You get where you can't sleep. You look in the mirror one day and realize you're rationalizing hurting people before they can hurt you."

Mia stayed with her cool and unruffled act, but her fingers were white, pressed fiercely against her briefcase. "I have to go."

"I'm not stopping until I know what's going on."

She walked steadily to the door. "I'm sorry about Tatro and what he did to that girl in New York," she said. "I wish he'd never made it out of Colombia. But he's not my responsibility. He never was."

"You know Tatro didn't pull off this kidnapping by himself. He's being manipulated by the same person who's manipulating you."

"No one's manipulating me." Then she added, the barest whisper, "Not anymore."

"Mia. Trust me."

She glanced back at him. "I used to trust everyone."

"The marshals are going to want to talk to me. The FBI. It won't just be Juliet."

"You know what you can and can't say." Her green eyes were as hard as emeralds now. "If I didn't trust you, you wouldn't be talking to the marshals at all."

"You're not scaring me, Mia."

"I'm not trying to. I've already given you my advice. You don't need to find another fire to put out. Go home, Major Brooker.

Visit your family. Mourn your wife. It's time."

After she left, Ethan stood in the middle of his fancy suite and tried to conjure up Char. The feel of her, the taste of her. The bubble of her laughter.

He could see her dark eyes, filled with regret and a sense of inevitability.

"I'm losing you, Ethan."

Had she actually spoken those words, or did he just imagine them?

Her death wasn't his fault. Everyone had said so.

He hadn't found Bobby Tatro in Colombia, and now Tatro had killed a doorman and traumatized a teenager.

Not your fault.

"Bullshit."

Ethan tossed his things into his suitcase, then headed down to the lobby and checked out, assuring the desk clerk that he had, indeed, enjoyed his stay. It'd just been premature to think he was due for any kind of a break.

Nobody congratulated Juliet for taking Bobby Tatro into custody. She'd have punched anyone who did. He'd barged into her building and killed a man. He'd pushed his way into her apartment and scared the hell out of a teenage girl. *Her niece.*

It was too much. Too damn much.

But she tried to keep herself from pacing and looking as horrified and livid as she was. What Wendy needed right now was a calm, controlled aunt, not a wild woman who wanted to put her fist through the wall.

Wendy had crawled onto the double bed in the small bedroom and had tucked her knees under her chin and wrapped her hands tightly around her shins. At least, Juliet thought, the bedroom was free of dead fish, sopping plants, FBI agents, NYPD detectives, marshals and crime-scene types.

She'd have taken her niece out of the building altogether, but she didn't want to risk Wendy seeing Juan's body. The crime-scene workers would be upsetting enough. Passing through the lobby after everyone was gone and everything was cleaned up — Juan's body safely at the medical examiner's office — would be traumatic enough.

Let Joshua be the one with her when she had to face that reality.

"Do you want some tea?" Juliet asked, her jaw tight with unreleased tension.

Wendy shook her head, her eyes downcast, as if she were counting the squares in Juliet's quilt.

"Water?"

Another shake of the head.

Because a federal agent was involved, the FBI was on the scene — Special Agent Joe Collins. He'd investigated the shooting of the two marshals in Central Park in May, and Juliet had ended up on the wrong side of his suspicions, which had brought him to her apartment to question her. He obviously didn't like being back under similar circumstances. Collins was an experienced agent, a red-faced man in his midforties. People sometimes assumed he was laid-back, coasting toward retirement, but that was a mistake.

He'd grimaced when Juliet had told him about Ethan and Tatro and the picture of her. "Brooker again? What is it with you two?"

She'd had no good answer.

She sat on the edge of the bed. Right now, she needed to concentrate on her niece. Brooker, Collins, Rivera — they all could wait until Joshua arrived and took over care of his only child. "Your dad should be here any minute."

Wendy shrugged her small shoulders.

"It'll be okay —"

161

"I saw him yesterday."

Juliet felt a sudden chill but took a mental step back from her own emotions. "Saw who, Wendy?"

She raised dark, tearless eyes and managed to settle her gaze on her aunt. "He sat next to me at the diner where I had lunch right after I got here."

"Wendy, who . . . ?"

"The man who — who was in here." Sniffling, she pressed her chin into her knees, her eyes glazing over again. "He knew my name. At the diner. I didn't tell him. He must have overheard me talking to Juan when he had me show him my ID."

"Did you see him here?" Juliet asked. "In the building? Out on the street?"

She shook her head, her chin still mashed into her knees. "I didn't notice him until he sat next to me in the diner. That doesn't mean he wasn't here. I just — New York's full of people. I just didn't notice."

"It's okay." But Juliet had stiffened, realizing that Bobby Tatro had been in the neighborhood yesterday, twenty-four hours before he'd killed Juan, broke into her apartment and terrorized her niece. "Wendy, did you tell Special Agent Collins or one of the NYPD detectives about the diner?"

"No. I didn't think of it until now." She averted her eyes, her lips chapped and swollen from biting down on them. "I should have told you about him sooner. I knew it wasn't right that he knew my name."

"Do you remember what he said to you?"

Wendy repeated their conversation at the diner in a toneless voice, as if she were reading lines for a part she had in a play just to get them memorized and would add the emotion later.

"He didn't use your last name?" Juliet asked.

"No."

"When you talked to Juan, you clearly stated that you were my niece?"

"I had to."

"Of course, you had to, honey. That's not what I meant. Bobby Tatro and I have a history. He's the guy I told you about last night. I arrested him when I was working in Syracuse. He just got out of prison. He was a free man. He had a chance to pull his life together. Instead, he decided to come after me." Juliet tried to sound comforting, but she could hear the tension and regret in her voice — the anger that this man would traumatize a seventeen-year-old girl to exact his revenge. "You got caught in the cross fire, Wendy. I'm sorry."

"Juan . . ." She couldn't seem to say more than that.

Juliet could see him slumped in his tiny office, smell his blood. "It looks as if he got caught in the cross fire, too."

"I should have told you," she whispered. "I should have told you about the diner yesterday."

"That might not have changed anything. We don't know."

Rivera rapped a knuckle on the open door. "Your brother's here, Juliet. The girl's father."

But Joshua was already pushing past the chief deputy, ignoring him and his sister as he went straight for his daughter, grabbing her into his arms. She crumpled, sobbing into his wool shirt. He was a big man, and he filled up Juliet's small bedroom.

"Thank God you're okay," he kept repeating, his voice hoarse.

"I shouldn't have come back here," Wendy sobbed. "That man might have seen me get off the subway and followed me here." She raised her head, her face splotchy, tears and snot running down her cheeks, into her mouth. "Juan might still be alive if I'd stayed on the train."

"Tatro wasn't after you," Juliet said. "He'd have —"

Joshua glared at her. "Stay out of this, Juliet."

"Dad — stop. Juliet saved my life."

But Juliet understood her brother. If she'd taken up landscaping the way everyone had expected — if she'd stayed home in Vermont — his daughter wouldn't be in New York in the first place. She wouldn't have had to use her wits to get out of a bad situation with a sadistic ex-con. She wouldn't have to deal with murder.

Never mind that Joshua was a state trooper who faced similar risks — then, he was in control. For the past twenty-four hours, he'd had no control whatsoever. He was powerless, and Juliet knew he hated that feeling as much as she did. At the moment, with his frightened daughter in his arms, maybe more.

Rivera motioned to her with one hand. "Come out here with me."

Juliet left her brother to console Wendy in his way and joined the chief deputy out in the hall.

"Joe Collins found a fish under the couch," Rivera said, leading her back to the kitchen. "It ended up in this little puddle, just one of those things. He's proud of himself for saving it."

"Good for him," Juliet said dully.

"And he found this." Rivera pointed to a small tin on the counter. "It looks likes somebody's ashes."

"What? Mike, for God's sake —"

"You look. You'll see what I mean."

Juliet frowned at him, but he reached past her and lifted the loosened lid off the tin.

Ashes, indeed.

She moaned, sinking against the counter.

Teddy.

"Ah, hell, Mike." She fought a surge of unwanted tears. "The ashes have got to be Wendy's dog. He died a few weeks ago. Sixteen-year-old golden retriever. They had him cremated."

"Must be what she came back here for." Rivera rubbed the back of his neck, looking pained. "Kid's been carrying around her dog's ashes. I've got five daughters, Longstreet. Trust me. The father's not going to understand."

"About the ashes or about my work putting Wendy in this situation?"

"Take your pick."

"If she'd been a boy maybe he wouldn't freak out."

"You see a seventeen-year-old boy taking

166

off to New York with his dead dog's ashes in a cracker tin?"

Juliet sniffed back any tears. Damned if she'd cry in front of Rivera. "Wendy's a gentle soul."

"Well, she handled herself admirably today. She got through this thing alive. That's all that matters." He sighed at the tin. "She'll want to know the ashes are intact. Her father's your older brother, right?"

"All my brothers are older."

Rivera squinted at her, as if he was suddenly seeing her for the first time since arriving at her apartment. "Do you need to see a doctor? That bastard twist your arm or anything? Sometimes you don't feel it until later."

"I'm fine."

"That's what you said in May when you had a couple of cracked ribs and a road rash from hell."

She didn't want to remember. "I've never liked ambulances and stretchers."

"It was hell, listening to you with that son of a bitch through the phone. Knowing he had your niece scared for her life. That you had no backup. I'm sorry I couldn't get here sooner."

"It helped knowing you were listening

167

in." She mustered a small grin. "Kept me on my toes. Don't want to mess up with the chief eavesdropping."

He shook his head in mock despair. "Where the hell did we ever find you?"

"Mike —" Juliet took a breath, the momentary injection of humor helping her to stay focused, keep her bearings on what she needed to do. "Wendy ran into Tatro yesterday."

Rivera listened without comment as Juliet relayed Wendy's story about the diner. Then he sighed heavily, nodding almost as if in response to something he was thinking.

"Collins will want to talk to her again," he said. "We don't know enough about what happened with the doorman. Don't go hanging that one on yourself just yet, okay?"

"Too late."

"Your friend the theater lady won't be thrilled when she finds out about today."

"I'm supposed to move out soon, anyway. Freda's due back from L.A. before Thanksgiving. I should begin looking for a new place."

As he started down the hall, Rivera's wet shoes squeaked on the floor. He glanced back at her. "Your neighbors'll breathe a collective sigh of relief when you pack up. The fish tanks flooded the place underneath you. The couple who owns it already tried to get past the NYPD to talk to you."

"They're ticked off?"

"Upset."

For now, Juliet thought. When the full impact of what had gone on in their building today hit them, they'd be questioning how a federal agent had ended up house-sitting for an apartment in their building. There were rules, after all. They'd figure out a way that she and Freda had broken them.

"In all my years on the job," Rivera said, "I've never had anyone break into my home and scare the hell out of my family. It wouldn't hurt for you to take some time off."

Juliet bristled, automatically defensive, but she told herself he was just trying to be helpful. She grabbed Teddy's ashes off the counter and remembered him as a cuddly puppy galloping after Wendy wherever she went.

"Vermont must be beautiful this time of year," Rivera said.

"I get your point, Mike."

She went back down the hall and stood in the bedroom doorway. Joshua turned to her, but he hadn't eased up even a notch. He raked a hand over his fair, close-cropped hair, his eyes as haunted and tired as she'd ever seen them, even when they were kids and a trooper had arrived at the door to tell them their father had been shot.

Wendy leaped off the bed and snatched the cracker tin from Juliet and held it tight, sobbing.

Joshua looked as if he, too, wanted to put his fist through the wall.

"Wendy has something to add to her statement," Juliet said.

"She told me." Suddenly, his eyes shone with tears, but his voice didn't crack — nothing else about him showed that he was about to lose it. "She'll talk to whomever she needs to. Then she wants to help clean up before we leave."

"That's not necessary —"

"She knows that."

Wendy lifted her eyes to her aunt. "You can come back to Vermont with us."

But it was Joshua who shook his head. "Juliet's got a job to do."

Nine

~:☙❦❧:~

He couldn't eat, he couldn't sleep.

As he picked out clothes in his walk-in closet, Ham kept catching his reflection in the full-length mirrors and wincing. Even before his kidnapping, he'd looked emaciated. He was skinny as hell. A string bean. A spaghetti noodle. *Unnaturally* thin, his mother had told him time and again.

Since his ordeal, his ribs poked out, and his skin color reminded him of a dead trout.

"Bobby Tatro's in custody. You can rest easy now."

Mia O'Farrell had delivered the news herself, reaching Ham on his private line at his parents' home in west Texas. She said she'd had nothing to do with Tatro's arrest and had no details. Before Ham could ask about Ethan, she'd ended the call.

A bolder person wouldn't have let her hang up, or at least would have tried to call her back.

Ham might be brilliant, but he wasn't bold.

He turned away from the mirrors and walked out into his bedroom suite with his clothes in his arms, wearing just boxer shorts, his knobby knees and bony feet all that kept his legs from looking like stilts. And the insect bites, still healing.

The diet those jackasses in Colombia had fed him was just enough to keep him alive. Unripened plantains, canned beans, pork fat. He didn't know how he'd survived nearly three weeks.

Thank God they hadn't tortured him. The threat was always there, hovering over him like an executioner's ax. Money — that was what they said they wanted. But Ham wasn't convinced. Snippets of conversation, whispers in Spanish and English, demeanors, stances, weapons. Things just didn't add up.

Then, Major Brooker arrived on the scene.

Ethan, the son Ham's parents had never had.

Ham pushed back his sense of failure and resentment and gratitude, an unholy mix of contradictory emotions, and pulled on a pair of Land's End jeans and a threadbare rugby shirt. He'd bypassed his wardrobe of expensive pieces from Neiman Marcus. Because of his ordeal, his parents wouldn't comment about his sub-par attire this time. He was their genius son who didn't care about money. They'd never understand him.

Why should they? He didn't understand himself.

He slipped into his twenty-dollar moccasin sneakers. His hair was long, straight and stringy, another bone of contention. He'd never make a very good Carhill. Although Ethan was an army officer, not a capitalist, he was a West Point graduate. He'd fought terrorists. He'd captured bad guys.

Ham had gotten himself shoved into a jeep at gunpoint.

His parents didn't know he'd provided information to the government that had saved lives — not that they'd be impressed. They'd call him a do-gooder. They'd tell him that kind of work should be left to others. Risking his life on a daring adventure was one thing. He'd come across as devil-may-care and manly. But his work for Mia O'Farrell they'd consider an unnecessary risk — not just of his life, but of the family name, their privacy, their stability, their fortune.

Suddenly he felt claustrophobic, although his bedroom suite was three times bigger than Tatro's hut. It'd had no running water, no electricity. They'd used generators. And the bathroom facilities consisted of an outhouse swarming with insects.

Five years ago, Ham's parents had moved out of their house on their thousand acres in west Texas, razed it, then built their current monstrosity. It had a turret and towers, an art gallery, a media room with stadium seating and a popcorn-maker. Everything was very expensive and not all that tasteful.

If not for Carhill money, Ham knew he could never have afforded to spend the past two years in South America. His parents had expected him to stay in safe, rich enclaves, but he'd had his own agenda — his own dreams. Unfortunately those dreams had landed him in Tatro's hands, and now he was getting the big "I told you so." Not in as many words, because his parents didn't really know all the details. But he understood the subtext of what they were saying.

No more of this shit or he was out of the will.

They didn't know about Mia O'Farrell.

Ham walked down the massive curving stairs to the main level of the ostentatious house. If it glittered and sparkled and dripped — and cost a lot — his mother liked it. His father trusted her taste completely, which, in Ham's estimation, was a mistake.

His mother emerged from behind a Greek-looking statue. Ham had no idea if it was real or a quality fake. He felt that way about his mother sometimes. Faye Carhill, wife, hostess and benefactor. What about her was real, what was fake? Ham wasn't sure anymore.

She had on a pale pink knit suit with diamond studs in her ears. She was ash-blond, slim and agile from her private Pilates and yoga classes. Although she wouldn't admit it, Ham got his thinness from her side of the family. His height came from his father's side. The two traits didn't fit that well together, and the result was their awkward son. Ham didn't know where his IQ came from. Probably a genetic quirk.

"Luke and Dorrie Brooker are joining us for dinner tonight," she said.

Ethan's older brother and wife. Ham tried to look nonchalant. "Just them?"

"Yes, Luke's folks are in Denver."

"What about Ethan?"

His mother winced. Although she'd have claimed him as her own in a heartbeat, she liked to pretend that Ethan made her nervous, especially since Char's death and his brush with international killers — and, even worse, international headlines. If the Carhills feared anything, it was notoriety — getting sucked into the public eye in ways they couldn't control, becoming part of a media feeding frenzy.

"He won't be here. I don't even know where he is these days."

The Brookers were multigenerational Texas ranchers with a working ranch up the road. They weren't as rich as the Carhills, but few were.

Although he was still uncertain how much his parents had surmised about his ordeal, Ham knew they didn't want to talk about it. For them, it was over. He'd told them he'd run into some trouble in Colombia on a side trip to check out emerald mines. Whatever else they knew or had gleaned on their own, they at least pretended his explanation satisfied them. Beyond asking him about his health, there'd been no questions.

"Are you all right?" His mother touched a cool hand to his cheek. "I worry about you."

"You shouldn't."

"Your father's in the library if you want to see him."

"I thought I'd take a walk."

"It's hot out —"

"The heat won't bother me."

She looked pained, as if she didn't know what to say. For both his parents, Ham was an unfulfilled promise, someone they didn't quite know how to include. Explain. *Accept.*

"No," she said finally, "I suppose it wouldn't."

Pretending not to hear her, Ham detoured past the library, avoiding his father, and went out the back door, onto a terraced patio they seldom used. He walked to the edge of the kidney-shaped pool, its perfect, clear water shimmering blue under the late afternoon sun.

What had Bobby Tatro wanted in New York?

Why go to Juliet Longstreet's apartment? Ham knew all about her and Ethan from their earlier exploits. She was a marshal. What did Tatro consider worth the risk that she'd catch him?

Had he acted on his own?

The last was Ham's central question. In the days since his release, as he regained his health and grew stronger, less fearful, he found it more and more difficult to believe that Bobby Tatro had thought up, planned and executed Ham's kidnapping all on his own. That its only purpose was financial gain.

The emeralds.

Ham stared down into the shimmering water, wondering what his mother would do if he peeled off all his clothes and jumped naked into the pool. Maybe that was what his parents did when no one else was around — went skinny-dipping. He smiled at the thought. But it didn't do anything for the overwhelming guilt and embarrassment that had gripped him since Ethan had burst into his hut and rescued him. Ethan didn't deserve to get sucked into the mess that was Ham's life.

Now, home safe, everything felt wrong to him.

To his father, winning was everything. Johnson Carhill would do whatever he had to do to limit the effect of his son's ordeal on him, his wife, their reputation and their money. Correction; damage control wouldn't be enough. He'd want to come out ahead.

And as Ham well knew, the repercussions wouldn't matter. Only getting his way.

The five-hour trip from Juliet's apartment on the Upper West Side to Vermont was too long for Wendy to go without eating, but she refused to touch even the rice cakes Joshua had brought with him that morning. They were organic *and* vegan, but she said she wasn't hungry. That much he understood. He wasn't hungry, either.

It was dark when they arrived back at Longstreet Landscaping, the house lit, Spaceshot drumming up just enough energy to waddle out to greet them. One of Wendy's goals during her stay with her grandparents was to help their overweight dog slim down.

But she didn't move to get out of the truck, the tin with Teddy's ashes cradled in both arms as she stared out her window at the wooden trailer of pumpkins.

Joshua turned off the engine. "Wendy?"

"I'm remembering his knife," she said in a barely audible whisper, her voice calm, almost toneless. "There was blood on it."

"Wendy . . . honey, I'm sorry."

"The blood was still wet. It — it was Juan's blood. I'd just talked to him."

Joshua tightened his fingers around his truck keys, hating that his daughter now had such an image in her mind, hating his inability to erase it. "I can hook you up with someone to talk to about what you experienced."

She shot him a look. "Does that mean *you* don't want to talk to me?"

"I'll listen to you anytime, Wendy. I just mean that there are doctors who can help someone who's experienced a trauma —"

"I didn't experience a trauma." She whipped back around to her window, her shoulders stiff. "Juan did. He's the one who's dead."

"I'm sorry —"

"Why should you be sorry? You didn't kill him. If I'd only said something about the man in the diner. He knew my name. It was weird — I *knew* it was weird. If I'd only told Juliet — if I'd warned Juan someone might be spying on him —"

"It might not have changed a thing."

"That's what she said."

Wendy pushed open her door and jumped out, running for the house.

Joshua couldn't remember ever feeling so exhausted and damn helpless. He followed her up the driveway. His legs ached. He patted Spaceshot on the head. "You don't have any answers, either, do you, old boy?"

But he could hear how haunted he sounded. His daughter's wide-eyed trip to New York to see her aunt — her little act of rebellion, filled with optimism and possibilities — had changed her life forever.

At least the Longstreets, all of them, would understand that much. They'd seen their share of violence, accidents, traumas — they'd all had that moment of abrupt change, of lost innocence.

After a crisis, his mother liked to make chicken and dumplings, but when Joshua entered the warm kitchen, he saw that she'd dished up a plate of pasta primavera.

But Wendy had run into the half bath to throw up.

"It's vegan," she said, setting the plate on the table.

"It's not you."

She took a deep breath and nodded with an understanding she didn't want, had never wanted. People said Anne Longstreet could take anything. But she'd only asked for a simple life, cooking and knitting, growing things in her garden.

Joshua had called her on their way back to Vermont and told her they'd be back in time for supper. His family knew that Wendy had skipped off to New York and Joshua had gone to fetch her. Unless they'd had the news on, they wouldn't know about Bobby Tatro. In recent months, Juliet's life had become more complicated — and dangerous — than ever. Now it had affected the most sensitive and sheltered of the Longstreet grandchildren.

"Joshua?" His mother's eyes narrowed on him. "What is it? What's happened?"

Another car pulled into the driveway. Paul, the town cop. He'd probably know about Tatro by now. He'd have called Joshua's brothers and told their father, and they'd all be at the house soon, wanting details, providing support, hashing out anything any of them needed to do. Not just for Wendy. For Juliet, too. Except she wouldn't want their help. She never had because their help was always laced with criticism.

Joshua pointed to a chair. "Have a seat, Ma. We can wait for the others —"

"We're not waiting. Tell me now. Why is Wendy throwing up? Why are you as white as a sheet?"

He knew he couldn't keep silent and told her. She listened without interruption, Paul standing in the doorway, Jeff and Sam following him inside, then Will. And, finally, Will, Sr., the family patriarch, his limp more pronounced tonight.

Joshua had seen people overcome tragedy and violence in his own family.

He'd just wanted his daughter to be exempt, at least for a while longer.

Juliet called an Upper West Side pet store that specialized in rescuing unwanted animals and had them come for her surviving fish. They sent a sanctimonious college student who seemed to think she'd kicked the hell out of her fish tanks in some kind of rage. She didn't enlighten him, just let him scoop the survivors into plastic containers and bags. She gave him all her food and supplies and added a tip to the rescue fee.

Her apartment felt empty without the gurgle of the tanks and the rhythmic motion — even the variety of colors — of her fish. She didn't really know how she'd come to have so many. Freda hadn't seemed to mind.

The place smelled of fish water, Pine-Sol, wet wood and sweat. Bobby Tatro's body odor lingered. Juliet opened the living room windows to let in some air.

And she spotted Ethan getting out of a cab.

She phoned the private security guard the building managers had hired until they could figure out what to do about a new doorman, and vouched for Ethan.

When Juliet opened her door for him, Ethan sniffed the rank air and made a face.

"Smells like ultraclean dead fish. Let's get out of here. I'll buy us dinner."

"Plan on doing some talking."

He didn't answer, and she noticed that he was clean and not as ragged-looking. He had on fresh jeans, the brown leather coat, the silver belt buckle, the boots.

"I don't know why I trust you," she said.

"What did you do with the fish?"

"Sent them to a rescue shelter."

"There's a shelter for fish?"

"They take care of all kinds of animals."

"Only in New York."

She thought she heard a hint of humor in his tone, but it didn't show in his face.

"What about your friend who owns this place?" he asked.

"Freda didn't take the news well. She wants me out by the end of next week. The sooner the better." Juliet nodded to the damp floor. "The couple downstairs got flooded. They're not real happy with her or with me."

"Never mind the murdered doorman and the traumatized teenager."

"I don't think they're happy about them, either, but their waterlogged apartment is easier to grasp."

"You're nicer than I am."

She almost smiled then. "What have I

been saying ever since I met you?"

He took her face in both his hands, catching her by surprise. He'd never touched her that way before. There'd been sparks between them from the first, but he'd been on the trail of his wife's murderers, out of control, breaking all the rules. Juliet had warned herself — she'd warned *him* — that he needed to get a grip before his guilt and regrets destroyed him. He couldn't escape the cauldron of memories and questions and so many things he couldn't change. What he hadn't done. What he should have done. How far he and his now-dead wife had let their marriage suffer because of the demands of their work.

"Damn," he said. "I'm sorry about what happened today."

Juliet noticed that his dark eyes were soft in the dim light, perhaps an optical illusion. "It wasn't your fault."

"I don't know. Maybe it was." He wound a short, thick blond curl around one finger. "I'm glad your niece is okay."

He kissed her then, on the lips, gently, but not tentative — nothing about him, Juliet thought, was tentative.

Ethan stood back, studying her a moment. "Sorry. I shouldn't have taken advantage."

"You didn't." She straightened, rubbing the back of her neck, awkward, wanting to kiss him again. "I guess it's just as well we're going out for dinner."

"Or?"

"Never mind. I'm light-headed." She caught herself. "Not from the kiss, either."

"Whatever you say, Marshal."

That laconic Texas accent, that superfit body — she needed air, fast. She grabbed her jacket off the back of a chair and slung it over one arm, not feeling even remotely chilly. "We can go to the place where we met last night."

"Works for me. Your niece?"

"Safely home in Vermont by now." Juliet ripped open the door, pictured Tatro shoving Wendy into the apartment. "I don't know what I was thinking, having fish."

"Juliet —"

"Yet, if I hadn't — I don't know what would have happened to Wendy today."

"You know better than to go down that road."

She nodded, pushing out into the hall. "Would have, could have, should have. Yes. I do know." She banged the down button for the elevator, keeping her eyes on it as Ethan came up next to her. "We can't go

186

back and undo what's done. None of us."

He leaned against the wall. "Knowing I can't do a thing to change something that's happened doesn't make me feel any better."

"It's not about feeling better. It's about acceptance —" She broke off, wishing she hadn't gotten herself started. The man had lost his wife. Who was she to tell him how he should feel? All she needed to do was picture Wendy coming out of the bedroom with Bobby Tatro cuffed and muttering things into the floor. "Forget it. I don't know what I'm talking about."

She stayed a step ahead of him. The night air was cool and clear, with just a hint of autumn, a breath of nostalgia, although for what, Juliet couldn't pinpoint. The life she hadn't led, she supposed. The paths not taken.

At the restaurant, she asked for a table by the window and looked out at the pedestrians walking slowly on the street outside, enjoying the beautiful fall evening.

"Joe Collins and Mike Rivera both want to talk to you," she said without looking at Ethan.

He ordered Jack Daniel's on the rocks. "I figured as much."

She almost seconded his order, then

opted for sparkling water. "How was Washington?"

"I slept for twelve hours in a comfortable bed."

"You weren't there to catch up on your sleep."

He pointed to the menu. "I think you should order the mac and cheese. Comfort food. It'll be easy on your stomach."

"I'm not sure it goes with chardonnay."

"Mac and cheese goes with anything."

"Or chardonnay does," she said. "Collins and Rivera both think you're trouble. So do *I*, for that matter. Gee, I wonder why."

"You told them —"

"Everything. I play by the rules."

"No, you don't. You'd never have been in Tennessee that day if you played by the rules. You'd never have let me into your apartment last month. You wouldn't have told me about Bobby Tatro —"

"What I told you didn't help you. Don't pretend it did."

"It will yet."

She leaned over the table. "Stay out of this case, Brooker."

He shrugged, obviously not particularly affected by her intensity or her authority. "You're a little late with the orders, Marshal."

Calling her "marshal" was just to tweak her, to pull her out of her unfocused anger. But thoughts of Juan, Wendy, Tatro, the fish, the dead dog's ashes on her counter, the frustrated and terrified neighbors, the soon-to-be ex-friend in L.A. — began to weigh on her, and she knew she should be off on a five-mile run, not sitting in a restaurant with a man who'd spin her around until she collapsed before he told her one damn thing he hadn't meant to tell her.

"You've been through SERE training, haven't you?" Juliet asked him.

"Survival, Evasion, Resistance, Escape. Yes, ma'am."

"Ever been captured by the enemy?"

He didn't answer.

"Not something you want to talk about in an Upper West Side restaurant." She didn't feel her tension easing. "I'm not playing games with you, Brooker. I don't care what you can't or won't tell me. I'll find out what I want to know. A man was murdered today. *I'm* responsible."

His eyes flickered with sudden intensity. "You're not responsible."

The water and bourbon arrived. He ordered a steak. When Juliet couldn't make up her mind — couldn't concentrate on the damn menu — he told the waiter to bring her the macaroni and cheese.

Ethan picked up his drink, took a small swallow, then set it back down. "I thought by coming up here yesterday I might stop something from happening, not cause something."

"You had no idea Tatro was in New York?"

"No."

Juliet squeezed the juice out of the lime that came with her water, briefly wondering what it would be like to have a normal dinner with Ethan, if that were even possible. "Wendy ran into him yesterday afternoon, before I even knew she was here." She relayed what her niece had told her, watching him for his reaction. But there was none. Whatever he felt, he kept it under the surface, out of sight, out of her reach — perhaps out of his own. "When you saw Wendy at my building —"

"I didn't see Tatro." He picked up his glass and stared at his bourbon, as if it held answers he didn't have. "I was fucking clueless."

His emotion — his guilt — caught Juliet off guard. "You weren't alone."

"Doesn't help."

"Wendy can put Tatro in the area yesterday, but we don't know he actually overheard her with Juan and learned her name that way."

"How else?"

"A dozen different possibilities, none of them any more enticing. I'm trying to deal in facts, not speculation." Except she'd been mired in speculation for hours, frustrating herself, berating herself, getting nowhere. "From where you were standing yesterday, could you hear Wendy give Juan her name?"

He shook his head. "I was too far away. If I'd realized she was your niece, on her own, I'd have stayed put. Hell, I could have followed her to the diner. Either Tatro would have thought better of sitting next to her or I'd have caught him —" He set his glass down, bourbon splashing onto his hand. "A moot point now."

"I don't know why Tatro had to kill Juan. He could have just knocked him out cold." Juliet focused on a young woman, maybe twenty, walking a cocker spaniel. Living a normal life. "Killing him seems extreme."

"Tatro's an extreme person."

Juliet looked away.

"He was put away on a nonviolent charge," Ethan continued, "but he's not a nonviolent man."

"He thinks I broke the rules when I arrested him." She turned again, facing Ethan. "That's why he hates me so much. He thinks everyone should follow the rules but him."

"Is he right? Did you break the rules?"

"No. Not really. I just didn't run into him at Wal-Mart by accident. I had a source."

Ethan leaned back in his chair, studying her a moment. "You protected your source."

"It was an eleven-year-old girl, his girlfriend's daughter. Carmel. She plays the violin." Juliet ran a fingertip around the rim of her water glass, remembering the girl's terrified voice on the other end of the phone. "Tatro got mad at the mother. To punish her, he tortured the family dog."

"That was the last straw for the girl?"

Juliet nodded. "She begged me not to tell anyone. She'll be looking over her shoulder her whole life as it is."

"Eleven years old."

"I was climbing trees at that age."

"Tatro's a sadist. He knows you've seen through him, and he can't stand it." Ethan sighed, but there was no surprise in his expression — he knew there were people out there who tortured dogs in front of little girls. "Did the dog live?"

"Yes. And last I checked, Carmel was first violin in her high school orchestra."

"The makings of a happy ending." But nothing about Ethan looked happy — or finished. "Why did Tatro show up at your apartment when he did? You were at work. If he wanted to get to you, he'd have picked a time when you were more likely to be home."

"I suppose he could have planned to hide and wait for me —"

"With the dead doorman?"

"Juan was in his office. Given Tatro's grandiosity, he could have thought he had all the time he needed." Their meals arrived, steaming, giving off good, homey smells that made Juliet want to turn in her badge, pack up her belongings, move back to Vermont and plant tulips. "Wendy returned to my apartment this morning spontaneously — no way could Tatro have expected her."

"He could have been hanging around on your street and seized the moment when she showed up."

"Maybe."

"But you don't think so."

She tried the mac and cheese. It was hot and gooey, but she knew she wouldn't eat much of it. "He was hanging around yesterday. Could he have followed you?"

Ethan shook his head without hesitation. "No."

"Well, Tatro's not talking. He might yet, but we've got him for murder — he'll clam up, use whatever he can to cut himself any kind of deal. It won't work, but he's not going to be forthcoming anytime soon." She set down her fork, the rich food sitting like lead in her stomach.

Ethan dug into his steak with his fork and knife, but Juliet could see he wasn't any hungrier than she was.

"How big a payday did you spoil for Tatro?" she asked.

"I don't have a figure."

"A guess?"

He smiled. "I'm trying to deal only in facts."

"Could he have known you came to me for information on him?"

"Possibly, but I doubt it. As far as I know, he was out of the country when you and I were having our chat in the rain."

She remembered his comment about sun-kissed cafés and roses and bougainvillea, and felt a surge of warmth, but it didn't last. Uncertainty crept in, anger, frustration. It could all have been talk, utter bullshit, manipulation.

"I told Mike Rivera you were solid," she said. "He knows it. We all do. Rivera just has his doubts about your impact on my life."

"With good reason."

"Ethan —"

"I'm sorry, Juliet. Sorry for everything."

He gave up on his steak, took a small sip of his drink, his eyes shifting to an elderly woman making her way down the street on a cane, smiling broadly at no one in particular. He seemed transfixed. Juliet thought of their kiss, then quickly pushed it out of her mind.

"What happened today wasn't your doing," Ethan reiterated.

Juliet pictured Wendy scooping up traumatized fish and quickly took a gulp of water, but the wedge of lime somehow landed half up her nose. She almost dropped the glass, fighting tears, irritated with herself because she couldn't think straight, couldn't put together her questions, a timeline — anything that would help her figure out what Tatro wanted and what it had to do with the man sitting at the table with her.

She pushed her glass aside. "I have no right to blame you for anything."

"If Tatro wanted to kill your doorman or

your niece, he could have done it yesterday. He didn't have to wait until today."

"You're saying he wanted me, except that doesn't make sense because I wasn't there."

"I'm not saying anything. I'm just telling you what I know."

"No, you're not. You're not telling me *half* of what you know."

Their waiter stopped by their table to refill their water glasses, but took a step back in shock. Juliet made herself smile up at him. "It's okay. We're not —"

"You're the federal agent whose doorman was murdered this morning." He seemed both repulsed and fascinated. "But you got the guy who did it, right?"

She nodded. "We did."

He glanced around, as if expecting Juliet and Ethan might have attracted some other violent offender, then seemed to catch himself. "What a hell of a thing, killing a doorman." He took their dinner plates and retreated as fast as he could.

"We should go," Juliet said.

Ethan nodded, checking his watch. "We've got an hour before I have to be downtown to chat with Rivera and Collins."

She gave him a long look. "Like being a step ahead of me, do you?"

"I called Rivera from the airport. Just aiming to make your life easier."

"Ha. Where are you staying tonight? Got that figured out?"

"I was thinking your futon."

"Uh-uh. It's still soaked from the broken fish tanks."

He smiled at her from across the table. "How convenient."

Ten

~:⊙⊛:~

Mia's cell phone vibrated in her coat pocket, its ring on mute, as she sipped a very hot latte at the Barnes & Noble on M Street in Georgetown, not far from her apartment. It was jam-packed this Friday night. She'd extricated herself from her office at eight — earlier than usual — and had decided to indulge herself, pretend she had a normal life. But in Washington, that would just make her boring.

The number read out as private. Not unusual, but her heart still jumped.

"Dr. O'Farrell. How are you this fine evening?"

She recognized the voice on the other end immediately. "Was that you last night? Threatening me, trying to scare the hell out of me —"

"I'm not sure where your loyalties lie. You're conflicted. Your actions lack a clarity of purpose." He paused, then added, "Don't be surprised if people jump to the wrong conclusions about you."

She bit back a sharp retort — she didn't want him to hang up on her. "If you and I had a chance to meet, I might be able to alleviate some of your concerns."

"Where are you now? Holed up in some dank D.C. office building?"

"Look —" Mia glanced around at the crowded bookstore, but no one was paying attention to her. An urgent cell-phone call in D.C. Big deal. "It's time we met. You've made an extraordinary contribution to your country —"

"You were supposed to keep me in the loop about your Special Forces guy. He's not the hero you all think he is. He has his own agenda."

Mia frowned. "You were there? In Colombia when —" She stopped herself from saying too much. *My God,* she thought. *Was he one of the kidnappers? Had he played her to that extent?*

He gave a snort of pure contempt. "You said all the right words and pretended you trusted me. You used what I gave you. Then, when it mattered most, you kept me in the dark. Why?"

"It was out of my hands. I don't even know who you are — I have no way to contact you." Mia kept her voice low, trying not to look conspiratorial or unnerved; she wasn't eager to draw attention to herself. "I'm not in a good place to talk right now —"

"I gave you *everything.* You'd never have found your genius Texan without me. I'm the one who told you Brooker could ID him. I'm the one who told you Tatro was obsessed with a blond, female marshal. Hell, half the shit Carhill gave you was because of me."

Mia didn't know about that last comment. The rest was true. She dipped the top of her pinkie into the foam of her latte. She didn't have a name, a face, a recording of his voice. Background information. She had nothing. But the man on the other end of the connection had led her to Ham Carhill's kidnappers.

He'd manipulated her. And he was doing it again.

"What you need to understand is this," she said coldly. "I'm not on your side or any other individual's side. I work for the people."

"Now we're on the same page, Dr. O'Farrell. I'll be in touch."

"You don't make the rules —"

He disconnected.

Mia shakily returned her phone to her pocket.

She'd known her lofty words would ring true to him.

A righteous voice on the other end of the phone. That was all she knew about him.

But he'd given her useful information since he'd first contacted her over the summer. Mia had assumed that his extreme views of the world and human nature put him in places where he sometimes happened on interesting tidbits. Perhaps his success — his access to her — had emboldened him. It didn't necessarily make him more competent or dangerous.

She left a tip for her latte and bought a book on her way out, a special edition of *The Three Musketeers.* She preferred unambiguous good guys and bad guys. Her vigilante was neither.

The shrill ring of her telephone bolted Juliet out of a deep sleep. Reaching for it, she struck a warm, hard body and damn near screamed.

Ethan.

Oh, my.

He was naked, the early morning light catching the black graphic tattoo on his upper arm. He'd thrown off his half of the blanket sometime during the night. Or had never bothered with it, seeing how the two of them had heated themselves up quite nicely.

The memory of their lovemaking — wild, uninhibited — rushed over her. There'd been a lot of sex last night. Not a lot of talking.

No thinking.

He was wide awake. "Going to shoot me or answer the phone?"

She grabbed the sheet to cover herself, although she didn't know why. He'd touched every part of her only a few hours ago. She could still feel the sensation of his mouth and hands on her skin.

"Lord, Brooker. How much wine did I have last night?"

"You had sparkling water."

The phone rang again, and she reached across his chest and picked up the receiver. "Longstreet," she said, her voice raspy from sleep and what had turned into a very long day — and night.

"It's Rivera. You up?"

It was six o'clock in the morning. "More or less."

"Get down here. Your doorman gave you a phony ID."

Any sleepiness left her. "What?"

"Bring Brooker."

"What makes you think he's here?"

Rivera had hung up. Juliet clicked off the phone and dropped it at the foot of her bed, raking a hand through her hair. "I've got to think." She spoke more to herself than to Ethan. *"Damn."*

She still had the sheet with her when she climbed out of bed. Ethan ended up exposed, leaning back against his pillow, watching her. He was tanned and very fit and not at all awkward or self-conscious about being in her bed.

Juliet spun around at him. "Get dressed. We're going downtown. We've been summoned." She ripped open a drawer and pulled out jeans, a long-sleeved T-shirt, then dug in another drawer for socks. "Juan isn't who he said he was."

Ethan rolled out of bed without comment. He had his belt buckled and his boots on before she'd fastened her bra. "You don't waste any time, do you?"

He shrugged. "Habit."

She remembered the life he'd led for so long. "Are you on leave?"

"I guess. Technically."

What more hadn't he told her, Rivera and Joe Collins?

He withdrew a folded piece of paper from a back pocket of his jeans and opened it onto her bed. Juliet saw that it was a copy of Bobby Tatro's doctored picture of her.

She finished dressing. "You made a copy?"

"It seemed like a good idea at the time."

"You knew you were giving me the original — you figured you might not see it again. Ethan —" She sighed at him. "You don't want to annoy Rivera and Collins."

He smiled. "Too late."

"Meddling in or impeding a federal investigation isn't a real good idea. I don't care who you've got covering your butt in Washington."

He let her comment stand and tapped his copy of her picture. "No doorman in the background. I was thinking Tatro took the picture, but I don't know. Anything pinpoint the timing for you?"

"My jeans," she said.

"They look good on you."

"They're the same ones I'm wearing now. I bought them and my leather jacket in late August."

"In New York?"

She nodded. "They're expensive, but I indulged because they fit so well. You have no idea what it's like for a woman to find the perfect pair of jeans. I hate shopping, so when I do finally drag myself to a store,

I make myself try on stuff. If it fits, I buy it. Especially pants."

Juliet stared at her image, recalling the dressing room at Saks, checking the fit of the jeans in the mirror. Ethan had just exited from her life, again, after the capture of the international assassin he'd been hunting.

She'd spent too much money on clothes that day.

"I was still thinking I'd make it to Tennessee for Nate Winter and Sarah Dunnemore's wedding." She pulled on her holster and Glock. "Look at the angle of the shot. Whoever took my picture wasn't in my face." She got her leather jacket. "Sure it wasn't you?"

"No, ma'am." Ethan moved in close to her. "I'd have been in your face. You're grasping."

Juliet took a breath. What the hell was wrong with her? "Ethan —"

She shut her eyes a moment, the full range of emotions and physical sensations of last night rushing over her. He'd taken her with the mindless ferocity of a man with nothing to lose and nothing to gain — with no thought of the past or the future. To think they had a relationship — a romance — going, she knew, was pure self-delusion.

When she looked at him again, he hadn't moved. "You're right. I'm grasping. But if you took the picture and Tatro just happened on it and had his fun, it wouldn't be so damn creepy." She tried to smile. "It'd just be irritating."

They took her truck, traffic light early on a Saturday morning. When they arrived at the USMS office, Mike Rivera was scowling at a grayish cup of coffee. "My powder creamer didn't melt. It looks like a debris field."

Juliet perked up. "There's coffee?"

"If you want to call it that."

With that ringing endorsement, Ethan passed, but she ducked out, grabbed the Big Apple mug off her desk and headed for the coffeemaker. But even she couldn't drink its contents. Deciding against making a fresh pot and leaving Rivera and Ethan alone for too long, she switched off the power and rejoined them.

She sat on one of the plastic chairs in front of Rivera's desk. Ethan, she noticed, stayed on his feet. "Have you got a legit ID for Juan?" she asked.

Rivera shook his head. "Nothing's turned up. When did he start as your doorman?"

"First of September."

"Before or after Tatro was released from prison?"

"I'm not sure. After, I think, but only by a matter of days. The building managers hired him. They must have checked references —"

"Collins is looking into it. What kind of doorman was this guy?"

"Efficient, pleasant. We all liked him."

"Well, who knows. Being a John Doe doesn't mean he's tied into this thing." Rivera pinned his gaze on Brooker, who seemed to expect a higher level of scrutiny now that a man had turned up dead. "You got a look at the doorman?"

"Yes, sir. I saw him Thursday afternoon. Same time I saw Juliet's niece."

"Why'd you stop at her building in the first place?"

"In case she was taking the day off."

Rivera drummed his fingers on the edge of his desk. "You didn't want to try here first. Thought you might get lucky."

Ethan shrugged without answering.

"Or," Rivera went on, "you were on Tatro's trail."

Juliet angled Ethan a sharp look. "Were you?"

"Not specifically, no." He spoke directly to Rivera. "I was in New York to give Juliet the picture Tatro had of her."

The chief deputy didn't seem convinced.

Juliet shifted in her chair. "If Tatro wanted to hurt me, he could have beat me over the head or broken into my apartment any time during the past month since he got out of prison. Why wait until yesterday? Why wait until I wasn't home? Even if he and 'Juan' were working together, same thing. They had a month."

Rivera grunted. "If Tatro and the doorman were working together, the doorman must have done something to piss Tatro off." He picked up a pen and twirled it between his fingers like a baton. "As far as I can see, Major Brooker, you're the trigger — the catalyst. You and this rescue mission of yours."

Ethan had provided some details to Rivera and Collins last night. Colombia. The rescue of an American contractor of interest at the highest levels of the U.S. government.

He'd never used the words *hostage* or *kidnapping.*

And he never said who'd invited him to participate in the mission. He didn't define his role, but Juliet surmised that he'd led a handpicked rescue team — he was an officer, he was experienced, and he was the type. Their job was to get their guy out of there, not figure out what had happened and who was responsible. They hadn't had a lot of time, and there was no room for mistakes.

"Bobby Tatro didn't take Juliet's picture," Ethan said. "He was in Colombia. Check. You'll find out he took a flight from Newark to Miami to Bogotá on the Friday of Labor Day weekend."

Rivera lifted a brow. "We'll check. Return flight?"

"None that I'm aware of."

"You ever put your eyes on him when you were down there?"

Ethan shook his head.

"But you have confirmation —"

"No. Not the kind you mean."

"Your rescued American," Juliet said. "He confirmed Tatro's involvement in the kidnapping, didn't he?"

Ethan glanced at her but didn't answer.

"Unless he was deliberately misleading you —"

"You mean unless he was lying," Ethan said.

"Was he?"

"I don't know. My guess? He wasn't in any condition to lie, but he's smart — smarter than the rest of us. It's not out of the question."

209

"Where's your guy now?" Rivera asked abruptly.

"Home."

It was an insufficient answer, and Rivera took in a sharp breath through his nostrils, which was never a good sign. Juliet sat forward in her chair. "Tatro knew my niece's name in the coffee shop on Thursday," she said. "What if he didn't overhear her and Juan talking? What if Juan told him?"

"It'll be interesting to see what Tatro has to say." Rivera absently took a gulp of coffee, apparently having forgotten how bad it was, and nearly spit it out. He set the mug hard on his desk. "I want a name, Brooker. Someone in Washington I can call. Someone who can talk."

"I'll pass along your name and number."

Rivera swore under his breath but didn't push any further, then shifted his attention back to Juliet, his black eyes softening ever so slightly. "It'll ease your niece's mind to know your doorman didn't die because he was trying to protect her."

He didn't bother asking more questions, raising more possibilities, just kicked Juliet and Ethan out of his office and told them to stay in touch.

Juliet nearly ripped the door off its hinges climbing into her truck. She stabbed the key into the ignition. "I'm giving you the benefit of the doubt and concluding that the concussion you got in August when you fell into Ravenkill Creek affected your brain. That's why you slept with me *before* telling me you'd figured out the doorman was involved in this mess."

"I'm not that complicated, Juliet." Ethan pulled his door shut as the engine started. "Mostly I was just thinking about sleeping with you."

"There's more." She jammed the truck into gear. "There's a *lot* more you're not telling us."

"I think that's clear."

"This rescue mission was a black op. Off the radar." She jammed into Reverse and hit the gas too hard, screeching out of her space, then braking hard, glaring at him. "It's *my* niece who was terrorized yesterday, *my* apartment that was ransacked, *my* fish that are dead and put up for adoption —"

"Juliet."

She ignored him, shifted into second gear. "And I'm the one you just screwed."

"Maybe that was a mistake," he said quietly.

Her eyes burned with fatigue, frustration, unreasonable anger. "Maybe it was."

She wondered if Char Brooker had known even half of what her husband had done in the line of duty. An army intelligence officer herself, she still wouldn't necessarily be privy to his missions. Even with the post-9/11 intelligence reforms, operational security would still prevent him from giving her details she didn't need to have.

Juliet realized just how little she knew about the man sitting next to her.

Ethan said nothing on the drive back to the Upper West Side. Once in her apartment, he washed up and got his stuff together. Juliet looked at her rumpled sheets — the fitted sheet was half off — and tried to find it in herself to regret last night. But she couldn't, and she didn't.

She stood in her bedroom doorway, arms crossed on her chest as Ethan walked past her into the hall. "Wendy said Tatro's eyes were stone-cold with hatred. She'd never seen anything like them."

Ethan stopped and tucked a short curl, one of about a thousand sticking out, behind her ear. "You need a chance to clear your head." His voice was steady, without even a hint of an edgy undertone. "Take a shower, get something to eat."

"I'm making a pot of coffee."

She didn't ask him to stay. He didn't offer.

When he was gone, Juliet latched the dead-bolt behind him. Fatigue overwhelmed her. She pictured Wendy, alone, sneaking back for her dead dog's ashes and ending up in a fight for her life.

"Hell."

Juliet headed for the kitchen and the coffeepot. If making love to Ethan last night had been an act of madness, she thought, then so be it. She was entitled.

Eleven

～∴☙❦∴～

Spaceshot trundled behind Wendy to the apple orchard on the hill above the house, making her feel better because usually he would stay flopped down on the driveway in the sun. He seemed to sense that she needed company. He was uncritical, uncomplaining. And he didn't hover. Her grandmother, her father — they'd been hovering since she got back yesterday and barfed up her guts.

Her grandfather, who'd been shot when she was still a baby, told his wife and eldest son to give her some space. Wendy had never felt such a sense of solidarity with him. Usually he was all about Longstreet landscaping, drainage and plantings and what trucks and bulldozers were on the fritz, or about talking cop stuff — but he hadn't asked her to take him through what'd happened in New York yesterday. He had the story from her dad. That was enough.

Wendy set her half-bushel basket under a

tree laden with fat, ripe apples. Cortland, perfect for applesauce and pies. The air was crisp, the morning sun sparkling on the bright leaves on the hills around her. Her father had taken the day off and said he was there if she needed him for anything. But she didn't want to think about yesterday. She wanted to pick apples.

She patted Spaceshot's head. "Why don't you go find a rabbit to chase? The exercise will do you good." She made a face. "Just don't catch it and eat it."

But the dog dropped into the tall grass and stretched out, summoning just enough energy to wag his tail.

Wendy started collecting the apples she could reach by standing on tiptoe. She picked one, then another, then stopped, taking a deep breath. Tears formed in her eyes. She blamed the cool temperature and the breeze. Her hands shook slightly — she'd had oatmeal with chopped nuts and apples for breakfast. Her grandmother had offered to scramble her some eggs.

A cluster of perfect apples teased her, just beyond her reach. Determined to stick to her task — to not weaken and succumb to her fears — Wendy hoisted herself onto a rough-barked branch, working her way out to the alluring apples. The branch hardly even moved under her weight. There were tools she could have used to reach the apples high in the tree, but she wanted to use her hands.

Spaceshot stirred. "Easy, boy," a man's voice said.

Peeking through the leaves of her branch, Wendy saw Matt Kelleher stepping around the dog, who hadn't troubled himself to get up.

Kelleher, in jeans and a sports sweatshirt, squinted up at her in the tree. "Need some help?"

"Not really, but thanks."

He raised both hands toward her. "Here. I can take those apples and put them in your basket."

Sprawled out on her branch, her legs hooked around it for balance, Wendy lowered the two apples she'd picked down to him.

"These are beauties," he said.

"Aren't they? There are a couple more —"

"I can get them."

But any help took the fun out of her adventure. She didn't say anything as he reached up and plucked the two remaining apples from her elusive cluster, then dropped them into her basket. He was tall enough that he didn't need to climb up into the tree.

"I'm sorry about what happened yesterday," Matt said. "I hope you didn't go to New York because of something I said."

"No, I'd been wanting to do it for a while."

He didn't seem convinced. "Your grandmother asked me to check on you," he said.

"I haven't been gone thirty minutes —"

"She says it's been an hour. She can't help but worry."

Wendy sat up on her branch and sighed. "I suppose not. Is my dad back?"

"Just pulled into the driveway when I left."

Great, she thought without enthusiasm. Although she did want to see him. She couldn't explain it. He'd slept on the couch in the living room last night — he wouldn't go home and leave her there alone. But this morning, early, he'd gone to the state police barracks. He didn't say why, but Wendy figured he wanted to check if there was anything new on Bobby Tatro and Juan's murder. Her father wouldn't say so to her, but Wendy knew he questioned whether Tatro had worked alone — she'd overheard him and her grandfather and uncle Paul talking last night. They were all irritated Juliet hadn't told them the man who'd threatened her had just gotten out of prison. On the other hand, they also understood her reticence; law enforcement officers got threats all the time.

Reaching up over her head, Wendy grabbed another branch with both hands and swung herself to the ground, landing in a rut. She went flying toward the ground, but Matt caught her by the arm, steadying her before she could end up flat on her face.

Wendy brushed back her hair. "Thanks. I'm fine."

"I can see that."

He had a nice manner, and she liked talking to him. He wasn't bad-looking, except she didn't like his shaved head, and he was in good shape. A lot of the guys who dropped in from nowhere to do seasonal work tended to look more down-and-out. "I just want to pick a few more apples," she said. "Then I'll head back to the house. Tell Gram not to worry, okay? My dad, too."

"Sure, kid."

"Thanks."

But he didn't move.

She tilted her head back, wishing she

were taller. Her arm and leg muscles ached from carting her backpack and tote bag all over New York and pushing Juliet's bureau in front of her bedroom door yesterday — and from the tension of fighting off that awful man. She couldn't get his pale gray eyes out of her mind.

A killer's eyes.

"Wendy," Kelleher said quietly, gently.

"What?"

"You okay?"

"Oh." Suddenly she thought she'd be sick, but she made herself nod. "Yes."

"You've gone a little white there, miss. Are you thinking about what happened yesterday?"

"I didn't mean to," she whispered.

"Sometimes bad memories will pop up out of nowhere and won't let go. It's normal. Give yourself some time. Be patient."

She nodded at his understanding, the urge to vomit subsiding. She squinted at him. "I know I was lucky."

He seemed taken aback. "Lucky?"

"Not to be hurt."

"A guy you knew was murdered. Another guy tried to kill you —"

She shivered, suddenly cold. She could hear the fish tanks breaking, the water rushing out of them — it'd seemed like such a huge amount, more than she'd expected. Fish squirming. Glass everywhere. That man — Tatro — cursing her.

Matt Kelleher touched her elbow. "Wendy?"

"I'm okay."

"Sorry. I didn't mean to remind you. But 'lucky' is going to New York to visit your aunt and coming back with bags from Saks Fifth Avenue. I know what you're trying to say, but you don't have to pretend nothing happened just because you walked away."

"You're right." She brightened, focusing on her basket of apples, then scooping one up and shining it on her flannel shirt. "You'll tell Gram and my dad I'm okay? I'll be down soon. I'm making applesauce and apple crisp later."

Matt smiled. "Apple crisp is one of my favorites."

"Really? I'll make sure I save you some. Gram puts ice cream on hers, but I don't eat dairy products. But it's okay if you do. I mean, I'm not going to make a big thing about it."

"No wonder you're so skinny." He winked at her in a reassuring way. "Sure you're okay?"

She nodded.

"See you around, then."

After he left, Wendy realized her teeth were chattering. She touched her lips. Cold. It wasn't just the October weather, she decided. It was nerves. *Psychological trauma.* Even when she was trying not to think about yesterday, all of a sudden she'd remember Bobby Tatro whispering awful things to her through Juliet's bedroom door.

She stared at her apple and tightened her jaw muscles to keep her teeth from chattering.

His words were like a physical wound. Hadn't her father told her that, as a way to help her understand what she might go through in the next few days, even weeks?

An amputation, she thought, not of an arm or a leg — of her innocence. Her faith in people. Her belief in her ability to navigate a big city — to navigate life.

She plopped under the apple tree, tucking her feet against Spaceshot's chunky frame, wishing she'd brought her journal with her. Her mother had told her that writing poetry when bad things happened — when she was just feeling bad — was therapeutic.

Maybe later, after she'd finished picking apples and had made her applesauce and apple crisp, she'd forget about her college essays for a while and write a poem.

"The Amputation of Innocence."

She said the title out loud and nodded, liking it. It would be a private poem. She didn't need to show it to anyone.

Feeling better, not so alone and out of control and *crazy,* Wendy carried her basket to another tree and reached for a misshapen but otherwise perfectly good apple.

She had four lines of her poem set in her head when she saw her father walking up the lane. Spaceshot actually got up and stretched, then wobbled toward him.

Wendy could tell something had happened. Something new.

He put out his hand, and Spaceshot pushed his head under it, wanting to be petted. But her dad's eyes were on her. "I just talked to your aunt in New York," he said. "There's been a development. Something you should know."

"I'm picking apples."

"Wendy —"

"I don't want to know anything."

"All right," he said. "It can wait. Need some help?"

"Not really." But she saw the hurt and worry in his eyes, felt tears brim in her own eyes, and changed her mind. "Actually, yes. I'd like it if you could help. I was — remember when you used to put me on your shoulders so I could reach the apples?"

"You remember that?"

She nodded, relieved at the spark in his eyes. "It was such fun."

They filled the half-bushel basket to overflowing, and Wendy didn't protest when her father picked it up to carry it down to the house. She was tired, her eyelids heavy — she hadn't slept well.

As they walked slowly back to the house, the wind picking up, rustling in the tall grass and the bright leaves, he told her that Juan, the doorman, wasn't who he said he was. That it was unlikely he'd been killed because he was trying to protect Wendy.

"Then who was he?" she asked.

"We don't know."

"Why was he killed?"

Her father shook his head. "We don't know that, either."

"Are you working on the investigation?"

"No. I'm here for you, Wendy. That's it. You're my only concern."

"Aunt Juliet —"

"I'm not worried about her."

But he was — Wendy could see it in his eyes.

She thought up another line to her poem. When they reached the house, she left him in the kitchen with the apples and ran up to her room, wanting to start her poem while it was still fresh in her mind.

She grabbed a pencil and paper and sat in her window seat, but no words came. She stared at the hills, the brightly colored leaves, unaware she was crying until a fat, hot tear dripped onto her hand.

Twelve

꙳ ⦿ ꙳

Ethan pushed open the door to the car he'd rented at Lubbock airport and sat there in the driveway of his childhood home, breathing in the warm evening west Texas air. New York might have been on another planet. Juliet Longstreet might have been an alien sent to tempt him.

The front room of the sawn-wood-and-stone house where he'd grown up was lit. His older brother, Luke, had a place on the property, where he lived with his wife and two boys, five and seven. Ethan hadn't seen them since Char's funeral.

He wondered what his life would be like now if he'd never left home for West Point.

The ranch was five thousand acres of mixed terrain — mesquite flats, open prairie, rolling hills, canyons. Some of it was planted with wheat, some fenced off for cattle and horses. His brother was into native grasses. A spring-fed creek ran through the east end of the property, but fresh drinking water was scarce and a constant issue.

Off to the west, the silhouette of a solitary windmill stood out against a fiery-yellow setting sun and orange sky.

Jethro, the family's ancient coonhound, slowly picked himself up off a cool spot on the rock driveway and wagged his tail. Ethan got out of the car. "Hey, old boy." He scratched the dog's bony head, felt Jethro's recognition. "Yeah. It's me. I'm home."

The dog went to the car and peered into the open door.

Ethan felt a pang of physical pain. "Sorry, fella. Char's not here."

The hound looked around at him.

"You're right. It's my fault."

There was no one home. His folks were in Denver on ranch business. The lights were on an automatic timer, which amused Ethan because the ranch was isolated, the closest neighbors miles away. The closest neighbors being the Carhills.

He walked through the country kitchen into the living room with its huge stone fireplace and tall windows that overlooked cottonwoods and cedar, the sky darkening, no city lights or skyscrapers to mask the coming of night.

Amid family photographs atop the old player piano, he spotted Char's smile on their wedding day. He stood next to her in his dress uniform. It might have been a million years ago, but it was just five.

Ethan remembered how confident he'd been, so damn sure he could handle whatever came next in his life — that he could control it.

Jethro, who'd followed him inside, rubbed against his legs. Ethan hadn't called his brother, but he expected Luke would be checking on the house and the dog later.

A small framed picture of his parents on their thirtieth anniversary caught his attention. The Carhills had thrown a surprise party for them. Faye and Johnson were in the picture, smiling, good-looking, friends of the Brookers for life. Ham, still in high school at the time, hadn't attended the party. Ethan didn't even know if the Carhills had invited their only child.

He stopped fooling himself. He hadn't come home to make peace with his ghosts.

He'd drive out to the Carhills in the morning.

He was here for answers.

Juliet threaded her way through the content crowd of loud, overweight, drunk men and sat at the same grime-encrusted wooden table where she'd last met George O'Hara. The Bronx bar still smelled of stale cigars and urine.

O'Hara joined her, and she could feel the floor shift under her as he lowered his bulk onto the chair across from her. Tony Cipriani had been to a club to see his comedy act and said he was very funny. "You look tired, Deputy."

"It's been a long couple days."

"I heard about your niece."

It'd been in the papers and on the news, at least part of the story. Ex-con who threatened a marshal was under arrest for murdering her doorman, breaking into her apartment and attacking her niece. Nothing about Colombia or the clandestine photograph, his artwork. No hint of the involvement of a certain Special Forces officer.

"Wendy will be okay," Juliet said. "What do you know about my doorman?"

George lifted the collar of his expensive shirt, airing himself. "It's hot in here. How can you drink coffee?"

"It was a bad choice. The coffee's lousy. Want to order something cold? Look at you, you're drenched in sweat." She studied him a moment. "You're not scared, are you?"

"Hell, no."

"Because if you are — we can protect you."

He shook his head. "I'm not going that route. If I need protection, I'll hire my own." He waved a waiter over and ordered a pitcher of iced tea, unsweetened, then looked at Juliet and shrugged. "I've got to start somewhere to slim down."

"Juan the doorman," Juliet said. "Anything you can tell me?"

"I didn't know him, but I hear he wasn't from New York."

"Where was he from?"

George lifted his massive shoulders and let them fall. "I don't have anything definitive. Maybe Miami, maybe Texas."

"There's a big difference between Miami and Texas."

"Picky, picky. He was American, or so I hear. He and Bobby Tatro got hooked up after Tatro was released from prison. Looks like that was a mistake." George paused for the waiter to deliver his pitcher of tea, pour a glass and withdraw. "Your doorman wasn't the worst of the worst."

"You say that about everybody."

"I like most people. That's why I'm funny." But he didn't smile. "I didn't know about any doorman when we met last time. Not until yesterday."

"I understand, George. Just give me whatever you have."

"Your doorman was a vigilante-justice type, too. At least, that's what I'm hearing."

"When we met last time, you said Tatro had hooked up with that type. Believe me, if he did, it wasn't out of any sense of conviction. Not from what I saw yesterday. He had his own agenda."

"You," George said.

Juliet didn't respond.

"He doesn't like you. Holds a grudge. You knew that, right?"

Juliet nodded. "Yes, I knew."

George's eyes flickered with regret. "My people tell me he relished thinking he could pounce on you anytime he picked. He'd watch you come and go."

"For how long?" Juliet asked, keeping her voice steady.

"He started right after he got out of prison. Kept it up for a week or so, or so I've heard. Then lightning struck, so to speak."

The bartender, about half George's size, brought an insulated coffee urn and refilled Juliet's mug. The coffee smelled decent, fresh. After the bartender trudged off, George held his iced tea glass up to the light, grimaced, then took a long drink.

Juliet smiled at him. "You're a big guy, George. How do you manage all the cleaning?"

"I have a good crew now. I just manage them."

"No kidding."

He gave a self-satisfied shrug. "As I've told you, I make more money running a private cleaning service than you do as a federal agent, Deputy Longstreet."

Juliet settled back in her chair, not as put off by the nasty odors and atmosphere of the place as she had been. George was easy to talk to, a man with a genuine affection for people. He never discussed what had turned him around, and she never asked.

"Tell me about the lightning striking," she said.

"Bobby Tatro ran into a turncoat, somebody the vigilantes were after. That's how he got mixed up with them."

"What do you mean, a turncoat?"

"A traitor."

"As in —"

"Treason. This guy turned on his country. Even creeps like Tatro don't like traitors."

Juliet had no idea what to make of George's story. He had an active imagination, and he wasn't always right. She tried the coffee. This pot was hot, strong and reasonably fresh. "George, what are you talking about? Some traitor walks up to my building while Tatro's stalking me —" She shook her head in disbelief. "Come on."

"I'm just repeating what I've heard. You've got it about right. This traitor showed up at your building one day while Tatro was getting off on spying on you without your knowledge."

"Was Juan the doorman then?"

"Afterward." Her incredulity must have showed in her face, because George frowned at her. "I don't make up these things. I just tell you what I hear."

She drank more of her coffee, wondering if this time the caffeine would give her the jitters, since everything else in her life seemed to be changing. "Go on, then. How did Tatro find out this guy was a traitor? Someone must have told him. Who?"

"No idea."

"Not our mysterious doorman?"

"I'm sorry. I just don't know. Tatro disappeared a day or two after he spotted the traitor."

"All right. The traitor. What do you have on him? A name, any kind of description —"

"It's third-hand at best. I hear he's white

and skinny. Wears an expensive black cowboy hat. But supposedly he still looked more like a nuclear scientist than a Texas Ranger." George smiled. "I don't mean the ball team. The cops. Chuck Norris had a TV show playing one."

"Did this description filter down from Tatro?"

"I don't know. Maybe. Maybe the doorman."

"Any talk on what Tatro did with this supposed traitor after he spotted him?"

"Nothing solid on that, Deputy. Sorry."

Juliet took George through his story a couple of more times — everything he'd heard, whether it was rumor or umpteenth-hand or something he'd dismissed. He added only minor details. When they called it quits, she tried to pay for his drinks, but he insisted on picking up the tab for both the iced tea and her coffee.

"Come see me being funny sometime," he said.

She promised she would.

When she arrived back at her apartment, Mike Rivera fell in behind her and followed her into the lobby. "It's colder than a witch's tit out there. I was about to give up on you."

"It's not that cold."

"Maybe not to you Vermonters." He walked back to the elevator with her, rubbing his hands together as if it were the dead of winter instead of early autumn. "At least there aren't any protesters picketing to get you out of the building."

"The ones who want me out don't need to picket. They've got lawyers. You coming upstairs?"

"For a minute."

Rivera got into and out of the elevator first, as if he wasn't sure what he'd find and thought he might have to shoot someone. "How is your place?"

"It smells like bleach. I guess it's an improvement over dead fish and mud. And Tatro's sweat."

"You can always sleep on my couch if your neighbors make your life miserable and you need time to find a new place. My daughters are in and out at all hours. That's the only drawback, but you get used to it."

"Thanks for the invitation."

Juliet unlocked her door, cool air and the faint odor of bleach wafted out into the hall from her apartment.

Rivera acted as if he didn't notice. "No Brooker?"

"He left this morning."

"You two —"

"There is no we two."

Juliet could see the chief was skeptical, and he stood in her entry, awkward, until she walked past him and he could laser in on her with a look that reminded her he'd worked his way up the ranks to chief deputy and was known for his intolerance of BS.

"Nate Winter likes you," Rivera said. "He wouldn't want to see you burn out."

Winter was a good ally to have. "I'm not burning out." She gave him a dry look. "My work is my life."

"You and that mouth, Longstreet."

"Made you smile."

"No, you didn't. It was a grimace because of the smell in here. You didn't mix ammonia with the bleach, did you?"

"No." She was suddenly so tired, she wanted to sink onto her bed and sleep for days. At least the coffee hadn't given her the jitters — one constant in her life.

Rivera sighed. "All right. You look beat. I'll keep it short. We're trying to retrace Tatro's steps from the minute he got out of prison. It's not easy. Trail goes cold in about twenty-four hours."

"The flight to Bogotá?"

"That's when we pick him up again."

"I just got back from meeting with a source."

When she didn't go on, Rivera grunted at her. "And?"

As unemotionally as she could, she relayed what George O'Hara had told her about Tatro staking out her apartment and coming upon a skinny traitor in a black cowboy hat.

"Guy's not pulling your leg?"

She shook her head. "I don't think so."

"You know, if it'd been a white cowboy hat —"

She almost cracked a smile. "I thought you'd lost your sense of humor."

"I never had much of one." But he narrowed his eyes on her. "You want me to put a security detail on you?"

"*No.* Come on, Chief. That'd cook my goose for sure. It's bad enough I end up with a road-rash scar in the line of duty. I'll never live it down, even if I didn't save myself from Janssen's goons. A security detail —" She shook her head, emphasizing her dismissal of his offer. "No way. I can watch my own back."

He shrugged. "Just thought I'd offer."

Some of Rivera's concern she took as genuine; he liked her and didn't want to see her hurt. The rest was professional. He didn't want an out-of-control deputy on his hands. That she'd slept with Ethan

236

Brooker and he obviously knew it didn't boost her claim to exercise good judgment.

"Take a couple of days, Juliet," he told her. "Transplant orchids, take a walk in the park. Get away from this thing. Come back fresh. There's nothing you can do here."

"I was thinking about heading to Vermont in the morning."

He narrowed his eyes on her. "Why?"

"Chief, what? You don't trust me? I thought you wanted me to get away."

"You want to talk to your niece about your doorman."

"I do, but that's not why you're thinking I'm heading to Vermont."

"We still don't have a firm ID —"

Rivera didn't seem to hear her. "It's the FBI's investigation right now. You're personally involved. I'd advise you not to step on Collins's toes."

"I don't know, Chief. I think Agent Collins is warming up to me."

He sighed. "Where's Brooker?"

"He doesn't check in with me."

There must have been something in her expression, because Rivera rubbed the back of his neck and heaved another sigh, deeper, regretful. "It's none of my business, but a guy like that will break your heart."

For once, Juliet didn't argue with him or make a comment she'd regret.

On his way out, he stopped and looked back at the living room, shaking his head. "Seventeen. Your niece shouldn't be exposed to such violence at that age. Any age. No kid should be." Rivera's black eyes shone. "I'm sorry, Juliet. I'm sorry as hell."

Thirteen

Faye Carhill welcomed Ethan into her sun-filled breakfast room, kissing him on the cheek and insisting he sit down for coffee and warm pecan rolls fresh from the oven, baked from scratch by the family cook.

"Ethan, Ethan," Faye said, shaking her head as if she'd never expected to see him again. "You look good, Ethan. I had no idea you were home."

"I got in last night — spur-of-the-moment visit."

"Your parents won't be back from Denver for another few days. You'll stay to see them, won't you?"

"Depends." He didn't elaborate. "I saw Luke and Dorrie and the boys last night."

"Aren't the boys getting big? Luke, Jr., reminds me of you, always on the go." Faye tried to smile. "Although I think it would devastate your mother if he went off to West Point. One boy in the family is enough."

Ethan didn't take the bait. Military service was for other people, other families — not the Carhills. He wondered just what Faye knew about her son's activities in South America. But he wasn't going to ask, and he sure wasn't discussing his own family with her.

"Is Ham around? I'd like to say hello."

"He was." She lifted a pecan roll onto a flowered china plate, intent on what she was doing but Ethan had heard the catch in her voice. "He left yesterday afternoon. I'd hoped he'd stay awhile longer."

"When did he get home?"

"About a week ago. It was good to have him here."

She spoke as if he were a college student home on break. Ham had graduated at nineteen, earned his master's at twenty, his Ph.D. at twenty-two, then chucked it all and headed to South America. Faye was clearly in denial of the fact that Ham was no longer a kid, that he had his own life.

Ethan watched Faye carefully place the plate on the glass table, snatching a pecan that had fallen off one of the rolls. But the smell of butter, cinnamon and pecans didn't tempt him. He wasn't hungry.

"Ham's still drifting," Faye said.

"He's only twenty-five. He's got time to figure out what he wants to do."

"You were fighting terrorists at twenty-five."

Not that Faye would want her son to do the same — but not that she wouldn't want him to, either. In a way, she'd like it if Ham told her to go to hell and signed up for the Marines. She'd always been conflicted about her son. Protective, because he was gawky and awkward with people. Distant, because at the same time, she was determined to shove him out of the nest. She and Ham's father were generous with financial support, yet eager to see their son make it on his own. And always, mother and father both were not quite able to hide their disappointment in their only child.

"He was very thin when he arrived here," Faye went on. "Emaciated, really. He had these little welts all over him. I don't know — insect bites, I think. He refused to see a doctor."

"Ham's smarter than most of us, Faye."

"Too smart for his own good. These so-called adventures he's having — I thought they'd make him stronger, toughen him up. Now, I don't know. It doesn't look as if they're doing him or anyone else any good."

"Did he say where he went, when he's

241

coming back? I'm at a loose end. I'd like to see him."

She shook her head. "I don't even have his cell-phone number. I don't know if he *has* a cell phone. I can't reach my own son. What if something happened to John or me? What if the house burned down? We wouldn't be able to find him."

"It's not that easy to hide these days. Someone would find him."

"You could, I suppose," she said with sudden earnestness. "Find him, talk to him . . . I'd pay you. You said yourself you're at a loose end —"

"Faye, that's not why I'm here."

She lowered her eyes. "I know. What Ham's put us through —" She raised her eyes again, her liner smudged from moisture. "You can't imagine."

Ethan drank some of his coffee, which, of course, was perfect. He thought of Juliet and the rotgut she'd drink, then pushed her out of his mind, because it wasn't going to get him anywhere.

"It's very sweet of you to stop by," Faye said, on the verge of tears now.

"Faye," Ethan said, "I need to know everything."

She sprang to her feet. She wore trim white pants with a hot-pink-and-white top and hot-pink sandals, as if she'd deliberately dressed to cheer herself up. "More coffee?"

"Faye —"

"Just —" She spun around to him. "Just find my son, Ethan. Please. Find him and bring him home before he does something none of us can undo. I want him out of harm's way."

Ethan pushed aside his coffee. "Tell me everything, Faye, or I go quail-hunting."

She smiled wryly. "You don't hunt. Luke does, but you —" She took a breath, a sharpness coming into her expression. "I should say you don't hunt *quail.* People, yes. You're a search-and-destroy specialist. Isn't that what you are, Ethan?"

There was a superciliousness about her tone — a sarcasm combined with an almost romanticized take on what he did — that set Ethan's teeth on edge. He got to his feet. "Did you and John pay off Ham's kidnappers?"

She grabbed the plate of pecan rolls and brought it to the counter. "I don't know what you're talking about."

"All right," he said. "I'm leaving."

She tried to smother a sob, her back to him. "We'd have done anything, Ethan. Anything. If you haven't been in our position, you don't know."

Ethan didn't react to her emotion. "Go on."

"Someone contacted us." She didn't turn around. "Just a voice on the end of the phone. He promised to call us with details. He never did."

"How much did he want?"

She ripped open a drawer and pulled out a box of Saran Wrap, snapping it down on the counter. "Five million. We didn't balk. We didn't say anything at all. He didn't give us a chance to respond." Her tone was argumentative now, anticipating Ethan's reaction. "I don't expect you to understand."

"When did you get the call?"

"Three days before Ham turned up here."

Two days before Ethan and his team had freed her son. "Did you tell the authorities?"

"*What* authorities? Ham was being held in some rathole in Colombia, for God's sake! There was no one to tell. Low-life mercenaries in a foreign country had my son. They wanted money. What were we supposed to do?"

Take matters into their own hands, Ethan thought. It was what Carhills always did.

"I thought the voice might have been

yours," she whispered, tearing off a sheet of Saran Wrap. "I almost wish it had been."

"You wish I'd kidnapped your only son. For money." Ethan stared at her, truly stunned, then moved for the door. "I should go."

She started to cry. "I'm sorry for even thinking such a thing. I'd hoped — I knew if it'd been you, there'd have been a reason, a larger purpose."

"Don't count on it."

"You can't tell anyone about the ransom call," she said, spinning around at him. "Nothing came of it. We never got another call. John — he'll be furious I told you. We're worried about Ham, Ethan. No — we're *terrified* for him. I don't know what he's involved in. I understand we don't show emotions well, but we love Ham with all our hearts."

Mia O'Farrell would want to know about the five million. So would FBI Special Agent Joe Collins and Chief Deputy U.S. Marshal Mike Rivera. And Juliet, up in New York with her dead doorman and her dead fish and her traumatized niece.

If Faye and Johnson Carhill had been ordinary parents receiving a ransom demand for their son, they'd have called the feds the minute they hung up.

But, then, if they'd been ordinary parents, Ham might never have gone to South America in the first place.

Faye averted her eyes, her hands shaking. "Please, Ethan. Find my son."

He kissed her on the cheek, ignoring her tears. He had no illusions that she'd given him the whole story. The Carhills never laid out all their cards at once.

And, as he headed out of the huge house, Ethan reminded himself that Faye Carhill never said anything without her husband's approval.

When he was on the open road, Ethan turned a country-western music station up loud and drove fast, fighting an assault of memories. Ham Carhill as a little kid, tagging along with the Brooker brothers on a quail hunt, trying to rope a steer, asking a million questions in that annoying, rat-a-tat way he'd had. The skinny genius. Ham could tell them how many feathers were on a quail and the geological origins of a canyon. He could think things, smell things, see things that Luke and Ethan never could. But Ham could never get the quail — his brain was too busy. He couldn't focus in time.

And, as much as he pretended otherwise, Ham couldn't pull the trigger to actually shoot the bird.

How he'd gotten mixed up with Mia
O'Farrell didn't make sense on one level
— Ham didn't seem the spy type. On another level, it made perfect sense. He'd go
along for the ride, for the approval and the
mental stimulation, and never see the dan-
gers. He wasn't so much naive as oblivious.

Char had met Ham once, but she didn't
romanticize the Carhills. "They think they
live in the real world. One day they'll find
out they don't. It won't be pretty."

She hadn't liked Texas. Ethan would try
to impress upon her that it was a very large
state with a diverse population — didn't
matter. Their house in the country wasn't
going to be in Texas.

The thought of their plans — their dreams
— of a quiet, normal life in the country, with
babies and dogs, tugged at his preoccupation
with his unanswered questions about Mia
O'Farrell's little rescue mission.

On a day like today, Ethan thought,
Char would have bitched about the bright
Texas sun and the constant wind.

He smiled, surprising himself because
there was no bite of guilt this time — no
pain.

He was almost back home when his cell
phone rang.

"Where are you?"

Juliet. Ethan eased up on the gas. "I'm in my brother's truck, enjoying a fine Texas morning. You, Marshal?"

"You're in Texas?"

"I got in last night."

"The hostage you rescued is a Texan," she said. "Black cowboy hat, thin, smart-looking."

Gritting his teeth, Ethan pulled over to the side of the road. Perhaps he'd underestimated Deputy Longstreet. "You've been busy. I should remember that you marshals are good at finding people."

"Is he the reason you're in Texas?"

She was hammering him. There wasn't even a glimmer of the woman he'd made love to Friday night, gentle, eager, as in need of a few hours of forgetting as he was. He decided he could be as hard-edged. "I'm not doing this over the phone."

She didn't let up. "Your Texan in the black hat was in New York in late August. He showed up at my place. Tatro was out of prison, stalking me. Still no ID on the doorman, but he was hired about that time."

Ethan gazed out at the broken clouds in an endless autumn sky.

He hadn't known Ham Carhill went to New York in late August.

"I want a name, Brooker," Juliet said. "I'll get the big guns involved if I have to."

"He isn't here. I don't know where is he. His mother says she doesn't, either."

"You've talked to her?"

"Just left," Ethan said. "Juliet — *damn.* He could have realized I was in New York in late August."

"Hunting your assassin, getting knocked on the head." Juliet paused a moment, then said, only half out loud, "So he wasn't at my building to see me. He was looking for you."

Why? Ethan couldn't begin to guess. Ham Carhill had never needed him or anyone else. "Within a week, he ended up in Tatro's hands."

"Who is this guy, an army buddy, a drinking partner? Someone you used to rope steer with? Do you owe him money?"

Ethan didn't answer her. "Where are you right now?"

She bit off a sigh. "On my way to Vermont."

She didn't explain why, but Ethan didn't need to be in law enforcement to have a fair guess. On Friday, everyone thought the doorman had been killed while heroically trying to stop Bobby Tatro from getting into the building. Now that the picture had become more complicated, Juliet would want to know exactly what Juan and Wendy had talked about before Tatro slit his throat.

"Your niece —"

"Picking apples and trying to put Bobby Tatro out of her head. Brooker —"

"I've got to go. Sun's in my eyes."

He disconnected her, then dialed the number he had for Mia O'Farrell.

She answered on the first ring but didn't say anything, just breathed into the phone.

"Dr. O'Farrell?"

"Brooker," she said, sounding relieved. "I wasn't sure it was you. What can I do for you? Is everything all right?"

"Depends on your point of view. Do you have our skinny friend stuck in some cubbyhole?"

She obviously knew he meant Ham Carhill. "No. Why?"

"He took off."

"When?"

"Sometime yesterday."

She didn't respond.

"Tell me, Doctor," Ethan said. "This rescue mission is going to blow up in your face. How far will you go to protect yourself?"

"Go to hell, Major."

It was strong language for Dr. O'Farrell. "You set up a mission without giving the people who were putting their lives on the line all the facts —"

"I didn't set up any mission. I don't have that authority."

"That's cover-your-ass language. Who told you I could ID Ham? Who told you he was being held by a guy with a thing for the blond, female marshal?"

He could hear her shallow, rapid breathing on the other end, but she didn't answer him.

"You don't like making mistakes," Ethan went on, feeling only the slightest twinge of guilt at his unrelenting tone. "I'll bet you used to cry when you got less than a ninety on a test."

"You won't be able to collect on that bet." Her voice was icy, unemotional. "I never got below a ninety."

No wonder she and Ham ended up working together.

She hung up.

Ethan tossed his phone onto the passenger seat. He could have handled frightened, dedicated, intelligent Mia better — more diplomatically, at least. But he wasn't in the mood. Ham Carhill had taken off. His mother was worried about him — or maybe that the kidnappers would make another try for the five million. Ethan hadn't mentioned the ransom call to Mia. He needed time to think.

And Juliet. She spoke her mind and had the bluest eyes and the very tightest butt — but Ethan had the feeling she was flat out of patience with him.

Right now, she was en route to her family in Vermont. Landscapers, cops, traumatized vegan niece. Apples and pumpkins.

Ethan had never been to the Green Mountain State. It'd be pretty this time of year with the foliage. He wondered what airport he'd fly into and whether he could get to Vermont by nightfall.

Fourteen

✌ ᎒ᏮᏋ᎒ ᔕ

Wendy held up a knobby, misshapen apple, next in line for her apple crisp in progress. "It's kind of cute, don't you think?"

Juliet sipped coffee at the table in the Longstreet family kitchen. She'd arrived in the middle of Sunday lunch. Parents, brothers, sisters-in-law, nieces, nephews. They all were there. But after the last of the applesauce cake was gone and the dishes were done, everyone had cleared out, with excuses of homework and soccer games and wood to split.

Except Joshua. He had stayed and now was leaning stiffly against the sink, trying, Juliet knew, to keep his mouth shut — reticence was not a Longstreet family trait.

"The Yoda of apples," Wendy said, falsely cheerful, and put it aside, giving it a little pat as her smile evaporated. "I'm going to spare it."

A muscle worked in her father's jaw. "Wendy, it's not alive. It's an apple."

Ignoring him, she chose another apple

from the pile on the counter and took a deep breath before slicing into it with her paring knife.

Joshua glared at Juliet, as if she were to blame because his daughter was having trouble cutting up apples.

And maybe I am, Juliet thought, drinking more of her coffee.

Wendy peeled one of her apple quarters. She had on an oversize dark green sweatshirt that made her look even tinier. She finished peeling the apple quarter and sliced it into her deep-dish pie plate. She wasn't making her grandmother's apple crisp. Her recipe involved wildflower honey, expeller-pressed canola oil and steel-cut oats, all of it organic. No butter, no white sugar. Juliet wasn't sure how it'd turn out, but at least they all could eat something healthy and guilt-free.

"Wendy, I need to talk to you," she said. "About Juan. The doorman —"

"I know who he is."

"You talked to him on Thursday when you arrived at my building and then again when you came back to meet me, and on Friday morning when you —"

"I know when I talked to him."

"I'd like you to tell me everything he said to you."

Joshua stirred. "Whatever you remember, honey."

She reached for another apple. "I remember everything he said. I keep thinking about it." She set the apple on her cutting board and sliced it in half. "He let me practice my Spanish. He was — nice. I don't care if he's not who he said he was."

Tony Cipriani had called Juliet on her way to Vermont with an ID for their John Doe doorman. Juliet kept the information to herself. She didn't want that knowledge coloring her niece's memory of any conversations she and "Juan" had had in New York. Juliet had pulled Joshua aside after she'd arrived, giving him the basics, no details. He'd reluctantly agreed with her strategy.

"Take me through what you talked about," she said. "Something you think is insignificant could turn out to be important."

Wendy spun around, knife in hand, tears shining in her brown eyes. "Why? You have the man who killed him." She stared suddenly at her knife and went deathly pale. Her fingers opened, and she deliberately let the knife drop to the floor. "I have enough apples for my apple crisp," she mumbled, turning back to the counter.

Without a word, Joshua picked up the knife and rinsed it off in the sink.

Tatro's K-bar. The blood on its blade. That image had probably just materialized for Wendy. Juliet could see it herself, could smell Tatro's sweat, hear his taunts. "Wendy, if you could concentrate on Juan —"

"He asked about the tin with Teddy's ashes." Using both hands, Wendy scooped oats into a battered aluminum measuring cup. "I told him it contained loose-leaf tea."

"He searched your bags?"

She nodded. "He was following security procedures. He asked to see my ID." Frowning, Wendy dumped oats into her mixing bowl, then pulled the necklace she always wore from inside her sweatshirt and fingered its small polished rose quartz stone. "He commented on my necklace. I told him I don't like fancy gems. He said something like, 'No diamonds and emeralds for you, huh?' And then he said you didn't seem the type, either."

"He mentioned me specifically?"

"He said you never know, maybe you have a soft side that likes a little luxury. I think that's pretty close. I remember —" She released her necklace and pushed up the sleeves to her sweatshirt, then she dug into the bowl, mixing honey and oats and oil with her hands.

"And on Friday," Juliet said, moving forward despite Joshua's tight look. "What did he say to you?"

She continued to knead her mixture. "He just seemed surprised that I'd come back on my own. He let me use his key to get into your apartment. That was it, pretty much."

"How was his demeanor? Did he seem —"

"I know what *demeanor* means. He was friendly. He never seemed nervous or angry or anything, like that man — Tatro. It's not like Tatro had got there first and threatened to kill Juan if he didn't say the right thing and was in hiding, watching us." Wendy pulled her hands out of her bowl and scraped the excess oats and goo off her fingers. "I don't think that's what happened."

Wendy had already told Joe Collins that she hadn't seen any sign of Tatro on her return to the Upper West Side Friday morning — not until he was shoving her into her aunt's apartment.

Juliet abandoned her coffee. It was her sixth cup of the day. More than enough. "I know this has been hard, but there's something I need to tell you. We have new information —"

Joshua stood up straight. "I'll tell her."

Juliet didn't argue with him. After all, he was Wendy's father.

Wendy sprinkled the oat mixture over the apple slices she'd arranged in a ceramic pie plate. Pretending she hadn't heard the exchange between her father and aunt, she wiped off her hands with a damp dishcloth, then put the apple crisp in the oven and set the timer.

But when she turned around, her cheeks were flushed, rosy pink with emotion. "Tell me what?"

"I'll be outside," Juliet said quietly.

Walking outside only reminded her what an intrusion she was. The autumn leaves blazed against the bright afternoon sun. Spaceshot worked up the energy to haul himself to his feet and lick her hand. "Hey, buddy," she said, "it's been a rough few days."

She headed behind the small barn where her family had kept chickens and the occasional sheep or goat for as long as she could remember. The last of the dahlias and even a few hollyhocks bloomed against the rough-hewn barn boards. Vines of blue morning glories tangled on trellises, and the hard-to-describe pink of cone flowers reminded her of summertime.

No matter how protected they were in their warm spot against the old barn, a killing frost would get them. There'd be one before too long — this was Vermont, after all.

Joshua joined her. "She's gone up to her room while the apple crisp is baking. Says she's working on her college essays, but I doubt it."

"Joshua, I'm sorry I had to bring it all up again."

He shook his head, but everything about him was tight, emotionally unable to accept what had happened to his daughter. As an experienced law enforcement officer, he understood. As a father — never. "It wasn't your fault."

"It wasn't Wendy's fault, either."

"Yeah." He looked away. "I know."

Juliet sighed, wishing she didn't have more to tell him. "I need to fill you in on a couple things I didn't mention earlier. My partner, Tony Cipriani — you met him at my place on Friday. He's been doing some legwork. He's the one who called me on my way up here and told me the doorman's real name was Vincente Perez, that he was from Miami."

At her pause, Joshua's eyes narrowed. "And?"

259

"Cip's looking into his background. Right now, we know his name came up in a smuggling investigation down there. He disappeared about a month ago."

"That's when he took the job as your doorman?"

She nodded.

"What kind of smuggling?"

"South American artifacts and gems — primarily emeralds. Presumably drugs, too. I don't think Wendy needs to know these details, but that's your call."

"This son of a bitch Perez asked Wendy about you *and* jewels. Hell, Juliet —" He swore, kicking a loose rock, winging it against the barn. "Don't tell me this goddamn mess is about stolen emeralds."

"It's not that simple," she said. "I wish it were."

He inhaled through his nose, reining in his emotions, then sighed at her. "Go on."

"Ethan Brooker led some kind of black op mission to rescue an American Bobby Tatro was holding in Colombia. I don't have all the details."

"Brooker?" Joshua exhaled, shaking his head. "Damn, Juliet. I thought you were finished with him."

"Well — it's tough if some friend of his

gets snatched by an ex-con who threatened to kill me."

"That's who was kidnapped? One of Brooker's Special Forces buddies?"

Juliet didn't answer right away. Cip had produced a name for her. The Carhills of west Texas. Ultrarich, ultraprivate. A young, brilliant son reportedly into adventures in South America. She immediately thought of George's Texan in the black cowboy hat, but the information wasn't solid enough for her to share with her brother.

"I don't think it was a Special Forces type," she said. "Anyway, when Ethan and his rescue team showed up for their guy, Tatro had already taken off."

"He knew Brooker was on his way?"

"Maybe. I don't know. I'm trying —" She reined in her own scattered emotions. "I can't get my head around how and why Tatro got involved in this business in Colombia in the first place."

Joshua nodded in agreement. "It sounds like a big operation to pull off fresh out of prison."

"Then there's what he and Perez — 'Juan' — wanted with me. Tatro's had it in for me since Syracuse. He thinks I cheated to find him at the Wal-Mart parking lot."

"You didn't just happen to run into him?"

Juliet shrugged. "Does it matter?"

"Not to me."

She took a breath, then plunged in with the rest of what she had to say. "There's a picture." She paused, debating how much to tell her brother about the picture Ethan had found in Tatro's Colombian hut. But she told him everything.

"The sick fuck," Joshua said when she finished. "If the doorman, not Tatro, took the picture, then why did Tatro up and kill him? Complicates things, doesn't it?" He rubbed the back of his neck, sighed at the sky, then returned his hard gaze to his sister. "Wendy picked a hell of a day to sneak off to New York."

"I can't tell you how sorry I am."

"Yeah. Me, too. What are you going to do now?"

She tried to smile. "Take a walk down to the lake."

"Don't be too long." He almost managed to smile back at her. "Wendy's apple crisp will be out of the oven soon."

Nate Winter waited for Ethan on the small dock on the wide, slow Cumberland River. Ethan had called from the Nashville airport. Winter, a senior deputy U.S. marshal, and his new bride, Sarah Dunnemore Winter, were spending a long weekend in Night's Landing, where the Dunnemores had lived for generations. Sarah's parents had finally retired and were living there more or less full-time. But they were traveling now — India. Her father, a retired diplomat, had a touch of wanderlust.

The Dunnemores had been in the Netherlands in the spring while Ethan was posing as their property manager, after a tentative lead had taken him to Night's Landing. After months of no answers, no suspects in Char's murder, he'd decided to shake some trees on his own and see if her killers fell out.

Generous, decent people, surprisingly down-to-earth, the Dunnemores had never questioned his story about being a good ol' boy from Texas who was working as a gardener until he got his break as a songwriter.

Ethan had written a few songs during his weeks in Night's Landing. He'd given one to Sarah and Nate as a wedding present, intending it as a bit of a joke — but Sarah had told him she really liked it. And she wasn't one for polite lies. She'd meant it.

He passed the tiny cottage where he'd

lived, where he'd almost given up on finding the answers to Char's death — where he'd almost given up on himself. But Sarah's push for answers of her own — who'd shot her brother in Central Park, what did it have to do with her and her family — and her trust, her essential kindness, had helped Ethan to pull himself back from the precipice, from the point of no return.

Nate's intolerance for any bullshit hadn't hurt, either.

Sarah, a historical archaeologist, hadn't come out to the dock. She was up in the main house, its squared-off logs sawed by her great-grandfather, who'd figured a house would help him get a wife.

The car Ethan had hired at the airport waited in the driveway. He didn't have a lot of time before his flight north.

The landscape of old-fashioned flowers and shrubs and huge old shade trees was still lush and green in early October, the late afternoon sun casting long shadows.

Ethan walked out onto the dock, but Nate kept his back to him. Not long after he'd met and fallen in love with Sarah Dunnemore in Night's Landing, Nate was assigned to USMS headquarters in Arlington, Virginia. He and Sarah were living, temporarily, in a historic northern Virginia house rumored to be haunted by both Abraham Lincoln and Robert E. Lee.

Ethan had stopped for a visit in September, a week after Sarah's brother and his Diplomatic Security agent had captured Janssen's assassin. Sarah had served him sweet-tea punch and fried-apricot pie on the porch and talked about Abe and Bobby Lee and how happy she was, a week before her wedding.

Then her husband had whisked him away to a private meeting with President Poe and Mia O'Farrell, and it was off to Colombia to rescue Ham Carhill.

But Nate Winter had been there for the meeting. He knew about the mission.

"Sorry I missed your wedding," Ethan said. He didn't exactly know why, but he'd been invited. "I hear it was perfect."

A tall, dark-haired, rangy man, Nate was a no-nonsense law-enforcement officer. The fact that his wife was like a daughter to the president of the United States wasn't something Winter would view as an advantage — it just came with falling in love with Sarah Dunnemore.

Even at dusk, Winter's eyes were a piercing blue. "I take it you're not here for a social visit, Major."

"You remember you drove me to the White House the first week in September, before your wedding?" Ethan didn't wait for Nate to respond. He laid out the facts. "We met with the president and Mia O'Farrell. You didn't stay for the entire meeting, but I think you know the basics of what I was asked to do."

Winter wasn't the type to lay out what he knew. "Go on."

"We got our guy. He's safe. The rest of it's a mess. I'll assume you've talked to Mike Rivera or Joe Collins and know about Juliet Longstreet's ex-con."

Nate didn't say a word.

Ethan looked out at the water, remembered his frustration in the weeks before Sarah Dunnemore, sipping sweet-tea punch on the porch of her Tennessee family home, had learned that her twin brother and another marshal — Nate — had been shot. By the time Juliet arrived on the Cumberland River, all hell had broken loose. But it seemed like five years ago, instead of just five months. "Tatro's in jail, my guy's free," Ethan said. "But this thing isn't over. There's more to it —"

"And that's your business?"

He looked at Winter, his unchanging expression, his steady self-control. "Was it your business to come down here in May? You weren't supposed to investigate the shooting. You were one of the victims."

Nate sighed, some of his rigidness easing. "Fair point. Go on. What do you want me to do?"

"Mia O'Farrell's on her last nerve."

"I don't deal with her."

"You were there with her and the president, Nate. You can see he trusts her."

"Shouldn't he?"

"You just might want to let him know that she's hanging by a thread."

Nate had no visible reaction. "Why don't you tell him yourself?"

Ethan shrugged, smiled. "Poe doesn't show up at my house for fried-apricot pie."

Again, Nate didn't indulge in so much as a twitch of a smile. No jokes about his wife's friendship with John Wesley Poe. Or her fried pies.

"What does Juliet know about your meeting with O'Farrell?"

"Not as much as she wants to. She's about as big a hard-ass as you are, Winter. The no-stone-left-unturned type."

Nate didn't disagree, but he said, "O'Farrell's on her way to New York. She's meeting with Rivera and Collins in the morning. There's no need to keep them in the dark as much as she has been."

"You set up the meeting?"

He shrugged, not answering. "Brooker — you might want to be careful."

"With Tatro, Mia, Collins, Rivera or Juliet?"

A near smile. "All of the above. You must know by now you're not the type to be satisfied sitting on the sidelines. You want to fill in the blanks, find the answers. It's the way you're wired, Major." The hard blue gaze stayed on him. "It's why you ended up digging in the dirt here in Night's Landing."

Literally and figuratively, Ethan thought. He gestured toward the beautiful Dunnemore lawn. "The stuff I planted looks pretty good, don't you think?"

But Nate didn't let up. "Why is Dr. O'Farrell on her last nerve?"

"If I knew, I wouldn't need to be here, now would I?"

"You have an idea. Or you wouldn't have come all this way."

"When I was in Afghanistan, I helped put some psycho vigilante mercenaries out of business. It didn't make the papers, but it was a pretty big deal. Most of them got away. A few didn't, but they were low-level players." Ethan didn't like taking the kind of leap he was taking now, but he wasn't a law-enforcement officer — he was just a guy trying to figure things out. "I think some vigilante psycho could be manipulating O'Farrell."

"Does she realize it?"

"Now she does, at least to a degree."

"Same guys as in Afghanistan?"

Ethan paused. "Maybe."

"The president and I —" Nate hesitated, then went on, his tone more amiable, his manner more approachable. "We get along okay, but it's Sarah he has the bond with — he's one of her closest friends. She adores him, and Poe adores her."

"This one's not her fight."

A darkness came into Nate's eyes, and he was obviously remembering the caves and the snakes and the dead bodies from his first visit to Night's Landing that spring.

"I'll see to it Poe gets your message about O'Farrell," Nate said abruptly, then shifted immediately into southern-host mode — Sarah's influence, no doubt. Nate was another northern New Englander. "Do you have time to join us for dinner? Sarah made a congealed salad this afternoon that seems to involve coconut and fruit cocktail."

"I didn't think anyone ate congealed salads anymore."

"She says they bring back memories of her grandmother."

Ethan grinned. "It's a shame I've got a plane to catch."

"Do I want to know where you're headed?" Nate asked quietly.

"North."

Ethan only gave one word, but Nate obviously didn't need more. "Juliet's got a good career ahead of her, Brooker."

Ethan took the comment for what it was — a warning not to screw up her life.

He left Winter on the dock and headed across the lawn, the grass he'd tended warm and soft under his feet. Sarah had come onto the porch. She smiled and waved to him. She was a beautiful woman with honey-colored hair and a strength people often didn't realize she had.

With Juliet, people noticed her strength first.

Ethan waved back and gave her a cheeky smile that made her laugh. He'd damn near screwed up Sarah's life when he'd pretended to be a good ol' boy from Texas. Now he hoped it wasn't too late for him to avoid screwing up Juliet's life.

Mia pushed open the door to her hotel room and wheeled her suitcase into the small room, leaving it in the middle of the floor while she checked out her view. It wasn't much of one. Her hotel was located on Central Park South, but she'd balked at paying for a room with a park view. Hers looked out on office buildings. She looked down at the street ten floors below and saw a man in a dark business suit running, flagging a cab.

The FBI agent, Joe Collins, and the chief deputy, Mike Rivera, had offered to fly to Washington to meet with her. Nate Winter must have given them her name. He'd been at the meeting when she and the president had asked Ethan Brooker to volunteer for the rescue mission. Nate hadn't stayed for all the details.

She couldn't give the FBI or the marshals Ham Carhill's name or any details of the information he'd provided her, but there was a lot she *could* tell them. About Tatro and his henchmen. The timing of the rescue mission. How Tatro wasn't there when Ethan and his team arrived at the camp. She'd cleared everything with her superiors. And she'd talked to the president. Now that Ham was safe and they'd acted on his information — and Ham was done, no longer a viable candidate for covert work — she saw no reason whatsoever she couldn't cooperate with the FBI investigation.

Neither did President Poe, when she'd told him what she intended to do.

But she didn't tell him all of it. About the anonymous calls, the tips — her mounting concern that her caller had manipulated her.

Turning from the window, Mia called room service and ordered the soup of the day — wild mushroom — and a glass of red wine. She'd relax tonight. She'd put up her feet, order a movie and let her subconscious do its work, and maybe, by morning, she'd have a better idea of who her caller was and what he wanted and how to stop him. Because this guy was still pulling strings. He wasn't done.

Fifteen

✦

Ham watched a rerun of *Law & Order* while he thumbed through a free Vermont guidebook in his room in a fleabag motel off I-89. All the decent hotels, motels and country inns were booked solid. Leaf-peeping season. He'd seen plenty of leaves on his drive north from New York. Supposedly "peak" foliage wasn't until next weekend. He couldn't tell.

The guidebook listed fairs, arts-and-crafts shows, hay rides, scenic hikes. He wasn't interested, but he hoped pretending he was, going through the motions, would help keep him from going crazy.

Lennie Briscoe made one of his pithy wisecracks, and Ham switched to CNN. At least his motel had cable. But nothing was going on, and he lay back on his flat pillow and crossed his feet, running through his mind again what he'd say to Juliet Longstreet. Talk about threading a needle in a sandstorm in the dark. Except, in this case, one wrong move and someone could die. Himself, even. Never mind pissing off the national-security types. He'd come close enough to dying this fall to know he wasn't in the mood for it.

But what was he supposed to do, leave everything to Ethan? Hope for the best?

He glanced at the old bedside clock-radio. Midnight. He supposed he could wake Mia O'Farrell and ask her advice about what to do. Get another opinion. But he didn't trust her entirely. And who was he kidding, anyway? It was too late for advice — too late for permission. He'd already made up his mind what to do.

Bobby Tatro thought Deputy Longstreet had his ransom payment.

The emeralds.

That scenario was the only one that made sense. The only explanation for breaking into her apartment. Tatro must have figured that Ham had given them to Brooker — payment, maybe, for freeing him — and Brooker had given them to Longstreet. To silence her about what she knew? Keep her from asking questions? Ham didn't have that part of Tatro's twisted thinking figured out yet. But he was pretty sure he was on target about the rest of it.

And Deputy Longstreet deserved to know.

She was in Vermont. Ham had stopped at her building to talk to her. The security guard told him she wasn't around, refused to tell him where she was. When Ham guessed Vermont, the guard still kept mum, but his expression told Ham what he wanted to know. He rented a car and headed north to Vermont, getting lost twice before he found Longstreet Landscaping. He saw Juliet Longstreet patting a fat dog next to a trailer of pumpkins, but with a state police cruiser in the driveway and people all over the place, he decided to wait until tomorrow to pry her loose.

Ham tried to relax.

Tatro's in jail.

The bastard couldn't hurt him or anyone else, not anymore.

Ham could feel the emeralds under his pillow. They were cut and polished — beauties. They weren't raw crystals freshly dug out of the Andes. Emeralds were portable — a favorite with smugglers — and good ones were valuable. He estimated the worth of the emeralds he'd spirited away from his captors in the vicinity of a half-million dollars.

Beryllium and chromium...two elements that, together, produced an emerald. Yet they were brought together only under rare geological conditions. The Colombian Andes were a geological rarity. And Muzo, Coscuez, Chivor were Colombian mines known all over the world for their unique, high-quality emeralds.

The emerald was the birthstone for May, the gem of Taurus and Gemini. It was associated with kindness and goodness, and rumored to ward off panic attacks.

And there were those who still believed that emeralds could provide their wearer with the ability to see the future.

Ham wished the emeralds under his pillow could empower him just to see what tomorrow would bring. But perhaps because they were tarnished by violence and deceit, their mystical attributes were unavailable, at least to him. He couldn't put pieces together, make connections that he normally could, connections that had made him valuable to Mia O'Farrell and, in a way, had led him to Vermont.

In any case, Ham had no illusions. He was at the mercy of forces outside of his control, and no one could help him now. Not even Ethan Brooker.

Wendy sat in the window seat in her dark bedroom, wrapped up in a fleece blanket, and tried to work on a college essay. The question she was supposed to answer was straightforward — *Why do you want to be a doctor?* — and yet she couldn't think of a single reason why. She pictured herself sitting in a college chemistry class, studying nonstop, dealing with the competition and stress of being a premed student.

And the work itself. She liked the idea of helping people, but she didn't think she could look at blood and pus or even runny noses every day. She thought about the doctor who'd had to examine Juan after he was murdered. She didn't want to have to be around death and suffering all the time.

Wendy put the essay aside and glanced at her poem, which was awful. She tore it up and threw the pieces on the floor. How could she ever have thought it was any good?

With her knees tucked under her chin, she stared outside. It was a clear night, with just a sliver of a moon and stars everywhere. She spotted a flock of wild turkeys down by the barn, led by the fattest tom she'd ever seen. What were they doing traipsing around so late? She quickly put on her slippers and ran downstairs, her blanket wrapped over her shoulders. She made as little noise as possible so as not to wake her grandparents, who worried about her too much as it was — even before New York.

Ducking out the side porch, Wendy immediately realized it was colder outside than she'd expected. She tightened her blanket around her and walked out back, triggering the motion-detector light. But the turkeys were gone now, the night quiet and still. She walked a little ways up the lane behind the barn. She was in pajama pants and an oversize T-shirt, but she didn't have on any socks, and the blanket wasn't really warm enough — she should at least have grabbed a coat.

Her poem really was stupid, she thought, shivering in the night air. She wasn't being overly hard on herself. She didn't regret tearing it to shreds.

And her apple crisp. What a disaster. No matter what anyone else said, it was disgusting. The oats were hard. The apples had turned to mush. Her dad said it was good, but Wendy had noticed he ate his helping with a lot of vanilla ice cream. It wasn't the recipe — it was her. She'd done something wrong. Her mind hadn't been on making apple crisp.

She'd kept seeing Juan — Vincente Perez — smiling at her, trying to make the indignity of having her bag searched easier for her to take. She'd had no idea he was lying about who he was.

And that awful Bobby Tatro. The things he'd said to her while she was hiding in Juliet's bedroom. She kept hearing him, seeing herself, as if she were perched atop her aunt's curtains and was looking down at what was happening to her — watching herself pushing the bureau in front of the door, imagining her expression as she'd tried to block the evil, horrible words from entering her mind. He talked about what he'd do to her. What he'd do to her aunt. He'd *liked* the idea that Wendy was in the bedroom, frightened, at his mercy.

She stopped in the middle of the lane. She thought she'd heard something. The turkeys? She tightened the fleece around her and decided she should head back. The motion-detector light had gone off again, and she was out of its range, anyway. It was just too dark to go any farther. She'd start a new poem when she got back to her room. Writing helped quiet the memories of New York.

"Wendy?"

She nearly screamed, but Matt Kelleher immediately caught her hand and said, "No, no, it's just me. I thought you saw me."

"Where —"

"I was up at the cabin, out working on my camper."

Her heart raced, but she patted her chest, trying to get herself to calm down. "Did you see the wild turkeys?" she asked him.

"They just walked across the end of the driveway up at the cabin. Kind of late for them, isn't it? But they're fun to watch. Just don't want to get in the middle of a turkey fight." His shaved head stood out against the blackness of the woods behind him. "Thought I heard someone out here."

"I couldn't sleep," Wendy mumbled, not explaining further.

"Yeah. I can understand that."

"My aunt's here. Juliet. Did you meet her?"

"Briefly."

Wendy sniffled. "She had to talk to me about — about what happened. I know everyone's worried about me." She wiped her eyes with her fingertips but wasn't crying. "But I'm okay. Really."

"It's hard, I know, having everyone hovering over you, watching you for every little thing you do," Matt said gently. "Makes you feel claustrophobic, doesn't it?"

"That's it. Exactly. I know they mean well."

"I remember, when my wife was dying —"
He paused, caught up in his emotions,
then went on thoughtfully, "People did
their best, I guess, but sometimes I just
needed to be alone. To be honest, there
were times I didn't even want to be around
her. That made me feel guilty, but that's
just the way it was. I didn't want to be
alone all the time by any means — but it
was like people, circumstances, wouldn't
let me be normal."

Wendy nodded, amazed at his understanding. "My dad and my grandmother
keep looking at me like I'm going to suddenly fall into a million pieces or go crazy
or something."

Matt laughed a little. "Yeah. I know that
look."

She smiled. "Thank you for telling me
about your experience. I feel —" She hesitated, uncertain whether her train of thought
would offend him. "I think it'd help me
deal with what happened if I could —" She
stopped herself. "Never mind."

"If you could what, Wendy?"

"I've had a hard time saying goodbye to
my dog. Teddy. And here, when I know
you've lost your wife —"

"Your dog was a part of your life for a
long time."

"Since I was a baby. I went back for his ashes at my aunt's apartment. That's why — that's why I was there when that guy —" She blinked back tears, wishing she hadn't brought up New York. "It's not Teddy's fault. He didn't do anything. He's not even — I mean, I know he's dead. It's *my* fault I went back. It's *my* fault I can't give him up."

"I don't mean to butt into your business, Wendy, but maybe now's the time to scatter Teddy's ashes. He must have been a great dog, but — I don't know. At some point, we all need closure after the death of someone we love."

The tears spilled down her cheeks, but she wasn't embarrassed for Matt to see her cry. He seemed to understand her feelings, not take them as a sign of weakness, or typical teenage angst. "I'm not like the Longstreets."

He cuffed her gently on the shoulder. "Kiddo, you're more like them than you think you are. Probably more than they think you are, too."

His words made her feel better. She wondered if he'd meant them to. "I've been thinking about scattering Teddy's ashes in the lake. He loved the water."

"He was a golden retriever, right? I've

never met one that didn't love water —"

"Once, he jumped into the lake when the ice was still melting. It was *so* cold. I thought he'd die! But he loved it! When he came out, he had icicles hanging off his fur."

Matt laughed. "Dumb dog."

Wendy found herself laughing, too, and when she headed back to the house, she had a glimmer of an idea for a new poem. It would be about Teddy. She wouldn't name him — that'd be corny — but, still, he'd be the inspiration for what she hoped would be her best poem, ever.

And first thing in the morning, she thought, she'd scatter Teddy's ashes in the lake.

Juliet awoke with a start and lay very still in the pitch dark.

Where the hell am I?

Her eyes adjusted, and she made out the interior of her small tent. She had left the flaps up, just the mosquito lining separating her from the elements. She could make out the faint shine of moonlight on the lake.

Vermont. My five acres on the lake.

A raccoon or a wild turkey must have wandered past her tent — or the cold had jerked her awake. Somehow she'd managed to squirm halfway out of her sleeping bag, not that it was worth a damn. She'd had the bag since college, but at least it was hers. Most of her camping gear had been handed down from her brothers.

The night temperature had dropped to the low thirties.

A barred owl sounded in the nature preserve across the lake.

There. That's what woke me up. Suddenly she heard the crunch of twigs just outside her tent and sat up, reaching for her Glock.

"Don't shoot, Marshal."

She groaned, immediately recognizing the west Texas drawl. "Damn, Brooker. Scare the hell out of me, why don't you?"

"You don't scare that easy." He unzipped the mosquito lining and crawled in, blotting out what minimal light there was from the stars and quarter moon. "All nice and cozy in here, I see."

"What time is it? You were in Texas this morning —"

"I flew into Manchester and rented a car, found my way up here. I figured I'd get the lay of the land and go find a motel room, but some guy who looks like you —"

"All my brothers look like me."

"This one had just pulled up in a town cop car."

"Ah. Paul."

"We had a nice chat. He was checking on the family before heading home. I think you make them nervous when you're around."

"I make them nervous when I'm not around. They'd be happier if I'd stayed home to sell mums and pumpkins and design pretty gardens. It was what I thought I'd do." She didn't know why she was telling him this — or anything. "I'd have liked it."

"Ah. The path not taken. I was supposed to be a rancher." He sat at her feet, his head hitting the tent roof. "Your brother told me you pitched your tent out here."

"Lucky you didn't run into Joshua. The mood he's in, he might have just shot you. What time is it?"

Ethan pulled off his boots. "Around midnight."

At dusk, after Wendy's apple crisp, Juliet had driven out to the lake with her camping gear. Matt Kelleher spotted her and introduced himself, then helped her cart everything down the path to her clearing. She'd found herself interrogating him about his dead wife and Arizona and his camper, then backed off. She'd spend the night on the lake. Then she'd head back to New York first thing in the morning. She wasn't accomplishing anything in Vermont except upsetting her family.

"I told Officer Paul that I had a room at a hotel off the interstate."

"You don't, though."

He shook his head. "I'm just a poor exsoldier."

"Ha."

"Don't worry, I wasn't protecting your virtue. I didn't want a Longstreet posse hunting me down."

But Juliet had to admit she didn't want her brothers finding out Ethan had made his way to her tent, either. She'd never brought a guy home to Vermont. Even when she and Rob Dunnemore were together, they seemed to both know it wasn't a forever relationship.

"You're shivering," Ethan said.

Damn it, she *was* shivering. She had on a flannel shirt and boxer shorts. *Very sexy.*

What was she thinking? She was determined to send Brooker on his way. She pulled her sleeping bag back up to her chin. "It's a small tent."

"Luxury quarters compared to what I'm used to." He shifted position, setting his boots neatly next to the tent's entrance. "Better company, too."

"Ethan —" She couldn't believe how cold she was, even with him in her tent with her. "You can't stay here. Really. If you don't want to stay in a hotel, fine. You can find a spot on the lakeshore. Make a nice bed for yourself in some freshly fallen leaves. You're Special Forces — you'll manage."

"Going to send me out into the cold night?"

He didn't seem that troubled by the prospect, or at all convinced she was serious. Juliet sighed, no longer shivering. "Ethan, I'm not that good at flings."

He rolled onto his knees and crawled next to her, touching her chin. "Neither am I."

"But —" She didn't know how to say it. "But that's what this is. The year you've had..." She winced, aware of him next to her, so close. "You've been running from what happened."

"You mean Char," he said.

"She must have been some woman, Ethan."

"She was. We were good together. We didn't see a lot of each other the two years before her death. That got to her." He spoke very steadily, as if he were describing the particulars of a mission and wanted to get every word exactly right. "But we'd have got through it."

"I'm sorry about what happened to her."

He nodded, sitting down next to Juliet, stretching out his long legs next to hers. "I'm not here because of Char," he said quietly. "I'm here because of you. Now. If you want to go ahead and throw me out into the cold —"

"I don't," Juliet said quickly, catching her breath.

He wound his fingers into her hair and smiled broadly, and even in the near darkness, she could see the spark in his eyes. "I didn't think so." He kissed her softly, his mouth opening onto hers, nothing about him cold or shivering. "You're freezing," he said, trailing one hand down her back and picking up her hand. "Oh, Marshal. You touch me with those icy fingers —"

"I fell asleep outside my sleeping bag."

"Let's make sure that doesn't happen again."

He shrugged off his leather jacket and pulled it around her shoulders, then unzipped her sleeping bag all the way down to her feet, which were encased in SmartWool socks. She rubbed her toes together. "I wasn't expecting company."

"There's something sexy about a woman in a flannel shirt and wool socks."

"And what would that be?" she asked skeptically.

He laughed softly. "The mystery of what's underneath."

"You worked for that one, Brooker." But she laughed, too, liking the relaxed feeling that was coming over her, that had eluded her all day. "Besides, there's no mystery. Not after the other night —"

"Every night's a new night."

"You can't even say that with a straight face."

But a part of him was serious — she could hear it in his voice, the undercurrent of emotion and romantic yearning. He unbuckled his belt and pulled off his jeans, shoving them to the far corner of the tent, and worked on the buttons of his shirt, a dark, soft corduroy from what Juliet had felt of it.

She put a hand on his shoulder. "Ethan."

"You're not shivering."

"Ethan, I'm not going to ask for more than you can give. Just don't pretend —"

"I'm not pretending." His voice was low, and he brushed a curl off her forehead, let his fingers linger there. "When I was in

Colombia, I kept thinking that I didn't want to end up dead in some jungle never having made love to you."

"I'm glad you got out of there alive."

"Meeting you that day in Tennessee —" He paused, as if to lend weight to his words, to make her understand that he wasn't just talking to talk, saying things to get her not to zip back up in her sleeping bag and send him on his way. "I could have gone past the point of no return. I was close. But Sarah Dunnemore, Nate Winter came along and helped. You. Without you, I don't know where I'd be."

Juliet touched her fingertips to his mouth. "You stopped yourself from crossing the line. You'd never have gone completely off the deep end."

"You're good at what you do. You could have kept me from taking off."

"Hell, no. I had cracked ribs and that road rash from hell. I was in no shape. And you weren't sharing your gun, as I recall."

"Night's Landing was crawling with you law-enforcement types. You know damn well you could have made me stay put, held me for questioning. You let me go. Then in August — you could have thought of a few reasons to cuff me —"

"I can think of a few right now."

He grinned suddenly, taking her breath away. "Can you?"

"Damn, Brooker," she said, gulping for air. "But you know we have to discuss your Texan and your vigilantes and —"

"Later."

She smiled. "That's what I was saying. We have to discuss them later."

He caught an arm around her waist, and she fell back onto her skinny roll mat, taking him with her, relishing the heat of his body. She clasped her hands behind his back, under his shirt, and if they were still icy, he didn't complain, just found her mouth again, kissing her as he felt for the buttons on her shirt. He missed one and ended up ripping it off — it ricocheted off his belt buckle and disappeared.

"Friday night wasn't a mistake," he said. "I never should have let you think it was."

"That made it easier for me. Both of us."

He kissed her again. The contrast of the cold night air and his hot mouth, his warm body, made her hyperaware of her surroundings, the moment. The dark tent, the owl, the shadows, the brush of his soft shirt against her breasts. She grabbed at his shirt with both hands, but a jolt of reality stopped her from tearing it off him — what if it was his only shirt? There'd be no explaining a torn shirt to her brothers.

So she undid the remaining buttons one by one, painstaking in her efforts, and Ethan let her, but his breathing grew ragged by the time she finished and pulled the shirt off his shoulders. She could see the outline of the black graphic tattoo on his upper arm, the shape of the muscles in his shoulders and arms.

He groaned at her. "Juliet."

She cast the shirt aside and smiled. "Serves you right for torturing me."

"You're a little breathless there yourself, Juliet."

"I love the way you say my name. It doesn't come out like that when anyone else says it. I think it's the accent —"

"Juliet," he whispered. "Juliet, Juliet, Juliet. I'll say your name anytime you want."

He rolled onto his back, taking her with him. The sleeping bag twisted around her, but she managed to push it off her, no longer minding the cold air. He smoothed his palms up her stomach and over her breasts, and she fell onto him, the last of their clothes off in seconds, coming together in a frenzy of heat and raw, open need.

"Ethan —" She didn't care that she

couldn't breathe. "Don't stop. Don't *ever* stop. You're perfect just as you are."

Grabbing her hips, he pulled her harder onto him, thrust deeper into her. "I'm not perfect."

"Perfect for me."

She hadn't meant to reveal that kind of emotion, but the words were out, and she was exposed, to herself and to him. He seemed to sense her unease and he held them both still for a moment. The owl hooting, the night suddenly seeming darker, colder. "It's okay." He skimmed his hands up her arms and caught his fingers in her hair, bringing her face closer to his own. "I'm not going to get scared and run away because you're in love with me."

"I'm not —"

He smiled, kissing her. "You repressed Yankees."

She placed her palms on his shoulders and raised herself off him, moving in such a way he had no choice but to suck in a breath. She grinned. "I thought that'd shut you up." And when he responded, quickening his pace, she cried out in surprise, unable to focus on anything but the feel of him inside her, the release that was building in every cell of her body. When it came, she felt him moving with her, timing his own to coincide with hers, until they both collapsed, breathing hard, the sleeping bag shoved at their feet.

"Hey, Marshal." He dragged a finger across her back. "You're sweating."

Juliet reached for the sleeping bag, pulling it over them both as best she could. "We'll be freezing our butts off once our heart rates slow down." She snuggled against him, his heart beating rapidly, every inch of him toasty warm. "Although I think the temperature would have to get below zero to make you shiver."

"If I start shivering, I'll find a way to warm up." He kissed the top of her head, then held her close. "Sweet dreams."

"You're a complicated man, Ethan," she said.

He didn't answer her, just found her hand in the dark, intertwining his fingers with hers as she closed her eyes.

Sixteen

◡⋄◎◉⋄◠

Mia crossed her arms over her chest to ward off the cold out on the street behind her hotel. She'd slipped into jeans and a blouse but hadn't bothered with a jacket. She'd done her graduate work at Columbia — she was comfortable in New York. But not in the middle of the night, not for the reasons she'd left her warm bed and her third movie of the night. She'd known she wouldn't be sleeping before she saw the FBI and the marshals in the morning, but she hadn't expected a jaunt outside.

"You want to meet me? Be outside your hotel in twenty minutes. Back entrance."

How, how, how — how had he known she was in New York? How had he known what hotel she was in?

Had he followed her? Had someone else followed her? Had someone told him?

But who knew? Special Agent Collins, maybe Chief Deputy Rivera.

Her caller — she'd recognized the voice — once again hadn't given her a chance to ask any questions. He'd disconnected, leaving Mia to decide what to do.

She'd debated getting Collins out of bed, but not seriously. Her caller would sniff out the FBI, and she'd lose this opportunity to find out who he was, what he wanted, what game he was playing. He'd helped her in the past. He'd put Ham Carhill in touch with her. Even if this guy was a nut, Mia wanted to believe he was, in his own mind, at least, on her side. She knew she was taking a risk, but didn't see what other choice she had. She didn't own a gun, didn't even know how to use one.

Huddled now in the entryway in the back of her hotel, Mia waited. Within minutes, an SUV with New York plates pulled up to her.

Something's wrong.

Mia took a step backward toward the door. She already knew she'd made a terrible mistake, but a man leaped out of the back seat and caught her around the waist, his hand close to her mouth but not over it. "Quiet. Not a peep. Do as I say or I guarantee Carhill and Brooker die. Got it?"

She nodded, even as he threw her into the SUV, shoving her onto the floor. Her face hit first, the carpet scratching her right cheek, smelling of mud and a man's sweat.

The SUV sped up the street, putting more and more distance between her and all that she'd left behind.

The man straddled her prone body. She couldn't get a good look at him now, and she'd only had a glimpse of him as he'd grabbed her. He had dark curly hair; he was familiar, somehow. He patted her down, taking her cell phone, her small handbag. She'd left her briefcase in her room. Her movie was still playing, the lights were still on. Would anyone on the staff notice and check on her?

Mia tried to adjust her position to take the pressure off her right elbow, which was under her, but the man in back with her pushed a foot into the small of her back. "Don't move."

"I can't — I can't breathe with your foot on me."

"Too bad."

She lifted her rib cage up as much as she could and tried not to tense up, aware it would only make breathing more difficult. But she had no confidence in her ability to resist her kidnappers. She wasn't an operative, trained in self-defense or anything else. She did Pilates and yoga. She read books.

"Who are you?" she asked, trying to keep her tone curious, without fear or any sense of entitlement.

Without letting up on his foot, he leaned down close to her face, his breath hot and foul on her left cheek. "You fucked with the wrong people, Doc. These bastards don't like corrupt White House advisers."

"You're not —"

His foot pressed firmly into her back, quashing her ability to speak. "Shut up."

From the way the SUV was moving, Mia suspected they were on a highway. The Henry Hudson Parkway, probably. Who was driving? How many were there in the car? Where were they taking her?

Unable to breathe properly, she grunted, and the foot eased off her back slightly.

She didn't ask any more questions. She thought of her mother, ironing in front of the television. And her father, off early each morning, uncomplaining, glad he had work, glad it was something he didn't mind doing. Her parents, content with their lives.

She'd tried so hard to do the right thing, not wishing ill for others, trying never to lose sight of rules, standards, procedures, a process, ethics — she was a moral person. She wasn't idealistic so much as determined to believe no one was ever faced with only bad choices. *Always* there was, at least, a right choice, if not an easy one. But Mia had no idea what her choices were now.

The man in the back seat with her removed his foot from her back and had her raise up her head slightly, then slipped a bandanna over her eyes. It smelled like stale sweat. He tied her wrists together behind her, using what felt like flexible plastic cuffs.

He chuckled. "Life is full of surprises, ain't it, Doc?"

"Where are you taking me?"

"No questions."

"But I —"

He smacked her, hard, on the side of her head, pain slicing clear through to her teeth. Her stomach lurched.

She could feel his breath hot in her ear. "Nobody told me how pretty you are."

The movement of the car added to her nausea. Before she knew what was happening, she vomited.

When she tried to sit up, he hit her again, a slap on the left side of her jaw that sent hot needles of pain straight up her cheekbones and through her eyeballs.

"Up you go." He pulled her up by her

hair, turning her onto her back and sitting her up on the floor of the SUV. "I've got a little drink for you."

"No . . ."

"That wasn't a request, Dr. O'Farrell." He seemed to enjoy her suffering. He put what felt like a paper cup to her lips. "Relax. It's just water."

He started pouring, the lukewarm fluid spilling down her chin and throat, into her blouse. Her mouth opened involuntarily. Her jaw was swelling, bruised, the pain even worse now.

"Drink," he ordered. "I don't want you passing out."

Pulling her hair, he yanked her head back and dumped the water down her throat. She choked on it, coughing. Something was wrong — it had an off taste.

It's bad water.

"Come on. Up you go."

His voice seemed far away. He got her to her feet and slung her over one shoulder, and she couldn't make herself kick or flail — couldn't move at all. And she was sinking into unconsciousness. She knew it was happening but couldn't stop it.

He'd drugged her.

Panic fluttered through her, but there was nothing she could do, and she could feel her eyelids droop, her muscles relax, as the darkness came.

Joshua had finally just dozed off when someone pounded on his front door.

"It's me, Barry," his downstairs neighbor yelled. "Open up!"

"What the hell —" Joshua pulled on his bath robe and glanced at his bedside clock. It was 3:00 a.m. *Jesus, Barry.* He hoped the poor guy wasn't having a heart attack, although from the vigor of his knocking, Joshua doubted it. He staggered into his living room and out to the entry, the tile floor cold under his feet. He pushed back the dead bolt and opened the door. "You okay?"

"Yeah, yeah, fine. You got your TV on?"

"Barry, it's three o'clock in the morning. No, I don't have my television on —"

"You work odd hours sometimes. You never know." He pushed his way past Joshua into the living room and switched on his television, picking up the remote. "I was up with sciatica. Half the time I don't sleep regular, anyway. I'm used to it. How the hell you work this remote? Put CNN on."

"Barry —"

"That guy — what's his name? The one

who attacked your daughter in New York —"

Joshua felt gut-punched. "Bobby Tatro?"

"Yeah. Him. He broke out. Faked appendicitis or some damn thing, and they took him to the hospital — they figure he had help from accomplices —"

"Tatro escaped?"

"That's what they're saying on the news."

Grabbing the remote from the old man, Joshua clicked on CNN and caught the tail end of the report. It confirmed the outlines of what Barry had just told him.

"They had it as Breaking News at first," Barry said. "I hate to admit it, but I get an adrenaline rush when I hear the Breaking News music."

"When did Tatro escape? Did they give a time?"

"About an hour ago."

Not time enough for him to reach Vermont. To reach Wendy. Juliet. Joshua forced himself to concentrate on the report. Tatro had been taken to the hospital just before two o'clock . . . within fifteen minutes, someone complained of a noxious odor. A woman went into seizures. Another lost consciousness. In the resulting pandemonium, Tatro took off. One of his guards was found doubled over, puking his guts out due to the fumes; another had his throat slit, but he was lucky — doctors found him and stitched him up in time. Although the exact substance used to cause the nerve reactions was still a mystery, it hadn't caused any fatalities, the only good news of the night.

According to the news report a massive manhunt was under way. As yet, there was no sign of Tatro or his accomplices or any indication of who his accomplices were.

Barry was shaking his head in amazement, his thin white hair sticking out above his ears. He had on a pilled red tracksuit that was at least twenty years old. "What a hell of a thing to happen."

"You okay?" Joshua asked him.

"Yeah, yeah. My ticker can handle a breakout. You?"

"I'm good. I'm going to make a couple calls, see what I can find out —"

As if on cue, his telephone rang. Barry plopped down on Joshua's couch and motioned for him to go ahead and answer.

He expected it to be a fellow state trooper. "Longstreet —"

"Trooper Longstreet, right? Juliet's brother?"

"One of them. You're —"

"Mike Rivera. Chief deputy —"

Joshua's heart jumped. Had she gone back to New York and not told him? He warned himself not to speculate. "I'm Joshua Longstreet. What can I do for you, Chief?"

"I'm trying to reach your sister. I was hoping you could help me. Her cell phone's off or something."

"She's in the woods. No cell service out there. I just heard about Tatro."

"A dozen things could have gone wrong with Tatro's plan, but nothing did. Worked like a charm. He must have had it worked out in advance in case he got picked up, because he sure as hell didn't have any company while he was in custody." Rivera sounded grim, but he didn't need to go into detail of what federal, state and local law enforcement were doing to find Bobby Tatro — Joshua knew a national manhunt was in progress. "Juliet needs to know. How far out in the woods is she?"

"She's camped out on a lake a fifteen-minute walk from our folks' place."

"She's in a tent?"

Rivera sounded incredulous, which made Joshua smile in spite of his tension. "That's right. She owns five acres on the lake. She likes to camp there during decent weather."

"Well, Tatro can't know she's in Vermont, and it's unlikely he'd get there even if he does know. Juliet's on high alert as it is. She's brought us up to speed. What is it, one, two hours before daylight? Have her call me after sunup."

Joshua didn't argue with him. The chief deputy would have a clearer picture of the situation. He hadn't gotten the news from Barry Small and CNN. And Joshua had no desire to traipse out to his sister's tent. Ethan Brooker was in town, and Joshua doubted he was staying at a hotel.

"How's your daughter doing?" Rivera asked, his tone softening.

"Okay. Thanks for asking." But Joshua knew he didn't sound grateful — he sounded worried and irritated and helpless, because the man who'd terrorized his daughter was on the loose. "Who helped Tatro escape?"

"We don't know."

Joshua could imagine what was happening in New York. He raked a hand over his close-cropped hair. "I'll have Juliet call you."

After he hung up, he resisted an urge to kick the wall.

Barry sat on the edge of the couch. "Anything I can do?"

"Stay here. Let me know if anyone else calls. I'm going up to my folks' place and keep an eye on things there." He'd also get in touch with his colleagues with the state police and find out what they had on Bobby Tatro. "Barry, you okay? Not too much excitement for you?"

"Nah. I'll be fine."

When Joshua arrived at his folks' house, all was quiet. Lights out, doors locked. Using his key, he slipped inside, not turning on any lights as he made his way to the living room. Spaceshot didn't even trouble himself to bark. Having raised five sons and a daughter, his parents had no doubt heard his truck. But they'd figure he'd come over because he couldn't sleep worrying about his own daughter.

Let them roll over and go back to sleep, Joshua thought, stretching out on the couch. There was no reason to panic. He pulled a knitted afghan over him, thinking about his daughter upstairs in his old room, telling himself that their luck was due for a turn and the marshals or NYPD would pick Tatro up by morning.

Seventeen

Ethan had left the window cracked on his rented car, and when he climbed behind the wheel, he sat in cold dew.

Served him right, he thought grimly.

It was barely daylight, but Juliet had assured him her family was the up-at-first-light type. He'd left her standing on the lakeshore, staring into a white fog that would burn off with the morning sun, her toes practically in the water. She'd slipped out of the tent early, before dawn, and performed tai chi and karate warm-ups in her flannel shirt and a pair of sweatpants she'd pulled on. When a flock of wild turkeys trooped through the nearby woods, she abandoned her exercises and went to get Ethan up so he could see them, but discovered he'd been watching her. He'd pulled her back into the tent with him.

And now it was time for a quick shower, a change of clothes, a pot of coffee and honest answers to any and all questions Deputy Longstreet had for him. She'd made it clear she expected nothing less. "I swear I'll turn you over to Joe Collins, Brooker," she'd warned him, never mind that she was lying naked beside him, loose and warm from their lovemaking.

The dirt road led back out to the main road, which he took down to Longstreet Landscaping. Juliet would walk from the lake and meet him there. When he parked next to the pumpkins, the vehicles that had been there last night were gone, and one that hadn't been there — a spotless truck — was parked crookedly, its front left tire on the stone walk to the side porch.

An old dog got up slowly, stretched and greeted him with a head butt. Ethan patted him on the head.

"His name's Spaceshot." A tall, fair-haired man walked out from the side porch. Another brother. "You must be Major Brooker."

"Just Ethan will do. You're —"

"Joshua Longstreet."

The niece's father. He looked tense, exhausted. Ethan felt a wave of compassion for the man and decided not to bullshit him. "Juliet's on her way over."

"Bobby Tatro escaped last night."

He gave Ethan a few seconds for the words to sink in, then told him what he had. By the time he finished, Juliet was there, in her new leather jacket and jeans, her Glock in its holster on her belt. Joshua didn't go through Tatro's escape again. He left Ethan to do it and got in his truck, speaking to his sister through the open door. "I'll be back in an hour. I'll check on the status of the search. Sam's in the shed. The folks wanted to stay, but I made them go — they've got a big job they need to finish before winter." If anything, his blue eyes hardened as he shifted his gaze to Ethan. "Wendy's asleep. She doesn't know about Tatro. Tell her she can reach me on my cell phone."

He pulled his truck door shut, started the engine and backed out of the driveway. Juliet grabbed Ethan's arm, her fingers digging in. "Wendy doesn't know what about Tatro?"

And Ethan told her, without emotion. She didn't interrupt, but when he finished, she ground her teeth. "Son of a bitch. *Damn.* Rivera must be beside himself." She focused on Ethan. "I need to call him. Stay put."

She took the three steps onto the side porch in a single leap. Without waiting for an invitation, Ethan followed her into the warm country kitchen. There were no pecan rolls freshly made by a hired cook. How was he going to explain the Carhills and his relationship to them to Juliet? How would he make her understand his sense of obligation to Ham?

He headed back out to his car, fetched his overnight bag and found his way to a bathroom sink to get cleaned up. A long, hot shower would have to wait.

When he returned to the kitchen, Juliet was off the phone, putting on a pot of coffee. Her back to him, she scooped coffee from a five-pound can and dumped it into a filter. "Help yourself when it's done. Mugs are in the cupboard above the sink. Left side. I'm taking a shower and clearing my head." She hit the power switch for the old coffeemaker and spun around at him. "Rivera and Joe Collins are meeting with your friend from the White House this morning. Mia O'Farrell. Nate Winter's flying up from Nashville."

"Juliet —"

"Did this O'Farrell arrange Tatro's escape?"

He shook his head. "No."

"Well, someone did. He had outside help. The plan had to be set up in advance, just in case he was arrested. He didn't know I'd catch him at my apartment. He

didn't have any visitors in jail. Now —"
She broke off, inhaling. "*Damn* it, a police
officer was almost killed."

"Anyone you know?"

"Doesn't matter."

She stalked past him, stopping abruptly
in the doorway, turning to him. Her eyes, a
clear sky-blue, black-lashed, were wide
with anger and determination, and regret,
Ethan thought. She softened slightly.
"We'll talk. Then we'll head to New York
together."

"Juliet —"

The edge came back. "You don't have
any choice."

She about-faced and ran upstairs,
trusting him, at least, to stay put, drink
coffee and wait for her.

Either that, Ethan thought, or she'd keep
one eye on the bathroom window and
shoot him where he stood if he tried to
leave.

He poured himself coffee and drifted out
to the front porch, shaded by a maple tree
with leaves so red, so bright, he couldn't
take his eyes off them. But he kept seeing
the photo of Juliet, lying in Tatro's hut.
Had he been meant to find it?

Bobby Tatro was an instrument. A tool
someone was using to get what he wanted.

Ham Carhill — the same. Mia O'Farrell — the same. Means to an end.

Ethan picked up a single red leaf that had blown onto the porch and twirled its stem between his fingers. How long had it been since he'd led a normal life? Even if he went back to Texas and took his place alongside Luke on the ranch, Ethan had no illusions.

A normal life wasn't in the cards for him.

It never had been.

Ham tucked himself into a booth at a lunch-and-breakfast place down the highway from his motel. He drummed the Formica table with his fingers while he looked over the plastic-encased menu. A short, plump waitress about his mother's age took his order for pancakes and home fries.

"Any sausage or bacon with that?" she asked.

"No, ma'am."

"You like your carbs, huh?"

"Yes, ma'am."

She sighed and tucked the order pad into her apron pocket. "Wish they affected me the way they do you."

He didn't tell her that a week ago he'd been eating fatback and beans. If his captors had set snake meat in front of him, he'd have eaten it, too. She went to put in his order, then returned with a mug of coffee. Normally Ham didn't drink coffee. He hoped the caffeine would give him a buzz.

Two uniformed cops came in and took stools at the counter.

Ham wondered if he looked suspicious. Hell, he wondered about so many things these days, he couldn't keep his head straight. He wondered if Mia O'Farrell hadn't liked him taking off on his own after his rescue. He'd told her he couldn't talk and needed time to recuperate from his ordeal. She would cut him off at the knees if she felt national security was at stake.

If the cops found cause to search him, Ham knew he was doomed. No way could he explain the emeralds he'd hidden in his hip-pack. One emerald he could pass off as a present for a girlfriend. *But fifteen?* After Colombia, he'd transferred them to a soft suede drawstring pouch.

A big man in work clothes, his bulk oozing over the edges of a stool down the counter from the cops, asked if they thought the escaped ex-con would head their way. "That's the same guy who broke into Juliet's place in New York on Friday, isn't it? You worried about her?"

One of the cops — fair, tall, blue-eyed, in no mood — shrugged. "My sister can take care of herself."

"I heard she's in town. Did she pitch her tent on the lake like she usually does?"

The blond cop — Juliet's brother — bristled, obviously preferring this guy didn't broadcast details about his sister. "You see Tatro, give us a call."

"Damn right."

The other cop said, "Consider him armed and dangerous. Don't approach him."

"Hell, I'll just call Juliet." The big guy had gone a little pale but wasn't letting it get to him. "She used to sit in front of me in algebra. Even then she could beat the hell out of the rest of us. Must be having five older brothers."

The Longstreet cop didn't seem to think that was funny, but the other cop hid his smile in his coffee. Ham could only see some of what was going on from his vantage point, but it was easy to fill in the blanks. During his two years in South America, he'd enjoyed sitting in cafés and bars, watching people. He'd grown up isolated and alone, but he thought he had a decent eye for reading people.

The waitress brought him his pancakes on one plate and his home fries on a second plate. "Anything else?"

"No, ma'am. This'll be fine. Thank you."

The two cops swiveled on their stools and looked him over.

The Texas accent.

Ham had left his cowboy hat and boots at home, but he never thought about his accent drawing attention. At least Tatro wasn't a Texan.

Ignoring the cops, Ham emptied his little syrup pitcher onto his pancakes. They were practically floating.

The cops finished their coffees, paid up and left.

A lake.

Ham decided it couldn't be too hard to figure out what lake. Then he could find Juliet Longstreet and talk to her alone. He wasn't sure what all to tell her, but thought he'd start with the emeralds and how he didn't want anything else rotten to happen to anyone on his account.

Juliet sat on a wicker chair on the front porch of her childhood home with her coffee, the ends of her hair damp from a sixty-second shower that had settled her

315

mood if not cleared her head. "Tell me about the Carhills first," she said. "Then we'll get to vigilantes, smuggling and ransom."

Ethan was leaning against a post and the porch rail, legs stretched out, ankles crossed. "You've been busy."

"My partner did some digging for me. The Carhills are your Texas neighbors —"

"I don't know that I'd call us neighbors. By Vermont's distance standards, they'd live in Maine."

"That's an exaggeration."

Her serious tone didn't seem to affect him. He shrugged. "Of course it is. I'm a Texan." But when she didn't budge, he went on, "Johnson Carhill and my father went to grade school together. The Carhills are very private people. They don't court publicity — they value the opposite, in fact."

"Their son?"

"Ham's a bright kid. He's twenty-five but already has his Ph.D. in physics. He took off for South America and adventures. Mountain-climbing —"

"Is he into precious gems? Colombia is known for its emeralds."

"If it's a rock, Ham's interested in it."

Juliet noticed the distant look that had

come into Ethan's dark eyes, and tried not to think of them in the night, locked with hers. "How did he become a national security asset? Because of his science background or his 'adventures'?"

"I don't know. I've told you." His gaze settled on her, just long enough to make her realize that whoever Hamilton Carhill was, Ethan's loyalty to him had driven his actions, at least in part, over the past month. "I'm just a soldier."

"Fair enough. I believe you. Where's your friend Carhill now?"

"He left his parents' home in Texas on Friday without saying where he was going. He was a wreck when we got him in Colombia. He's thin by nature, but he was malnourished, covered in bites — scared as hell. He needs time to recuperate." Ethan turned to the sugar maple in the front yard and gazed up at it, the sun having burned off most of the fog by now. "Ham knows that not very many people give a damn about him."

"But you do," Juliet said.

"He'd follow my brother and me around when he was a little tyke. His parents —"

When he didn't go on, Juliet thought she understood. "They wanted him to be like you. He idolized you. Damn it, Ethan, how did he get mixed up with Bobby Tatro and national-security types?"

"That's what I'm trying to figure out, too."

"If it's true that Carhill was in New York in late August —" She hesitated, choosing her words carefully before continuing, "If he was in trouble, in over his head, would he come to you?"

"If he could find me."

"News reports had you hooking up with me in August over the search for Libby Smith. You haven't been that easy to find this past year. Maybe my source is right and Ham came to New York looking for you for some reason —"

"Such as?"

"Maybe he knew he was in over his head and was turning to you for help."

That seemed to make sense to Ethan. "It's possible."

"Bobby Tatro was out of prison by then, stalking me. If he saw your guy —" She stopped herself, frowning. "But how would Tatro know who he was?"

"Someone told him."

"Mia O'Farrell?"

"No. I don't think so. She's got a source, but whoever it is got in touch with her before Tatro was released from prison."

"She won't tell you who it is?"

He gave her that wry smile again.

Juliet sighed. "Ah. Yes. You're just a soldier."

"I doubt Tatro figured out Ham on his own. It'd be difficult to put a name and a face together out on the street like that, even with people you've seen before. And Ham's a Carhill. There aren't many pictures of him floating around in public, none recent."

"So, Tatro had help figuring out who Ham was."

Ethan obviously didn't like the idea any better than Juliet did, but he said nothing.

"How convenient," Juliet went on, "that you don't need a picture to recognize him. And you happen to be a Special-Forces type who could also rescue him."

"That's a lot to swallow in one mouthful."

"Sure is. You *happen* to be a Special-Forces officer. Your very smart, very wealthy friend and neighbor in Texas *happens* to get mixed up in national security. An ex-con who has it in for me *happens* to snatch him."

"Yes, Deputy," Ethan said, gritting his teeth. "A lot of coincidences."

Juliet didn't back off. "Did Ham start

doing covert work, or whatever he was doing, to impress you?"

"I didn't ask him."

"But what do you think?"

"Maybe it was a factor. I don't know. It doesn't matter. I agreed to get a team together and go rescue him. So that's what I did." Ethan dropped his feet to the floor and stood, his face lost in the shade and the shadows. "What else do you want to know?"

"Everything."

He stared at her, then grinned. "You don't intimidate easily, do you?"

"Were you trying to intimidate me?"

"No, but I wasn't not trying to, either."

"I've got five big brothers. They're all tall, they're all frank —"

Ethan took both her hands into his and lowered his face to hers, his eyes flinty with intensity and a flash of humor. "I'm not your brother. In case you need reminding."

He let her hands go and stepped back, and she took a breath and smiled at him. "Nope. No reminding necessary."

He turned, his back to her, and looked out at the front lawn, shaded by two old sugar maples. "Mia O'Farrell gave me the tip that Ham was being held by someone who had a thing for a blond, female marshal."

"It wasn't any more specific?"

"No. Once we had an ID, it was enough to help us find Tatro, and therefore Ham."

"Bobby's not subtle, and he's also very good-looking. He left a trail for you and the Colombian authorities and whoever else to follow. But now you're wondering if we've all been manipulated. Even Tatro."

"That's a big, tangled ball of twine to unravel, Juliet."

"Right now, we don't have to. We just have to find Tatro. That's one thing I like about fugitive investigations. I get a target, and I go after it. So — did the Carhills get a ransom demand for their son's release?"

"Juliet." Ethan looked around at her. "You're going where I can't take you."

"I'll take that as a yes. Did they pay it?"

He sighed. "Faye — Ham's mother — says no."

"Do you believe her?"

"I don't know."

"How much did the kidnappers demand?"

"Five million."

Juliet coughed. "Well, hell."

"It's not that much to the Carhills."

"Does Mia O'Farrell know?"

"She was never in touch with them."

"Meaning no, she doesn't know. And

presumably the Carhills didn't contact their local FBI agent. Is that how they found out about the kidnapping — from the ransom demand?"

"We didn't get that far. Faye's not one to dwell on the past. Right now, she just wants her son back home safe."

Juliet was still on the ransom demand. "Tatro? Was he the one who called?" She ran that one through in her mind and shook her head. "I just don't see Bobby Tatro calling up the Carhills of Texas for five million. I sure as hell can't see him breaking into my apartment thinking he'd find it under my futon. But he was looking for something."

"Maybe Ham can answer some of these questions when we find him."

Juliet regarded Ethan with as much objectivity as she could, considering she'd slept with him twice since he'd handed her the doctored picture of herself. He wasn't spinning tales, and he wasn't holding back much, if anything. He hadn't been playing by the rules in the year since his wife's death, but that didn't mean he'd done anything unethical or illegal.

"Juliet, Ham's a romantic," Ethan went on. "An idealist. If he thinks he did something to cause your doorman to get killed and your niece —"

"You're worried about him," Juliet broke in.

"Yes."

"Any reason anyone would think he's a traitor?"

"The way I see it, people don't need much of a reason to think anything."

"These gonzo mercenary vigilantes —"

"I rousted a group of American vigilantes in Afghanistan a couple years ago. Before Char's death. If Ham got mixed up with anything like them —" Ethan's eyes darkened perceptibly. "Let's hope that's not the case."

"All right." Juliet rolled to her feet, realized she'd only had a couple of sips of coffee, but, after last night, she was still energized, as if every nerve ending was alive, sensitized, on alert. Ethan had an effect on her — she didn't always like it or understand it, but he definitely had an effect. "I need to head back to New York. I'll get Wendy up and tell her about Tatro and bring her out to the shed with Sam until Joshua gets back. I don't want her waking up to an empty house and turning on CNN."

Ethan followed her to the door. "Ham

thinks his parents wished I were their son instead of him." He kept his voice level, but Juliet could sense the guilt he felt. "One way or another, I'm the reason he ended up using his genius-IQ for the government. He looked up to me. He wanted to be me."

"Ethan —"

"I've made a few enemies along the way, Juliet. More than a few. If one of them decided to play Ham to get to me —"

"Then that's one very nasty person."

"If I'd stayed home in Texas," Ethan said quietly, "Ham Carhill would be teaching physics at MIT and working on a Nobel Prize."

"He may yet." Juliet took a gulp of her coffee, knowing she should regret not getting more sleep last night — but she didn't. "I don't know, Brooker. I probably shouldn't have let you into my tent last night, knowing you were pals with one of the richest families in the country." She tossed the rest of her coffee over the porch rail into the grass. "You and the Carhills don't buy five-pound cans of coffee on sale, do you?"

"Juliet —"

"We'll find your friend, Ethan."

"Ham's brilliant, but I never pictured

him getting mixed up in anything involving national security. I want to help him. That's all."

She pointed her coffee mug at him, trying to dissipate some of his seriousness, his guilt. "What you want to do, Brooker, is not meddle in a federal investigation. Bobby Tatro's a federal fugitive. You hold back vital information, someone's going to toss your ass into jail."

He smiled at her suddenly, catching her off guard with the spark in his black eyes. "Do you ever mince words?"

She smiled back. "That *was* mincing words."

She led the way up the narrow, steep stairs and knocked on the door to her niece's corner bedroom. "Wendy? Time to get up." Juliet waited a moment, and when there was no answer, banged on the door. "I'm leaving for New York in a few minutes. I need to talk to you."

Again, no response. Ethan tried the knob. "It's locked."

"What? She never locks her door —" Inexplicably worried, Juliet gave it a kick. "Wendy!"

"She could have on headphones —"

But Juliet leaned her shoulder against the door and put all her weight into a single, hard push, springing it open.

Wendy's bed was unmade, torn pieces of paper were scattered on the floor. Lace curtains — her mother's addition after the boys had moved out — fluttered in the window.

There was no sign of her niece.

Juliet spun around at Ethan. "Where is she?"

He picked up a sheet of paper off her window seat, gave it a quick glance, then handed it to her. Juliet recognized Wendy's neat handwriting.

I'll be back soon — I hope before you find this note! Please don't worry. I'm not doing anything dangerous, and I'm not running away. I just need to do something for myself.

Love,
Wendy

"She's seventeen," Ethan said, as if that explained everything.

"What'd she do, melt through the walls? Her door was locked from the *inside*." But she noticed the closet door, half open, and groaned, knowing exactly what her niece had done. "Ah, hell. She went through the trap door."

Juliet marched to the closet and ripped

the door all the way open, Ethan looking over her shoulder as she pointed at the trap door in the ceiling. "Wish I'd had one of those when I was growing up," he said.

"Joshua and Sam shared this room. They used to sneak out when they were kids. They took out the hanging rod and put up hooks and shelves." She noticed the clothes on the floor, the scattered books and magazines. "Wendy's not as tall as they were. She must have climbed up the shelves."

"The trap door leads to the attic?"

"It's more like a crawl space. My brothers locked me up there once — they didn't think I'd have the guts to go out the window. It drops onto the back porch. It was nightfall before the little bastards realized I'd escaped."

"Bet you had pigtails then."

Juliet sighed, backing up from the door. "I'll go find Sam. I haven't seen him yet this morning, but if he saw her sneaking out the attic window, he'd have stopped her. For all we know, she's sitting in the shade, reading a book."

"What about her father?"

"If Sam hasn't seen her, then I'll call Joshua." She grimaced, heading back out into the hall. "It won't be easy telling him Wendy took off again."

Eighteen

Mia stirred but didn't open her eyes. She breathed. No pain, no nausea. She resisted the temptation to move. She wanted to get her bearings first. She was facedown on some kind of wood floor, blindfolded, gagged, her feet bound, her hands still cuffed behind her.

She thought she heard birds.

An owl, maybe?

Where am I?

She remembered her father kneeling at her bed with her, clasping his hands on her pink bedspread as they said the "Hail Mary" together. Whenever she prayed, it was his voice she heard along with hers, not that of the priests, the nuns. *"I'm a rough man, Mia. I swear too much, I drink too much. But I pray every day for strength and guidance."*

She couldn't remember the last time she'd been to Mass.

Her head throbbed, and her mouth had a funny taste. She desperately wanted water.

And she was cold. As she focused on her surroundings, she realized the floor had thick splinters, and she could feel cold air coming up through the cracks and gaps in the boards.

With a surge that was almost painful, she remembered the late-night call, the SUV, the foul-breathed man pouring water into her mouth. The kicks and slaps. No wonder she was so stiff.

Where had he — they — taken her? Had he handed her off to someone else?

They'd changed vehicles — or had she imagined it?

She couldn't be in Colombia. It was too cold.

"You're prettier than I thought you'd be." The man's voice. Had he been there all along? "Say thank you."

How could she when she was gagged?

She felt fingers on her face, and the gag was yanked down to her chin. "Now say thank you. Don't bother screaming. No one will hear you."

"Where —" She was parched, and her lips were chapped and split when she opened her mouth to speak. She shuddered in pain. "Where am I?"

"I didn't hear you say thank you."

"Thank you."

"Thank you for what?"

"Thank you for saying I'm pretty."

"Prettier than I thought you'd be. There's a difference."

She said nothing. *God, help me.*

"Where are my emeralds?"

"What?"

He slapped her across the left side of her face, sending her backward against her bound hands. Pain shot through her from the unnatural position. "Don't play dumb, Dr. O'Farrell. It doesn't suit you. You know what happened to them. It's your job to know these things." He got close to her. "I want my fucking emeralds."

She rolled onto her side, taking the pressure off her hands, and thought she smelled damp earth.

Bobby Tatro.

He was her captor. Somehow, he was out of jail. Somehow, he'd found her, taken her to this place.

I'm not getting out of here alive.

She coughed, tried not to think about the pain. "You kidnapped Ham Carhill for emeralds?"

"A half-million dollars' worth of emeralds. If you want to give me cash, I'll take it." He was sarcastic, sneering. "You shouldn't have double-crossed me."

"A half million? That's all you got?" She couldn't hide her surprise. The Carhills were worth over a billion. Ham was their only son. Why ask for only half a million? Unless the emeralds hadn't come from the Carhills. "Who gave you the emeralds? Was it your take —"

"Shut up."

But from his split-second's hesitation, Mia realized that Tatro didn't really know.

"You're a Washington insider," he went on. "You play games for a living. Don't think you can fuck with my head."

"I'm just trying to understand what's going on." She was so tired, and her head was spinning — but trying to put the pieces of her ordeal together kept her from focusing on her pain and fear. "How did you know about me? How did you find me in New York?"

He kicked her in the ribs, and she cried out, almost vomiting with the agony. He moved in closer to her. "You don't need to understand anything. Just tell me where my emeralds are. You don't want me to turn you over to my friend. He knows how to run an interrogation."

Mia was gulping in air, on the verge of hyperventilating, but she forced herself to stop, get control of herself. *Think.* She tried to lick her lips, but her tongue was parched. "I need water. Please."

"That's better." He seemed to enjoy having her plead with him. "Sit up."

He didn't help her as she struggled to a sitting position, fighting pain, nausea, fear. Her shoulders ached constantly from how far he'd yanked them back to cuff her wrists, and she could feel the bounds cutting into her ankles. The blindfold was disorienting but not painful. She didn't know if it was night or day.

"Two sips. I don't want to clean you up after you pee in your pants."

He was sadistic, she realized. He enjoyed watching her suffer. She took the two sips, not caring if the water was drugged — she'd almost prefer unconsciousness to this misery and fear.

"That's a girl."

He replaced her gag, and in another few seconds, she heard a door creak.

Alone in the dark, she curled up into a fetal position. She had to get free. If she didn't, he'd kill her. It didn't matter if she could or couldn't lead him to the emeralds. She was dead.

Hail Mary, full of grace, blessed art Thou amongst women . . .

Comforted, she was able to relax her muscles, and to think.

Wendy dropped behind a huge granite boulder that was half in the lake, half out, and sat in damp, rotting pine needles. She could taste their acid mustiness. The boulder was in the woods along the clearing where Juliet had pitched her tent, still on her land. Wendy's jog through the woods down to the lake had sounded thunderous to her — every crunch of leaves and twigs, every gulp of air, seemed magnified, threatening to alert anyone within miles to her whereabouts.

Which would have been okay, but she really wanted to be alone.

Her heart was racing, thumping hard in her chest, but just from exertion, she thought, not fear — not like Friday with Bobby Tatro. She'd accomplished her first goal of getting out of the house and away from her dad and her aunt and everyone. She couldn't believe her dad had come at the crack of dawn and slept on the couch. She was up early and halfway down the stairs when she saw him, and she tiptoed right back up to her room. His overprotectiveness was going to drive her crazy.

Matt was right. She needed to scatter

Teddy's ashes and let him rest in peace. It would help with her sense of restlessness and failure, her guilt over Juan. No matter who he was, no one deserved to be murdered.

She'd crawled up into the attic and out the window while her aunt and her dad and that army guy were out in the driveway. Wendy didn't like Ethan Brooker being in Vermont. She'd seen him arrive last night. She'd finally warmed up after going out after the turkeys. She didn't recognize him at first — she'd met him only briefly in New York. But after he left, she checked with her uncle Paul, and he told her who he was, said not to worry and sent her back inside before she froze.

She didn't want to think about how nuts they'd all be if they found her gone. She planned to be back before that happened. She'd decided it was her responsibility to find a place to scatter Teddy's ashes. He was *her* dog, and she'd wanted his burial to be just between the two of them. So far, she'd made it to the lake without being seen.

Uncertain about what to do next, Wendy watched freshly fallen yellow birch leaves floating on the water, and her eyes teared up as she imagined sprinkling Teddy's ashes on the lake, watching them disappear. She let herself take in the play of sunlight burning through the last of the morning fog, bright golden rays catching the stunning fall foliage. Although her cousins, who weren't homeschooled or only children, whose parents weren't divorced, didn't give her credit for knowing *anything* practical, she knew her way around the lake.

She didn't want to scatter Teddy's ashes just anywhere. It had to be the perfect spot. She wasn't going to rush her decision. If her dad or aunt got suspicious and beat down her door, her note should keep them from going totally nuts and bringing in search dogs or anything, even if they wouldn't understand. Wendy knew she could tell her dad about her mission, but she didn't want to — her sentimentality embarrassed her.

And the truth was, she didn't want her father to help her scatter Teddy's ashes. It was for her to do, on her own.

Feeling reenergized, she set the tin on top of the boulder, on a flat, shady spot where it wouldn't fall. She'd leave it there until she'd picked out Teddy's final resting place. She was so afraid of tripping on a tree root or something and dropping the tin, having the ashes dump out in the ferns or dead pine needles.

The spring.

She smiled, remembering it was one of Teddy's favorite spots on the lake.

Ducking under a low hemlock branch, Wendy pushed through ferns until she came to a narrow path that would take her through the woods to the spring. The nature preserve had made a sign for it and carved out a little picnic area on the lakeshore, where hikers and paddlers could take a break, before or after hiking the hundred yards back up another path to the spring to refill their water bottles.

On a happier day, Wendy thought, she'd sit and watch the ducks that were often there, and dip her toes into the water. Teddy would come with her sometimes, and he'd leap off the rocks into the water. She pictured him paddling like mad, his tongue wagging. He'd scare the ducks, but he never meant to.

Maybe that was where she'd scatter his ashes.

As he dipped his paddle into the soft lake water, Ham felt almost like a normal tourist. He'd stopped at a wilderness outfitter, whose name and address he'd spotted in his Vermont guidebook, and found out about the small lake and the nature preserve out by Longstreet Landscaping. He'd had to be direct with some of his questions. No way around it. With Tatro's escape in all the news, he wanted to get on with finding Deputy Longstreet and talking to her.

But everyone seemed to know she was involved in Tatro's arrest, and what he'd done to her niece, and Ham didn't want to attract attention to himself. He decided to rent a kayak — prove that his interest in the same lake where Deputy Longstreet owned land was purely coincidental, and all he wanted to do was to spend the day on a quiet lake that didn't allow motor-operated watercraft.

He'd had to rent a roof carrier, too. He headed out to the nature preserve, alert for any sign of Deputy Longstreet's campsite as he drove up the dead-end dirt road. He passed a small lake house, a cabin up on a hill on the other side of the road, then, back on the same side of the lake, a sign for a spring, a rustic old barn, another lake house, and, finally, the turnaround he'd read about in his guidebook, where he could leave his car and launch his kayak.

He hoped he'd be able to see the marshal's campsite from the water.

The autumn scenery was breathtaking, and Ham was able to lose himself in the peace of a solitary paddle in an isolated Vermont lake. This was where he should have come to restore body and soul, he thought, not home to Texas, not into the middle of all the secrets he and his parents kept from one another.

The long, slender kayak was easy to maneuver, tracked well, forgiving of his lack of physical conditioning. But there was no wind, just a bit of fog to contend with, and it was dissipating fast. Ham paddled through a thick patch that hovered in the middle of the lake. When he came out of it, he was just ten yards from shore.

A girl was standing under a giant pine tree on a narrow, rocky point, mouth agape as she stared at him as if he'd just emerged from a cloud of doom, the devil himself.

Ham smiled and waved to her. "Good morning!" he called cheerfully, noticing another sign for the spring, this one on the lake, presumably to alert paddlers like himself. "I'm just stopping for water. That sign's right, isn't it? There's a spring here?"

At first the girl looked as if she might bolt, but then she nodded, although still tentative. "It's a short walk through the woods."

She looked about seventeen. Ham wondered if she was the marshal's niece who'd had the run-in with Tatro. What was she doing out here alone, with that sick bastard on the loose? Didn't she know?

Ham kept smiling, paddling, feeling the strain in his shoulders. He didn't have much upper-body strength. "Great. I need to stretch my legs." He did, too. He hadn't taken the time to adjust the seat properly, and his knees were almost up to his chin. "My name's Ham." He didn't know what else to say, then added, lamely, "I'm here on vacation."

The girl watched him, suspicious, as he pushed his kayak onto a muddy, grassy spot just a few yards down from her pine tree and climbed out, splashing into the water in his moccasin shoes, yelping at how cold it was. That made her smile.

He gave a small, awkward laugh. "I'm not used to Vermont lakes." He laid the paddle across the top of the kayak's cockpit. "Ah. Sorry if I startled you."

"That's okay. I didn't see you in the fog."

"Are you from around here?"

She nodded.

He glanced around at the small clearing, surrounded by blueberry bushes, a simple wooden picnic table sitting in the shade of an oak tree. A pretty spot. "Would you freak out if I asked you to show me to the spring?"

"I can't. My dad's meeting me here in a few minutes. He's a state trooper. My aunt's coming with him. She's a federal marshal."

The kid was nervous. Ham didn't blame her. He smiled. "Wow. A trooper and a marshal in the family."

"I have another uncle who's a town police officer."

Probably the guy at breakfast. Ham squinted at her in the bright sunlight. "Cool."

Cop's daughter that she was, she narrowed her eyes on him. "Where's your water bottle?"

Fortunately, the outfitters had insisted he take basic supplies with him, and he was prepared. He got his hip-pack from where he'd stuffed it down into the cockpit, unlatched it and pulled out a brand-new neoprene water bottle that he'd bought from the outfitters, hoping to keep them from becoming suspicious.

He held the bottle up toward the girl. "It's right here." He gestured toward the woods, grinning at her. He had a fair idea of what Tatro had put her through the other day and didn't want to scare the hell out of her. "Any lions, tigers and bears back there?"

She seemed to relax somewhat. "Maybe a bear, more likely a fisher cat or a fox, and probably some wild turkeys, but they won't bother you."

"Good to know."

Ham had no doubt he looked out of his element. Never mind that he'd climbed mountains all over South America, he figured he'd always look like a mad, nerdy scientist. Since he *was* a scientist, he didn't shatter anyone's stereotypes, even when he wore his black cowboy hat and cowboy boots. He had on cargo pants and a sweatshirt and had pulled his hair back into a neat ponytail, but the bug bites on his face couldn't help his cause. Since now he really was thirsty, he figured he'd fetch some water from the spring.

"I'll be back in a few minutes," he said.

"Nice meeting you. I need to go meet my dad."

Ham silently applauded her for sticking to her obvious lie. The kid was taking care of herself. It was better than he'd done for himself in recent months. He shambled off onto the path amid yellow-leafed birches and young pine trees, knowing she'd be long gone when he got back and he'd missed his chance to ask her where her aunt had pitched her tent.

He stopped abruptly. *Hell!* He'd been so damn concerned about reassuring the girl he'd left the emeralds behind in his pack. To go back now would just draw more attention to him. He'd just make quick work of his jaunt to the spring.

Wendy waited until Ham was out of sight on the path to the spring before she scrambled off her rocky point and over to his kayak, recognizing the logo of the place where he'd rented it.

She'd been watching the ducks on the other side of the point when he'd materialized out of the fog. Ham — what kind of name was that? Was it his real name? Who was he?

Trust your instincts.

It was what her father had always told her.

Her instincts were on high alert, as if they were trying to tell her something that she just wasn't *getting*.

She didn't feel safe.

She noticed that the main compartment of Ham's hip-pack was still open in the cockpit. She squatted down and glanced behind her, but she didn't see him — it was a good hundred yards to the spring. She didn't want to get caught snooping, but why hadn't he just waved to her and kept paddling? It seemed odd that he'd come to shore the way he did, even with the spring right there.

He'd shoved a mess of stuff into his hippack, but sitting right on top was an unopened bottle of store-bought spring water.

He hadn't needed to stop at the spring.

Her ears were ringing from tension and indecision.

What was going on?

She gingerly moved aside a couple of crushed granola bars and pulled out what looked like an airline boarding pass and a battered wallet.

The boarding pass was issued to Hamilton Carhill. *Ham.*

Okay, so that really was his name. Feeling a little more reassured, Wendy opened the wallet and saw a Texas license with a photo of the man who'd just headed off to the spring.

Maybe she was just paranoid.

"Wendy! Wendy — run!"

She shot to her feet. The yell came from the woods. Ham, but she couldn't see him.

Acid rose in her throat. How did he

know her name? She hadn't told him. She *knew* she hadn't.

It was like the diner in New York all over again.

"Get out of here." It was more of a shriek this time. "Call the police. I'm —"

She heard a grunt, then nothing.

Trust your instincts.

Moving fast, Wendy shoved the hip-pack out of the way, pushed the kayak into the lake and ran in after it, ignoring the shock of the cold water. She floated the kayak into water up to her knees, then grabbed the paddle and dropped into the cockpit butt-first. The bow struck an underwater rock, but she pushed off from it with the paddle, using it for leverage to get her farther from shore.

Paddling as quickly as she could, she steered the kayak past the rocky point that she loved so much, ducks ignoring her, in their own peaceful little world in the shallow cove. She stayed in deeper water. She was headed in the opposite direction of Juliet's campsite, but she didn't care — her first priority was to get out of sight of anyone on the path to the spring.

As she passed the point, Wendy heard thrashing in the woods, as if a bear were tearing out toward the lake.

What if Ham was being attacked by a wild animal? She should help him.

But he'd screamed for her to run, and to call the police, and it wasn't a bear who'd told him her name. Unless he'd known it all along and the shouting and the thrashing were some big fake-out.

Her instincts told her they weren't. Besides, it didn't matter; she wasn't going back there.

Wendy paddled furiously. She focused on using her shoulders to power her strokes, careful to maintain her center of gravity and not overturn the kayak. She didn't look back.

She needed to get to a telephone.

There were two houses on the lake, one behind her — past the spring — and one up ahead. She couldn't remember if either had a phone, but the one up ahead was closer. It was owned by a family from New Jersey. They'd had some landscaping done over the summer, and Wendy had helped her uncles plant apple trees and fix a problem with drainage. They were nice people. And yes, she thought, they had a phone — she remembered Uncle Will asking to borrow it, because his cell phone didn't work out there.

By the time she reached the house,

Wendy's shoulders ached, and she was gasping, totally out of breath. She lifted her paddle out of the water and let the kayak glide toward shore, then felt it scraping the rocks, until it finally hooked among them and stopped. She jumped into knee-high water and grabbed Ham's hippack, slinging its wide strap over her shoulder as she waded onto the shore.

The house was painted a dark evergreen and had a screened porch that overlooked the lake. Wendy tried the porch door. Of course, it was locked. She went around back to the glass door there, but it, too, was locked. She didn't hesitate — she found an empty clay flowerpot and smashed the glass on the front door, then gingerly reached in and flipped the simple lock on the knob.

She was shivering, her pants soaked from her thighs down. As she pushed open the door and ran inside, she felt her running shoes squishing, tracking up the rugs and wood floor.

When she reached the kitchen, which opened out onto the porch, Wendy grabbed the telephone off the wall next to the stove.

It was dead. Not even a dial tone. The owners must have had it shut off for the season.

She fought back tears. The receiver fell off the hook, and she just left it hanging as she set Ham's pack on the kitchen table. Now what? She needed to get her bearings.

She took out the bottle of spring water and opened it, her hands shaking. She hadn't had anything to eat since the apple crisp last night. She gulped down the water, digging deeper into the pack, in case Ham had a cell phone that she could get to work.

She came up with a soft, drawstring bag made of suede in a deep maroon. It looked as if it'd come from a jewelry store.

Odd.

Almost grateful for something else to think about, Wendy tugged the bag open and saw that it was stuffed with what looked like little bubble-wrapped packages. Using her thumb and forefinger, she pulled one out. It was taped shut, but she could see a shiny green stone inside.

She dumped out more of the little packages onto the table. Each one protected a green stone. She pried the tape off one and unwrapped it, and a smooth, beautiful, spring-green stone rolled out onto her palm. It felt incredible against her skin. She held it up to the window and saw a bluish tint, but the green was deep and clear.

An emerald?

Was Ham a *thief?*

She was tired and hungry and thirsty, and now she wished she'd left the pack back at the spring. What if Ham thought she'd stolen it?

Wendy returned the emerald to its packaging as best she could and stuffed them back in the suede bag, which she tucked into the hip-pack. She took a Nutri-Grain bar with her, and the water, but left everything else on the table. She'd get her dad or her aunt and let them figure out what was going on.

She went out through the porch, figuring she'd explain to the owners later what had happened and fix the door she'd broken.

But she didn't go back down to the lake. The kayak was no use. The other lake house wouldn't have a working phone, either. And it was farther away — the wrong way, too. She'd be faster on foot — she'd reach her grandparents' house before she could paddle back across the lake.

She walked up the dirt driveway to the road. She didn't hear any cars, or anyone yelling, or any thrashing.

What had happened to Ham?

A slight breeze stirred atop the huge maple tree at the corner of the driveway, most of its leaves still green. Wendy's teeth were chattering now. She hoped she wouldn't get hypothermia — she'd had basic first aid and knew the signs. But she didn't dwell on the possibilities.

Patting the old maple's rough trunk, as if somehow it could comfort her, protect her, she forced herself to start down along the road, staying within the cover of the woods, in case she had to hide. She only wanted to see her dad or her aunts and uncles, her grandparents — Matt. It wasn't that far to the cabin where he had his camper, to the lane back to her grandparents' house. *Someone* would be around to help her. Help Ham. And she'd been gone a long time now. She wouldn't mind so much if her father had sent out a search party for her.

Low, dead pine branches poked at her, but even with no one in sight, she refused to go out onto the road. Her hair caught on a thorny Japanese barberry, an invasive species, and her eyes teared up, but she didn't cry out.

Not that far to go.

She pictured Teddy shaking himself off after an autumn swim in the lake and fixed that image in her mind, and kept moving.

Nineteen

꜀꞉ᏬᎧ꞉꜁

Ethan waited for Juliet out on the side yard, next to a wooden trailer loaded with pumpkins and decorated with dried corn stalks. Sam Longstreet hadn't caught their niece sneaking out of the attic or seen her at all that morning. Neither had Matt Kelleher, a temporary employee who'd apparently taken a liking to Wendy. Now Juliet was inside calling big brother Joshua. Ethan didn't envy her that one.

Kelleher approached the trailer, picking up a couple of pumpkins from the hundred or so laid out in the side yard. "No word yet on Wendy?"

"Not yet," Ethan said.

"She'll turn up. She wouldn't stay out and get everyone worked up."

"I hope so. Kids that age don't always think things through."

"That's for sure." Kelleher placed the pumpkins on the trailer and stood back, appraising his handiwork, but the display looked exactly the same to Ethan. "I only started work here a few days ago, but I gather she's had a hard time. Her mom, her dog, then that business in New York. She's got to be reeling. Sometimes, all you want to do is escape your own skin."

Since Kelleher's words described what Ethan had been doing for most of the past year, he understood, but he said, "Nobody's judging her. They just want to find her."

Spaceshot, the family's chubby mutt, roused himself from the driveway and nudged Kelleher, who patted the dog. Kelleher's shaved head was bare, but he had on a heavyweight black sweatshirt over a dark red turtleneck, jeans and trail boots. He was fit, agile. He'd told Ethan he'd hit the road after his wife's death, fulfilling his promise to her. Smarter, Ethan supposed, than diving into the world he had since Char's death. Murder, extortion, illegal weapons, spies, federal agents. Except for his weeks in Night's Landing, he'd seldom slept in the same place for more than a few nights.

But he'd met Juliet, who spoke her mind and liked her work and had energy and optimism and a strong, beautiful body. That bad things happened every time he showed up in her life was something they'd have to work on. Unless he just was snakebit. Then — he didn't know.

Kelleher straightened, Spaceshot flopping down onto his feet. "I heard on the radio that the guy in New York escaped last night. You don't think Wendy knows?"

"I doubt she'd have taken off if she knew."

"He's not —" Kelleher rubbed the back of his neck, as if he didn't want to show any sign of panic. "The police don't think he's headed here, do they?"

Ethan shrugged. "They don't tell me what they think."

"He'd be stupid to show up here. I don't know if you've noticed, but these Longstreets don't come small — except for Wendy." Kelleher winced, his humor falling flat, even for himself. "I'm glad she wasn't here to hear that. She told me she sometimes feels like a mutant because she's so small." He quickly changed the subject. "This your first trip to Vermont?"

"It is. It's pretty country." Ethan pointed at a giant, pale orange pumpkin among the corn stalks at one corner of the trailer. "That guy's a Charlie Brown pumpkin, isn't it? It's so big, the orange ran out."

Kelleher chuckled. "It's huge. I don't think I've ever seen one that big. Not real pretty, though, is it?" He sighed, awkward. "I should get to work. Good talking to you. I'll keep an eye out for Wendy."

As Kelleher walked back across the driveway toward the greenhouses, Ethan was half tempted to find some work to do himself. He was talking pumpkins in Vermont, and Bobby Tatro was on the loose. Ham Carhill was off on his own when he needed to be lying by the pool, letting the Carhill cooks and maids wait on him, resting, indulging himself, forgetting he'd ever heard of Mia O'Farrell and Bobby Tatro — or had ever met the Brookers. He was in no shape — physically or mentally — to take on the unanswered questions of his kidnapping, or whatever the hell he was doing.

Ethan's cell phone rang, or tried to. He answered it, but, with the lousy coverage, could barely hear Nate Winter on the other end. "Mia O'Farrell didn't show up for her meeting," Nate said. "We're checking her hotel. Has she been in touch?"

"I left a message for her. I haven't heard back."

Winter said something, but Ethan only made out Juliet, New York and Tatro.

"Her niece took off out the attic window." Ethan had no idea if Winter could hear him. "Once we find her, we're heading to New York."

"We?"

The senior marshal's skepticism came through just fine. "I think she doesn't want me out of her sight."

"Told you she's got a good career ahead of her." But, with the bad connection and work to do, he didn't linger. "Let me know if you hear from O'Farrell."

Ethan tucked the cell phone back into his jacket pocket, noticing Juliet on the grass, stepping over the array of pumpkins. She looked as impatient as he felt. "Joshua's on his way."

"How'd he react?"

"As you might expect. Exasperated, pissed off, worried."

"I'll help you all look for your niece."

She nodded, her thumbs hooked on the pockets of her jacket, as if to control some of her restlessness. "Makes sense to check the lake first. We can walk. We'll cover more ground we would driving, and if we find her sitting under a tree writing poetry, I can pack up my tent. My truck's still there." She squinted out at the sun-washed hills surrounding the picturesque spot where she'd grown up. Without looking at him, she asked, "Who were you talking to?"

"Matt Kelleher —"

Juliet shifted her gaze to him, clearly aware he'd known what she meant. "On the phone."

"Nate Winter."

Winter was a senior deputy and one of her champions in the USMS, but also a man she admired and respected. Her expression didn't change. "And here I was thinking you'd come clean and told me everything."

"He and I bonded in May when we saved you and Sarah Dunnemore from certain death."

That drew a roll of her blue eyes. "You didn't save us from anything. What did he want?"

"He says O'Farrell didn't show up for her meeting this morning."

The cop expression was back. "Do they know each other?"

"Sort of."

"I swear, Brooker, if I thought thumb-screws would work on you —" Juliet sighed, dropping her hands to her side. "Let's go."

She spun around so hard, her heels kicked up little stones in the driveway. Ethan let her lead the way to the barn, where two hens had escaped their pen and were pecking in the grass, and onto a grassy lane, an apple orchard up to their right, woods and hills and the lake to their left. Juliet walked fast, bearing left, maneuvering comfortably over exposed rocks and tree roots, tall grass and wildflowers slapping against her jeans. She had strong legs. She worked to stay fit. For the past year, Ethan thought, he'd mostly worked at finding fresh distractions to keep him from thinking about Char's death and life without her, to keep him from acknowledging that he hadn't been a good husband and their marriage had sputtered and faltered long before she'd ended up in an Amsterdam morgue.

"Does this remind you of Texas at all?" Juliet asked abruptly, with a quick wave of her fingers that seemed to take in all of her surroundings, the hills, the orchard, the fields and woods and stone walls, the vibrant fall colors against a cloudless sky.

None of it was like west Texas at all. Ethan smiled. "No."

"I have a friend from the Midwest who says Vermont makes her claustrophobic. She likes nice, flat, straight roads. She says the roads around here are narrow and twisting and that the trees grow too close to the road."

"I don't get claustrophobic."

"Probably wouldn't have made it into the Special Forces if trees overhanging a road got to you." Even as Juliet continued along the lane at a healthy pace, distracting herself with her talk of Texas and Vermont roads, Ethan could see that she was scanning constantly for any sign of her niece. "Do you have barbecues with the Carhills?"

"They're not that type."

"Is Texas their sole residence? With that kind of money —"

"It's their main residence. I don't even know what else they own, but west Texas is definitely home."

"Could Ham have gone to another of their properties to recuperate? Maybe his mother got on his nerves."

"I don't know where he went."

She gave Ethan a sideways glance. "Are you worried about him, especially now with Tatro on the loose?"

"Ham goes his own way. He doesn't fit anywhere that easily, which makes it hard to know whether I should worry or not."

"An unlikely spook."

Ethan didn't bother with a denial.

"The thought of that creep Tatro —" Juliet tightened her hands into fists and picked up her pace, the lane in the woods now, taking them along the bottom of a hill. "Let's hope Wendy doesn't know he escaped. If she's off on a little adventure, throwing pebbles in the lake or catching frogs or writing poetry — maybe an hour or two on her own in peace will do her good."

"Maybe," Ethan said, neutral.

She stopped when they came to the dirt road, postcard perfect with the morning sun and the autumn foliage, the sprinkle of freshly fallen red, orange and yellow leaves. The fog had burned off, and an intermittent breeze cooled the air. She stood next to Ethan and sighed at the quiet scene. "There are a million places she could be."

"We can split up. Just point me in the right direction."

"Sam's gone up to the orchard to look. We know she didn't take a car, and her note says she'll be back soon. We're all probably overreacting, but we'll find her." Juliet cast him a wry smile. "In the meantime, the Marshals Service can conduct a manhunt without me."

Ethan knew he didn't need to remind her that it was a manhunt for Bobby Tatro this time.

"I wonder what she was wearing," Juliet

said, half to herself. "It's warming up now, but it was cold when she —"

"Wendy knows Vermont. She'll have dressed for the weather."

"Ethan — I don't like this. Your Texan's missing. Mia O'Farrell's missing. Tatro's escaped. Wendy picked a bad time to sneak out." Juliet glanced up the road, toward a cabin tucked on the wooded hillside. "What did Matt Kelleher say when you talked to him, before Nate called?"

"Not much. He said he hasn't seen your niece."

"Apparently he and Wendy have hit it off." Juliet thought a moment. "If Wendy thinks he understands her and the rest of us don't, maybe whatever it is she's up to involves him. She could be sitting in his camper writing poetry. I'm not suggesting he's aware —"

"Let's have a look," Ethan said, heading up the road to the steep driveway.

The cabin was built into the hillside amid tall evergreens and a few birch trees, their yellow leaves and white bark a contrast to the pines and hemlocks. Stone steps led up from the driveway to a deck and sliding glass doors. Huge rhododendrons had taken over the front windows. And the Longstreets were landscapers, Ethan thought, amused.

Kelleher's fifth-wheel camper stood in front of the one-car garage. His truck, an older vehicle with Arizona plates, was parked alongside the camper, in the shade of a massive hemlock.

Juliet knocked on the dented camper door. "Mr. Kelleher? It's Juliet Longstreet." When there was no answer, as expected, she tried the door, but it was locked. She stepped back down onto the driveway. "Wendy! Are you here?" She sighed, nodding to the cabin. "I'll check up there, just in case. You'd think she'd know to turn up before her father gets back. Never mind worrying the rest of us."

But she left it at that and mounted the steps to the cabin, trying the slider, but it, too, was locked. "I guess she's not here," Juliet said, disappointed.

Ethan had remained by the camper. "Your brothers check out this guy, Kelleher?"

She headed back down the steps. "I doubt it. He hasn't been here that long."

"He just shows up out of nowhere and asks for work, says his wife died?"

"It happens —" But she frowned, her eyes reaching Ethan's as she joined him on the driveway. "But maybe not this week."

"Yeah, maybe not." Without asking her permission or telling her what he was about to do, Ethan raised his right leg and gave the camper door a hard, snapping kick with the heel of his boot. It popped open. Easy. He shrugged at the federal marshal next to him. "The door's dented. I'm buying him a new one. Have to take the old one off first."

"You don't trust anyone, do you, Brooker?"

"Do you?"

Not answering, she climbed into the camper ahead of him. The interior was shabby but immaculate. Wendy wasn't tied up in a corner. There was no kiddy-porn laid out on a stained mattress. Juliet checked the refrigerator — no alcohol, not so much as a six-pack. The shelves were crammed with protein bars, soy milk, carrot juice.

"No wonder he gets along with your niece," Ethan said.

She ignored him and pulled open the door to the tiny bathroom. He noticed two mugs and two plates in the strainer, not enough to sound any alarms, but curious.

He heard Juliet suck in a sharp breath and swear. She backed out of the bathroom, her expression grim, her color off. "Tatro's here," she said tightly, on her way to the door.

Ethan checked the bathroom himself. Shaving gear for two men, two toothbrushes and cargo pants and a T-shirt hanging on a hook on the door.

He joined Juliet outside. "Recognized the clothes?"

"It's what he wears. Whoever helped spring him must have had clothes for him. The pants are the wrong size for Kelleher. And the smell — Tatro has this smell."

"What do you want me to do?" Ethan asked her quietly.

She fixed her eyes on him and thought a moment. "Check down by the lake. Check my tent. If Tatro knows I spent the night there —" She abandoned that train of thought, too disciplined to let herself spin out of control. "I'll take my truck and head back to the house. Joshua should be back by now. He needs to know."

Time to call out the troops, Ethan thought.

"You're not — are you armed?"

"No. It's okay, Juliet. Go." He winked at her. "I'll be stealthy."

"There's a spring —" She held her breath a second, as if pushing back her emotions. "It's through the woods — you'll see the path near my tent. There's a picnic area. It's one of Wendy's favorite spots.

362

And if she didn't bring water with her and got thirsty —"

"I'll take a look."

"Kelleher —"

"He said he was going back to work. I saw him head toward the barn, but I didn't see if he went inside."

Her gaze focused on him. "Who is he?"

"We'll find out." But Ethan thought of Mia O'Farrell, her tips, her fear, and wondered if, somehow, the Longstreets' recent hire was the reason she was on her last nerve, hanging by a thread.

Juliet had walked over to Kelleher's truck and raised the hood. "Do you know how to disable a truck? I don't want this bastard going anywhere."

"I'll take care of it. Go on. Go raise the alarm with your family."

Her eyes shone. "Ethan — *damn*."

"It'll be okay," he said, although he had no idea whether it would or not, just wanted to cut through her palpable sense of dread. "Wendy handled herself well in New York, and this is her turf."

"Tatro —" She shut her eyes briefly. "Let him come after me. Not her."

Ethan kissed her, and she brushed her fingertips along his jaw, their eyes connecting, just for an instant, before she pulled away and headed back down the driveway. But that split second of eye contact was enough, a wire tripped, launching them onto a different plane. It was as if he'd seen into her soul.

She turned, walking backward. "Stay safe, Brooker."

Then she spun around and trotted down the road, out of sight. He returned to the camper and got a sharp knife from Kelleher's tool kit.

In less than two minutes, he had the ignition wires on the truck cut.

When he reached the path to the lake, Juliet's truck was gone — he'd seen her head up the dead-end road, undoubtedly to see if she could spot Wendy before turning around and heading home. He ducked onto the narrow path, noticing the play of light and breeze and shadow on ferns and wildflowers, and tried to think like a seventeen-year-old girl with too much on her mind.

Before leaving that morning, Juliet had zipped her tent up tight. Ethan unzipped it now and crawled inside, thinking that it was small for the two of them. But not, as he recalled, *too* small. Wendy wasn't taking a nap atop the sleeping bag, nor did he see any sign that she'd been there. As he crawled back out, he took one of Juliet's gold-wrapped chocolates with him. Juliet could operate just on caffeine. He needed food.

He walked down to the lake, glistening in the morning sun, the water rippling with a cool, steady breeze.

"Hell."

The cracker tin. Ethan made his way over to a three-foot boulder just into the woods and took the tin, pulled off the lid. The dog's ashes were still there.

He carefully replaced the lid and set the tin back on the boulder.

Okay, so Wendy had been there. Where was she now? Hiding? They'd met for only a few seconds in New York — she wouldn't necessarily recognize him. If he was a teenage girl and saw him marching through the woods, he'd hide, too.

"Wendy? It's Ethan — Ethan Brooker, your aunt's friend."

Nothing, just the rustle of leaves in the breeze.

He'd check the spring. He found the path, less used than the one from the road to Juliet's clearing, but it was a short walk through the woods to another clearing, with a picnic table, some kind of red-leafed bush, and a wooden sign, which just read, prosaically, *Spring.*

But no Wendy Longstreet, sitting in the shade with a book of poetry.

If she was out here, she was being damn quiet about it.

Ethan got his chocolate out of his pocket and unwrapped it, popped it into his mouth. It was dark chocolate, filled with gooey caramel. Thick.

He didn't know Vermont. He didn't know the Longstreets. Teenage girls. He was so damn far out of his element, he was eating Vermont-made chocolate.

A flutter of paper caught his attention, and he picked it up, then saw a wallet — a man's wallet. And tracks in the grass and mud. A canoe or a kayak had been there, and recently.

The paper was a boarding pass for Ham's flight from Dallas to LaGuardia.

And the wallet belonged to him.

Ethan took a breath. A red squirrel chattered at him from a hemlock branch. Somewhere in the thickets, a duck squawked. Ham was a genius, but he was also a romantic and an idealist. If he believed his parents had paid off his kidnappers on the sly and in so doing had endangered others, he'd want to make up for their narrow-sightedness, their willingness to put themselves ahead of anything — anyone — else.

Ethan tucked the boarding pass and the wallet into his jacket pocket and walked out to a pine tree on a rocky point where he had a better view of that end of the lake.

He stood under the pine tree.

The squirrel had quieted. He'd scared off the duck.

Something bobbed in the water out by a small lake house tucked on the shore.

A kayak.

Ham sank onto his knees in the tall grass and waited for another poke from Tatro's walking stick. They'd left the path to the spring and had taken another one, less well-traveled, up to an old board-and-batten barn. It looked empty, long abandoned. They were behind it, on the side overlooking the lake, in what had once obviously been a small field but now was overgrown with briars, grapevines, barberry, honeysuckle and poison sumac — probably poison ivy, too.

The blow came, hard to the small of his back, but Ham didn't moan or make any noise at all. The last time he'd collapsed, Tatro had threatened to knock him out cold or kill him. Ham had no reason to doubt him. The bastard enjoyed inflicting pain.

Soundlessly, Ham staggered to his feet. As it was, he'd be pissing blood for a week.

Tatro leaned in close to him, his foul breath on Ham's neck. "I want my emeralds."

"I'm here to see Juliet Longstreet. The marshal. I told you." Ham kept his voice low, just as Tatro had. "I'm not lying."

"That bitch. Did you give her my emeralds? Did Brooker give them to her? I know you stole them, you asshole. Left me with rocks. What did you do, use them to pay Brooker?" Tatro snorted. "I like that. Stealing from me to pay for your rescue."

"That's not what happened."

"I know people who can make you talk."

"Yeah? Well, remember, they're willing to die for the cause. I bet you're not. You're just in this for the money. They're using you. Don't you see that?"

Tatro shoved the stick into Ham's kidneys again, but grabbed him by his waistband to keep him on his feet. Ham's head spun. No way would he ever tell this bastard that the emeralds were in his kayak. Thank *God* he'd left his hip-pack behind, after all. Taking Tatro back down to the lake, trying to buy himself time, was out of the question. Too risky. He didn't want them to run into Wendy. Let her get to safety. Let her get to the *cops.*

And once Tatro got the emeralds, Ham would be floating facedown in the lake or dead and buried in some rocky Vermont hole.

A door to the barn opened. It was a regular door, to Ham's left toward the far end of the barn. In the middle was a wide door — for animals and wagons — but it was boarded shut.

"Hang on, Bobby." Another man's voice came from inside the barn, quiet and soothing, with an undertone of authority. "Let's think this through."

Ham breathed through his clenched teeth, his deep breaths only worsening the pain.

Tatro eased off. "You told me to get this fuck —"

"I know, I know. But we have a problem. Wendy Longstreet took off this morning. Her family's out looking for her."

"She was at the lake." Tatro poked Ham with the stick, but not as hard. "This fuck yelled for her to call the cops. I figured I'd dump him back here and go find her."

"I'll go. The girl trusts me."

With that gentle, reassuring voice, Ham thought, anyone would. "Don't hurt her," he said. "It's my fault —"

"Shh, shh. Don't worry, Mr. Carhill." The man tucked a finger under Ham's chin and lifted his head. "I think some of those bites are infected."

Tatro grunted. "He stole my emeralds. I told you —"

The man came out of the barn, showing himself. He was lean and fit, with a shaved head. He continued to address Tatro. "And I told you that you shouldn't take matters into your own hands. That's how you landed in jail. I can buy us some time. Once Wendy's back with her family, she'll tell them everything. By then, we'll be gone. I don't believe in taking innocent lives."

"What about the woman and this bastard?"

"We leave them. We shut down. We can't risk trying to take them with us."

"Then it's all for nothing?"

"We can come back after things cool off here. Chances are no one will think to check the barn. Either way, we'll know."

"They'll die without food and water —"

"Then they die." His voice hardened. "Traitors deserve death."

Ham coughed. "Traitors?"

Both men ignored him. Tatro said, "I thought you wanted Major Brooker."

"I do. And you want Deputy Long-street." The other man's voice was soothing again. "Patience, Mr. Tatro. That's what I've learned in recent years. Patience."

In the haze that was his brain, Ham put pieces of what they were saying together and came out with a bad ending for himself and whatever woman was already in the barn.

The guy with the shaved head opened the door, and Tatro shoved Ham inside, pushing so hard he practically pinwheeled across the floor.

He landed against a wall that smelled like hay.

It was dark inside, but some daylight came through cracks in the walls.

In short order, Tatro tied Ham's hands and feet, then gagged him with a ban-danna, but didn't bother with a blindfold. He grinned. "Have fun."

The door slammed shut.

Ham managed to sit up. Did these bastards think he was going to take a nap and wait for them to get back?

Hell, no.

His eyes adjusted to the semidarkness. He could make out the outlines of the two doors. And whoever owned the barn had

never bothered to clean it out entirely.
There were rusted antique farm tools that
could probably pull in a fortune on eBay
hung on nails and pegs, and there were old
barrels, car and tractor parts, a wagon
wheel, wooden apple crates. Even if Tatro
and that other guy had locked him in,
Ham figured he could find something in
this mess to get himself out of there.

Turning, dizzy, he blinked rapidly, trying
to make out what was in the far end of the
barn.

A giant meat hook hanging from a rafter.
A thick rope shaped into a noose.

What was this place?

There were car batteries lined up side by
side on the floor under the meat hook.
There were jumper cables. A bucket of
water.

Mesmerized, shocked by what he was
seeing, Ham didn't move.

He thought he heard something. A muf-
fled cry, a moan.

His stomach lurched. He didn't want to
throw up with the gag on.

The woman Tatro had mentioned.

She was tied to a chair, her feet bound,
her mouth gagged, her eyes blindfolded.

Oh, my God, he thought, making a gut-
tural noise to get her attention. She

flinched. She had to be terrified.

But who was she?

Ham's pulse raced. Mia O'Farrell. It had to be.

There was nothing either of them could do but wait.

When she saw Matt on the road, Wendy almost cried with relief. She ran out to him, her knees buckling under her. He caught her by the arm, steadying her, and she kept gulping in breath after breath, trying to get control of herself.

"Easy, Wendy. Just take it easy. Your family's looking for you —"

"He's got Ham." She got the words out, felt her fingertips and her cheeks go numb. "Someone. I don't know who. I didn't see him. I was at the lake. I decided to scatter Teddy's ashes, like you said and — and —"

"Who's Ham?"

"I don't know. A guy. He was in a kayak. He's from Texas. The army guy — Brooker. Aunt Juliet's friend . . . *he's* from Texas, too." But she couldn't seem to speak to make herself coherent and was sure Matt didn't understand what she was saying. "Please. We've got to call nine-one-one. I need to tell my dad."

"Okay. We will."

She started to cry. "I didn't mean to worry anyone. That's why I snuck out of the house. So I *wouldn't* worry them. Now — I'm scared, Matt. The pack — Ham's pack. There are emeralds in it. The doorman, Juan. He asked me about precious gems. Why would he do that? Why would he and Bobby Tatro think that Aunt Juliet had emeralds? Who —"

"Wendy — whoa, honey. Slow down. We can get all your questions answered. Let's concentrate right now on getting you to your family and calling the police. Okay? Makes sense?"

She took a breath, nodding, and made herself stop blurting things out.

"Where are the emeralds?" he asked.

"What?"

She stared at him, her heart pounding, that buzzing, alert feeling happening again.

Something was off.

She heard a noise in the woods behind her. "Hey, little girl." Bobby Tatro stood under a maple branch. "Why don't you take me to the emeralds?"

Matt looked pained. "I'm sorry, Wendy. I like you. I really do. But I can see now this just isn't going to work." He shifted his attention to Tatro. "Stay in the woods, out of sight. Don't hurt her unless you have no other option. Bring her back."

Tatro had an assault knife, exactly like the one in New York. Wendy didn't know which was worse, looking at the knife or at his eyes. "Where's Ham?" she asked.

"See that barn?" Tatro pointed with the tip of his knife. "Your new pal is locked inside. He's tied up. Gagged. He has no food and no water. If you want him to live, little girl, you'll bring me to my emeralds."

Wendy felt herself going very still inside. These men wanted the emeralds in Ham Carhill's maroon suede bag. She knew where they were.

That was her leverage, she thought.

She remembered her note, her locked bedroom door, Teddy's ashes — and knew she'd been away too long. Matt hadn't lied. Her family *was* looking for her.

All she had to do was stay alive until someone found her.

Twenty

⁓∶ⓄⒼ ∶⁓

Joshua nearly ran over a damn pumpkin when he pulled into the driveway. He couldn't see straight. He had no business being behind the wheel of his cruiser, but he'd turned down another trooper's offer to drive him. When he'd asked her what his daughter could possibly have been thinking to sneak out through the attic, she'd just smiled. "Thinking? She's seventeen, Trooper Josh. I've heard stories about you at seventeen."

When he'd left the house that morning, he thought Wendy was asleep in her room. It had never occurred to him she'd taken off. He'd stopped back at his place, checked on Barry, who'd rolled off his couch at some point and was out on the porch having coffee as if it were summer. Joshua had headed out to the barracks to get an update on Tatro's escape and the search for him.

Joshua scratched Spaceshot's head. "Where's your girl Wendy, hmm?" With one foot, he shoved the pumpkin out of the middle of the driveway. "Quiet around here."

He saw that Brooker's rented car was still in the driveway. He didn't know if that was a good sign or a bad sign — or no sign at all. His sister's problems had infected the rest of the family, that was for sure. If his head knew not to blame her, his emotions didn't.

But Joshua tried to get control of his thinking, as well as his feelings. Wendy loved her grandparents' place and felt safe there, and she'd always been one to take off on her own. She'd led a sheltered life, at least until this past week.

Sam joined him out on the driveway. "I checked the apple orchard," he said, not bothering with any preamble since Joshua knew his brother meant Wendy. "No sign of her. Matt Kelleher's gone to look for her. Juliet and that guy, Brooker, are out looking. Rest of the gang's on the way here."

"I'm sorry," Joshua said tightly.

"What for? You didn't climb out the window. Wendy's got a lot on her mind. Juliet showing up yesterday asking more questions didn't help. Then Brooker turning up in the middle of the night."

Sam obviously didn't like any of the recent developments. "Anything on Tatro?"

"Nothing new."

"The marshals must have her place in New York staked out, but you'd think he wouldn't be dumb enough to show up there. Or here."

Paul drove up in his town police car and jumped out. "I just got a call from Eddie Sherman." Eddie ran a popular local outfitters that catered to tourists. "He said a skinny guy asked about the lake, said he heard it was up near Longstreet Landscaping. He made small talk about Juliet."

"Not Tatro —"

"He rented a kayak and gave the name of Ham Carhill."

"Carhill?"

"He's from Texas. He was at breakfast this morning. He's damn skinny, Eddie's got that right. He looked like death warmed over."

Joshua felt a stab of pure, primal fear. "If Wendy's on the lake —"

Paul looked at his oldest brother. "Want to take my car out to the lake or yours? We need to find this guy."

"Go," Sam said. "I'll fill in the gang when they get here."

Not trusting himself behind the wheel,

Joshua climbed into his brother's cruiser. Paul glanced at him but said nothing, just backed out and headed for the lake.

Fifteen emeralds in all.

Juliet had dumped them out of their little suede bag onto the table and liberated one of them from its bubble wrap.

Although she knew nothing about precious gems, the polished stone she held in her palm was stunning.

She'd pulled over when she saw the broken window in her neighbors' door. The wet, muddy footprints on the steps told her the break-in was recent, and she'd slipped inside to check it out, following more prints into the kitchen. The hip-pack definitely looked out of place on the kitchen table, and she'd unceremoniously dumped out its contents. Granola bars, protein bars, matches, a free Vermont guidebook, a local map.

And emeralds.

No wallet, no passport — but she found a checkout receipt from a local motel in the name of Ham Carhill.

Ethan's friend, Mia O'Farrell's covert agent, Bobby Tatro's former kidnap victim.

George O'Hara's Texan and purported traitor.

Juliet returned the emeralds to their drawstring bag, not bothering to rewrap the one she'd liberated. She squatted down, examining a perfect footprint.

A running shoe for a foot smaller — way smaller — than her own. Unless Ham Carhill was a tiny man, it wasn't his print.

Wendy.

Clutching the suede bag, Juliet followed the footprints out the back door onto the porch, then down the steps, where they disappeared into the lawn.

She heard ducks down by the lake.

And she saw a kayak bobbing in the lake, scraping on rocks.

Whose kayak?

She walked down to the lake. The paddle was half in the water, half in the mud, as if whoever had dropped it there didn't care if it floated away. She leaped onto a flat rock about four feet into the water, but there was nothing in the kayak — no hint that her niece had been there.

"Aunt Juliet!"

Wendy. But the tone of her voice, laced with terror, chilled Juliet.

Bobby Tatro pushed Wendy out of the woods, onto the lawn near the lake. He had one arm around Wendy's waist and the other around her neck, a knife held to her throat. "My turn, blondie. Hands up where I can see them. If you move a single muscle toward your gun, I'll slit her throat. You know I will."

Juliet raised her hands above her head, and she noticed his gaze follow the one that held the drawstring bag. "Let Wendy go, Bobby. I've got your emeralds. I'll trade them for my niece's safety."

"Your gun, blondie. Toss it into the lake. Then we'll deal." He brought the knife even closer to Wendy's throat. "Try anything, and you watch little Wendy die."

"Okay. Just stay cool. I'll use my left hand —"

"Do it."

Juliet took her gun by its handle and dropped it into the lake.

"Very good, blondie."

"It's a muddy bottom here," she said. "I'll dump the emeralds out and all fifteen of them will disappear into the muck. It'll take you forever to find them. You don't have that kind of time. It's a dead-end road, Bobby. Cops are on the way. You need to get your ass moving."

He obviously didn't like the idea of the emeralds disappearing.

"All you have to do is let Wendy go. Then you get the emeralds."

Wendy's eyes widened, but she didn't say a word.

Juliet focused on her niece. "When you're free, Wendy, run into the house. Barricade yourself in and wait for your dad to get here. Don't run away. I don't know who else is around here."

"Matt," she whispered. "Matt's around."

So, she knew her friend wasn't who he'd claimed to be.

"The emeralds first," Tatro said. "Then the girl."

Juliet shook her head. "Not a chance. Let Wendy go."

With a sudden burst, he shoved Wendy, so hard that she fell onto her hands and knees, but she got up, scrambling for the house as Juliet had instructed.

"Toss the bag on the ground," he ordered. "I know you're a black belt. But I'm good with a knife."

That Juliet knew. She'd wait for the right moment to get it away from him. Not only didn't she want to get killed, she didn't want to get killed in front of Wendy. She flipped the suede bag onto the lawn. "If I were you, I'd take your emeralds and get moving. Never mind me."

"What makes you think I won't cut your throat?"

"No fun for you in that, Bobby."

"Where are the keys to your truck?"

"Left coat pocket."

"Jump over here. Do anything, and I'll kill you, then I'll kill the girl."

Juliet jumped lightly from her position on the rock, landing in the soft, wet sand. "Where's your friend, Kelleher? Any other accomplices trying to blend in around here and take advantage of people's good nature?"

Tatro ignored her. "Get your keys."

Juliet dipped her hand into her pocket.

Without any warning, Ethan leaped out of the woods, and Tatro, distracted, turned, giving her the opening she needed. She went for the arm with the knife, latching on to it, immobilizing it, as Ethan got Tatro around the neck with one arm and, at the same time, reached around with his other arm and latched on to the same forearm she had. But he snapped it, breaking the bone. Tatro yelled out in pain, and the knife dropped out of his hand.

Moving fast, Juliet picked up the knife. "You're under arrest, Bobby."

He rolled on the ground, holding his broken arm.

Ethan, breathing hard, stood up and dusted himself off.

"Nice distraction," Juliet said, barely aware of her words. "I had him, one way or the other. I have another gun and pepper spray in my truck, and a black belt in karate —"

"You have another gun? I could have broken into your truck instead of sneaking through the woods. The ducks are pissed at me. I've got pine pitch all over me." But he took the knife from her and touched her shoulder. "Juliet."

She nodded. "I'm okay."

"Go to your niece."

But Wendy ran out of the house, the porch door banging shut behind her. "He's got Ham! He locked him in the barn! He'll *die!*" She stopped dead in her tracks before she got too close to Tatro. "Please. Juliet. Do something."

"Go, Brooker." Juliet took the knife back, keeping her eyes on Tatro. "I'll be there as soon as I can. You can take my backup gun —"

"What kind?"

"Snub-nosed revolver. My Glock's in the lake."

He made a face. "Keep it. You might need it." He withdrew a steak knife from his jacket. "But I'll switch knives with you. I think you can handle this creep

384

with a steak knife, don't you?"

"Ethan, I think you were right." She tried to smile. "I am in love with you."

He winked. "I knew it," he said, and trotted off with the K-bar.

By the time he reached the barn, Ethan had a new appreciation for the cool Vermont breeze. Trekking back and forth along the lake had him sweating. But concentrating on his breathing, on not tripping on a root or slipping on a mushroom and stabbing himself, kept him from worrying about Ham.

The two doors — one wide, one regular — on the front of the barn were boarded shut. He went around back, finding a mirror image of the doors on the lake side. The regular door was padlocked. He noticed the trampled brush and grass.

At least he knew he had the right barn.

Since it was Vermont, he had no trouble finding a rock, and the cheap padlock broke with two good whacks.

When the door opened, Ham Carhill was in the doorway, on his back, poised to kick whoever came through, never mind that he had his feet and hands bound.

"Twice now," Ethan said, pulling off Ham's gag, a red bandanna soaked in drool. "Next time, you get to rescue me."

Ham grinned weakly. "Always so humble." But his eyes flattened with pain and fear. "Wendy?"

"She's with her aunt. They're fine."

"Tatro —"

"Under arrest."

"The other guy, the one with the shaved head?"

"Don't know."

"That's not good."

Ethan quickly cut the ropes, first on Ham's hands, then on his feet. The rope had dug into his wrists and ankles, opening up insect bites still healing from his Colombian ordeal. "Ham. Jesus." Ethan felt his throat constrict. "You're skin and bones. You've got to learn to pick better friends."

"Me?" Clutching Ethan's shoulder, Ham got to his feet. "Mia — we need to help her. She's in a bad way."

Hell.

With energy that surprised Ethan, Ham darted back into the barn. Ethan glanced out at the pretty, idyllic landscape. There was no way he could cover his tracks with the broken padlock. He tried closing the door, but it popped back open. Well, he thought, he could use the light. He followed Ham inside.

Mia O'Farrell's situation wasn't just bad. It was dire.

She was blindfolded, gagged and tied to a chair, and even in the semidarkness, Ethan could see she was deathly pale, barely conscious. But, worse, she was sitting on a bomb. He could see the wires wrapped around the legs of the chair.

"It's a tumbler switch," Ham said.

Ethan nodded. The switch was suspended by the wires, a single line attaching it to her.

Ham brushed his mouth with the back of his hand. "If she moves —"

"I know." And from her stillness, so did Mia. She didn't need reminding. If she moved, she'd set off the device. Ethan moved toward her. "Mia? It's Ethan Brooker. Ham Carhill's here, too. We're going to get you out of this contraption, okay?"

She let out a sound, too weak to be a groan, but an acknowledgment of her understanding, nonetheless.

"The tumbler's a plastic pipe," Ham said. "There's a lantern battery under the chair. You've got wires running from the positive lead into the tumbler. The negative runs into the igniter —"

"Ham."

The igniter was inserted into a roll of

detonator cord. The cord was wrapped around a thick metal pipe, undoubtedly filled with some kind of shrapnel — nails, BBs, metal shavings. Any of them would prove lethal.

A plastic ball inside the pipe, if rolled to either end by any movement, would set off the bomb.

Ham squatted next to Ethan, his breathing ragged, his eyes dark and puffy. "I could disarm it, but I don't trust myself." He opened and shut his hands, working his stiff fingers. "I'm shaking."

"Mia," Ethan said, "Ham's not touching you. I'm going to disarm the bomb. I've done it before." He turned to Ham. "I want you out of here. Understood?"

From his expression, Ham definitely understood. If Ethan had miscalculated, or the bomb was improperly constructed and went off, he didn't want Ham to get blown up, too. But Ham shook his head. "I'll stay. I can talk you through what to do if — you know, if it gets complicated."

Ethan's mind flashed back to a quail hunt with his brother, Ham tagging along, chattering about the migrating habits of quail, the geology of the area, trying not so much to impress them as to fit in.

"All right. Thanks." Ethan wanted to

comfort Mia with a touch, take her gag off, but he didn't want to risk startling her. He took Tatro's knife, isolated one of the wires and glanced back at Ham. "Don't move, don't say a word."

The trick was to disarm the bomb without tripping the tumbler.

"Here goes." Carefully, but using just enough strength, he cut the wire. Then he breathed. "Got it. We're good, Mia. You're safe."

Her shoulders slumped. Ethan quickly pulled off her blindfold and gag, but she didn't react. He cut the ropes binding her hands and feet, speaking to her softly.

"He's coming back," Ham said. "That shaved-head nut. He hates all three of us. Thinks we're traitors."

"I'm not —" Mia's voice was very weak, but her eyes fluttered open. "I'm not a traitor."

Ham was staring at her. "Man, Dr. O'Farrell. I didn't expect you to be so beautiful."

She gave him a faltering smile, then shifted to Ethan. She still hadn't moved. "He believes we conspired to get a multi-million-dollar ransom for ourselves. He's — he's interrogating me. Ethan, I don't know what he's talking about."

Ham frowned. "Multimillion? The emeralds are worth a half million, tops."

Her eyes managed to focus on him. "Where did they come from?"

"They're the ransom my parents paid. I switched them at the last minute, and Tatro ended up with worthless rocks. That's why he's so pissed. He thought I paid off Brooker for rescuing me, and that Brooker gave them to Juliet —"

Ethan got Mia to her feet, holding her up, and said, "We'll sort out the whys and wherefores later. Let's get out of here."

Ham went to one of the apple crates.

"Ham, what are you doing?"

"Seeing what's in this crate. No wonder he trussed us up." He rummaged in the crate and turned around, awkwardly holding an MP5. "We could have shot our way out of here."

Ethan frowned. "What else is there?"

"Ammo. Want me to load this thing?"

"That's okay. I'll do it. Bring me a gun and a clip, okay?"

Mia tried to clutch his sleeve, but her fingers couldn't hold on. He continued to hold her up. She said, "He's my source. He gave me the tips — about the marshal, about you being able to recognize Ham. He wants you. Because of Afghanistan."

"He wants to kill me —"

"Or convert you to the cause."

Ethan helped her, half carrying her as they moved toward the door.

Ham joined them. He had two guns and two clips. "Ethan, you need to go after this guy. Now, before he has a chance to strap someone else to a booby-trapped chair."

"I know." Ethan took one of the guns, an MP5, and jammed in a clip. He handed it to Ham. "This place will be filling up with cops any minute. Kelleher is the name of your shaved-head wingnut. Matt Kelleher. If he shows up, shoot him."

"Okay."

But he was pale, and Ethan took the other MP5. "Don't you two get into some big long analytical discussion. Just point the gun at his chest and pull the trigger. Go for body mass. Don't try to shoot him in the head."

Mia sank onto the floor next to the door, clearly too far gone even to hold a weapon. Ham was in only marginally better shape. But he took the MP5, nodding. "I've got it, Ethan. Don't worry."

"Be sure it's Kelleher. Don't just start shooting —"

"Just go," Ham said. "Get this bastard."

Mia dug her fingers into Ethan's hand.

"Don't — don't shut the door. Please."

He nodded. "I won't."

He shoved a clip into the second MP5 and, without another word, ducked out of the barn and into the woods.

Mia sat in the sunlight, her back against an apple crate Ham had dragged over to the door. She could smell water on the breeze. "There's a lake nearby?" But Ham didn't hear her, or was too preoccupied with his own thoughts to respond. She felt weak, listless, the drugs and the bruises and the fear — the awful fear — having merged into a kind of numbness. And she was thirsty. But if she asked Ham for water, she was afraid he'd start digging through more crates and forget about Kelleher. "A nice, smart, rich guy like you. I'll bet if you'd cut your hair, you'd get all the girls."

He heard that. "Really?"

She smiled. "Yes, really. I wished we'd met under better circumstances."

"Me, too." His brow furrowed as he stared down at the submachine gun in his lap, but Mia didn't think that was what he was seeing. He looked up again, his eyes almost vacant. "The emeralds actually came from Kelleher. He used them to manipulate

Tatro. I should have known. I thought my folks made a deal with him. He — I was on to him. Kelleher. Remember I told you I was on to an emerald-smuggling ring?"

"Ham . . ." But he had her interest, and she nodded, grateful for the distraction. "Yes. I remember."

"Kelleher was smuggling emeralds and using the profits to support his vigilante mercenary work. I figured my folks gave him the emeralds because that's what he wanted."

"He'd know what to do with them."

Ham didn't seem to hear her. "Kelleher put us in touch with each other. Indirectly, because I never met him face-to-face. He knew I was friends with Ethan. He'd been watching me. And you —" Ham thought a moment. "He liked playing the white knight with you."

"He did provide some useful information. Obviously he turned on me."

"It's my fault. I got scared," Ham said without embarrassment. "I went to New York to find Ethan — I think Kelleher wanted me scared, wanted me to go to Ethan for help. I was in over my head."

"Why didn't you come to me?"

"I knew for sure I could trust Ethan."

Kelleher had manipulated Ham, confused him to the point he'd go to the one person he knew he could trust — Ethan Brooker. Which was exactly what Kelleher wanted. *Why?* Mia shut her eyes a moment, but she still felt the blindfold and opened them again quickly, relieved at the sunlight. "What about Tatro?"

But Ham bolted to his feet, and then she heard it, too, understood why. A rustling sound outside. He got his MP5 into a ready position that looked authentic to her. Then he grinned at her, and relaxed. "It's the Longstreets."

Juliet Longstreet entered the barn first, followed by a tall, handsome, fair-haired man, both of them armed. Ham was yapping at them a mile a minute, but Mia couldn't focus on what he was saying. She tried to stand. The fair-haired man caught her around the waist. She'd always been so self-sufficient, so confident and determined. But she sank into his strong arms and started to cry.

Juliet knew she wouldn't find Brooker unless he wanted her to find him.

She ran up the road, using trees as cover, having nixed the idea of Paul's police cruiser. Let Kelleher wonder if they were on to him.

Paul had stayed with Wendy and called for backup. Wendy hadn't wanted her father to stay. It wasn't rejection — it was, Juliet realized, a necessity. An assertion of identity more than independence. And an acceptance of him, the man he was. Now he was at the barn with Ham Carhill and Mia O'Farrell, both in tough shape, physically and emotionally. Joshua would protect them, and he would protect the crime scene.

Kelleher had constructed his own personal torture chamber and vigilante minibase in the days he'd been here.

Juliet's only regret was that she hadn't thought to take an MP5 for herself. She had her snub-nosed revolver. But it would do, and her primary goal was to isolate Kelleher and contain the situation until the cavalry arrived.

Ham Carhill had looked at her with a clear, calm gaze. "He wasn't sure about your role. Kelleher. He came to Vermont to learn more about you and your role in the conspiracy he had us all in. He positioned himself to get Ethan, through you, and to expose us as traitors, get money." The young Texan had frowned then, his certainty faltering. "I thought it was just the emeralds he was after. I don't understand the multimillions."

Juliet hadn't taken the time to sort out what he was saying with him. But she would, later, when Kelleher and Tatro were behind bars, when her family was safe.

Twenty yards before reaching the cabin's driveway, she started up the steep hill, moving at a diagonal, staying out of sight, even if she wasn't as stealthy as Brooker. Every crunch made her wince, but the bed of pine needles and freshly fallen leaves helped soften her approach.

She ducked under a monstrous rhododendron on the edge of the driveway and peered through its oversize branches. The hood to Kelleher's truck was up. He stepped down out of his camper, an MP5 cradled in his right arm.

And Ethan, coming into Juliet's line of sight, shut the truck's hood. She was within earshot.

What the hell was he up to?

He had an MP5 in his right hand. Kelleher got his weapon in ready position and said, "Keep your weapon lowered. Raise it an inch without my permission, and I'll shoot you."

"No problem. It's cool." Ethan nodded to the truck. "Ignition wire's been cut."

"Longstreet?"

"She's not with me. I've seen your setup

in the barn. Good deal, Kelleher. I never trusted O'Farrell. And Ham Carhill — a means to an end."

Kelleher seemed satisfied with Ethan's remarks. "What happened in Afghanistan? I've wanted to believe you were with us. Then, well, because of you, we lost valuable contacts and information that would have helped this country."

"I did what I could to help. How do you think you and most of your team escaped?"

Staying within cover of the rhododendron, Juliet crept closer to the driveway. She knew Ethan would keep Kelleher talking this nonsense as long as possible.

"I heard you were operating in Colombia." Ethan went on, his tone and stance casual, as if he had nothing more serious on his mind than a hike in the woods. "I encouraged Ham to go there. I made an opportunity for you."

"O'Farrell — were you on to her?"

"Not for a long time."

"Me, neither." Kelleher sighed, deeply disappointed. "I provided her with solid intel. A White House adviser. A smart woman with the president's ear. And she turns out to be a traitor. I was worried you were in on her scheme."

"No. I missed it. Carhill's in on it?"

"Definitely. People in my business some-times have to work with unsavory characters, do unsavory things. I was involved in a complicated moneymaking operation."

"Emerald smuggling."

He nodded. "Carhill was on to me. I was *that* close to getting tossed in a Colombian or U.S. prison. He knew he was in over his head and went to find you —"

"In New York. I'm sorry I missed him. I could have helped you unravel this thing sooner."

Kelleher gave a sad laugh. "Instead, I had to work with the likes of Bobby Tatro."

"You paid him to kidnap Carhill and hold him?"

"Then I told O'Farrell the truth, that you were one of the few who'd recognize Carhill on sight." Kelleher, alert, scanned left, then right. But he seemed to relish talking about his accomplishments. "I gave her the tip that would lead her to Tatro — not his name. I didn't want to raise her suspicions by giving her too much."

"You manipulated Tatro with the promise of his blond marshal. The picture —"

"He loved it. I got it to him, and he did his little drawings. He knew the doorman — Vincente — was my guy, but the stupid bastard killed him, anyway. He was out of control, breaking into Longstreet's apartment. He was convinced you'd given her the emeralds. Vincente had already been through the place and searched the niece's bags, but Tatro had to see for himself." Kelleher gave a hiss of pure contempt. "There was no need to terrorize that girl."

This from a man, Juliet thought, who had just tied Mia O'Farrell to a bomb.

"You called the Carhills with a ransom demand. Five million. The money's supposed to fund —"

"A training facility. I'm working with good people, Major. You'd be impressed. But we're all scattered right now." He nodded down toward the road. "We need to get this done."

"What's your plan?"

Kelleher didn't answer, and Juliet saw his expression — and so did Ethan. Kelleher didn't believe his camaraderie pretense. With lightning speed, Ethan dove behind the truck, and she fired at the same time he did.

Kelleher fell, his weapon clattering onto the driveway.

Juliet launched herself out from under the rhododendron and charged over to Kelleher, her gun on him as she picked up his MP5.

Ethan, right behind her, dropped down and checked Kelleher for a pulse. "Names, Kelleher. Who are you working with? Who broke Tatro out of jail? Who —" He stopped, looking up at Juliet. "He's gone."

"Damn. You're quick with a gun."

"An MP5's better than that thing you have."

She didn't want to admit that her knees were soft, and that she hadn't been at all sure her revolver had the accuracy at that range. She didn't know if her shot had struck him. She cleared her throat. "You had the drop on him, didn't you? When you got here —"

"I wanted information."

"You should leave that sort of thing to civilian law enforcement."

"I knew you'd end up under a rhodie. Monster, isn't it? You Longstreets are like the cleaning lady who doesn't clean her own house."

"Ethan —"

He brushed the back of his hand on her cheek. "Are you okay?"

She nodded, letting the breath go out of her. "You?"

"Just keep your brothers from arresting me."

But his smile didn't reach his eyes.

Twenty-One

~:෧෨:~

Wendy used her grandmother's old hand-cranked can opener to open three cans of organic red kidney beans, one after another, aware of Ham Carhill pacing behind her. She'd kicked everyone else out of the kitchen. The Longstreets had descended. Uncles, aunts, cousins, grandparents. And town cops, state troopers. Juliet and Ethan were at the hospital with Mia O'Farrell. Ham had been taken by ambulance to the emergency room, but he refused to stay — he had little round bandages over some of his cuts, and he was in obvious pain when he moved. Wendy couldn't kick him out of the kitchen, because that would be rude. But she just wanted to make chili.

She dumped the cans of beans into a colander in the sink and rinsed them. He looked over her shoulder and made a face. "I don't think I can do beans. I had enough of them in Colombia to last me."

"Was it awful?"

"Pretty bad. I knew I was worth more

alive than dead. That helped."

She switched off the faucet. "Matt . . ."

"Never saw him. Didn't have a clue. The thing about him I realize now —" He thought a moment as Wendy carried the colander of beans over to the stove and dumped them into her pan of sautéed onions, peppers, garlic and carrots; she didn't think anyone would notice the carrots when the chili was finished. Ham sighed and said, "He wanted it all. The glory, the violence, the money, the risk, the sneaking around. So he ended up biting off more than he could chew. It all got away from him."

Wendy didn't respond. She opened cans of tomatoes, dumped them in her pot. She added spices, fresh herbs from her grandmother's garden. The steam and the smells filled the kitchen, and one uncle drifted in, then another, and another, until they all were there, and it was Uncle Sam who noticed the carrot shreds. "Wendy — carrots?"

"They add sweetness," she said.

Her grandmother backed her up, and she and Uncle Will got bowls down from the cupboards while Wendy grated cheese for those who wanted it. Most of her cousins and aunts and the extra cops had left. She put the cheese on the table and dipped out the chili, noticing that Ham had left. Too many people for him, she thought.

"I liked Matt," she said in a half whisper when she sat at the table. "I trusted him."

Her father took her hand. "We all did. We all got taken."

"He was a likable guy," Uncle Sam said.

"You can't live your life not trusting anyone," her grandfather added.

Uncle Jeff concurred, then grunted. "But the next guy who shows up for temporary work gets checked out."

They all seemed to enjoy the chili. Wendy liked it, too — it had worked out a lot better than her apple crisp.

A car sounded in the driveway, and she felt her heartbeat quicken. Her grandfather went to the window, his limp more pronounced today. "Ah." He turned to his family at the table. "The feds are here."

He greeted them at the door, and they introduced themselves.

Joe Collins, Mike Rivera and Nate Winter.

Wendy smiled tentatively at Special Agent Collins and Chief Rivera, and their serious expressions softened when they saw her. Her father squeezed her hand. "They'll want to talk to us," he said.

"Both of us?"

"Oh, yes."

Aunt Juliet followed the three men into the house and made a face. "If someone had handed me a picture of all you guys here in the kitchen when I was seventeen," she said, "I'd have stuck to landscaping."

"You and that mouth," Chief Rivera said, but he was grinning.

Then Ethan Brooker walked in, and from her aunt's look, Wendy decided that no way would Juliet have been happy planting lilacs.

Juliet joined Ham on the porch. It was early evening, the temperature falling fast. "We're losing sun," she said. "In a few more weeks, it'll be dark at three o'clock."

He smiled at her. He looked tired, pale and very sore. "That's an exaggeration."

"Okay, three-thirty."

He lifted his eyes to her. "They want to talk to me now?"

She nodded, knowing he meant Collins, Rivera and Winter. "You can tell them everything. What's classified will stay classified."

"I just —" He got awkwardly to his feet, picked at one of his little bandages. "I just told Dr. O'Farrell stuff I heard. It was never that big a deal."

"From what I understand, you prevented

some rotten things from happening."

He shrugged, obviously pleased, but not wanting to take any credit. "But I almost caused —" He broke off, then continued, his head lowered, "If I hadn't switched the emeralds."

"Bobby Tatro's a violent man, Ham. If he'd walked away with the emeralds, who knows who else he would have hurt."

"Yeah. That's what I tell myself." He pulled open the porch door, glancing back at her. "How is Dr. O'Farrell?"

"She got pretty beat up, but she's okay. The mental scars are going to take the longest to heal."

Ham nodded, his eyes distant. "He'd have tortured her —"

"I know, Ham. Don't dwell on what might have been." Juliet gave him an encouraging smile. "Go talk to Agent Collins."

"I don't understand why Kelleher turned on Dr. O'Farrell." Ham frowned, shaking his head, muttering to himself as he went inside.

Juliet sat on the porch steps, a cold wind whipping through the bright leaves of the sugar maple. When the door creaked open behind her, she knew it was Ethan and didn't look up. He sat next to her, stretching his long legs down the steps and leaning back on his elbows. "I think Officer Paul wants to skin your mother."

"Why?"

"Apparently your fed friends can't find a room for tonight, and she offered to let them stay here."

Juliet nearly choked. "She did what? Oh, hell. I'm not going back to New York until tomorrow. The last thing I want to do is run into Joe Collins on the way to the bathroom in his boxer shorts."

Ethan was clearly amused. "No tent tonight?"

"Uh-uh. Not after all the sneaking around in the woods I did today."

"That's not it." He settled his black eyes on her, studying her, and she had the feeling he could slice right through all her defenses and see straight through to her soul. "You want to be close to your family. You might not ever live full-time in Vermont again, but it's still home."

"Oh, heavens," she said. "I'll become a flatlander."

He grinned. "The flatlands aren't so bad." A gust of wind scattered orange leaves at his feet. "Ham's parents have chartered a jet for him, and he's offered me a ride to wherever I want to go."

Juliet nodded. "You'll go back to Texas."

"Maybe."

"Ethan —"

"I don't know what comes next for me, Juliet. I have to figure that out. For the past year, I haven't thought much beyond getting through the next twenty-four hours."

"When do you and Ham leave?"

"As soon as he finishes up with the big three in there."

She smiled at him. "Maybe I'll land on your doorstep next time."

Twenty-Two

Mia wore slim pants and a sweater to her meeting with President Poe one week after her ordeal in Vermont. She couldn't bear to put on panty hose, tuck in a blouse, find the right brooch, the right earrings. Her doctors had told her to give herself time. They didn't understand the world in which she operated.

"I recommend you not let Ethan Brooker slip away. He's too good to lose," she told the president. They were in a windowless room, at a surprisingly rickety table. "He's finished with active military duty, but he'll never be a rancher."

Poe didn't speak for a moment. Then he asked softly, "What about you?"

She raised her eyes to him, again noting what a remarkably handsome man he was. And a decent one. "You have to cut me loose."

"Why?"

"Mr. President —" She looked at him as if he were being dense on purpose. "I got information from a vigilante mercenary. I was tortured. I endangered —" She stopped herself and added simply, "I screwed up."

"You have a different perspective now. Your work isn't all theoretical. The lives you and Mr. Carhill saved are the lives of real people." He drummed the table for a few seconds with all ten fingers. "We only have the tip of the iceberg. We need to find Kelleher's associates, the men who followed you to New York, who engineered Bobby Tatro's escape. I realize you're not an investigator, but we have a lot of work to do."

Mia didn't know what to say. She thought of Vermont and pumpkins and apples, and the Longstreets, especially Joshua, whose kindness to her, whose uncomplicated principles, continued to bring her comfort, and she found herself unable to speak.

"Mia?"

"I'm sorry . . ."

"No." President Poe got to his feet. "No, I'm sorry. You've been through hell. Take some time off. All the time you need. Then, if you want to, we can talk."

Joshua picked fallen leaves off the pumpkins he and Wendy had set out on each step to his porch. She hadn't wanted to carve them. The air was frosty and clear, and the leaves were dropping fast, leaving behind the burgundy and rusts of the oak trees, the evergreens. The leaf-peepers had gone home, the skiers hadn't yet arrived. The media and the federal investigators had finally left town. His corner of Vermont was quiet again.

And Wendy was going to be all right. Her mother had charged down from Nova Scotia but only spent a few days with her, because their daughter wanted her to go back — wanted, she said, for her to finish her yoga study, go after her own dreams. The three of them — mother, father, daughter — walked down to the lake one morning and scattered Teddy's ashes together. Before her mother left, Wendy announced to both her parents that she didn't want to be a doctor — or a cop or a landscaper, or a yoga teacher.

She didn't know what she wanted to be.

That was fine with Joshua and his ex-wife. Wendy was just seventeen. Neither of them had realized just how much their daughter had anguished over her decision.

He dumped the stray leaves onto the yard. He didn't know why he bothered. By morning, more leaves would have blown onto the steps, the pumpkins, up onto the porch. Barry swept every morning, but couldn't keep up. But it gave him something to complain about.

A car pulled up to the curb in front of his house. A woman. Small, with dark auburn hair.

Mia O'Farrell.

She got out and smiled at him over the top of the car. "I like the pumpkins."

It'd been three weeks since she'd collapsed into his arms. She looked strong, and the terror and pain had gone out of her eyes. Joshua walked out to her. "What —"

"I'm not here on business," she said quickly. "I took some time off. I've been staring at the walls of my apartment too long."

Joshua was at a rare loss. "Um . . . come on in."

"I hope I'm not interrupting —"

"Not at all."

Barry came out onto the porch and assessed the situation. "Are you inviting her to the football game?"

"That's Barry Small, my downstairs neighbor," Joshua said to Mia. "My nephew's playing football tonight at the high school. Wendy and I are going. She's bringing apple cider, and Barry's making

411

some kind of vegetable casserole." He smiled. "I hope you like eggplant."

"It all sounds wonderful."

"Good."

"Thank you." The tension seemed to go out of her. "I should have called, but I didn't know if I'd get here and turn around and drive straight back to Washington."

"I'm glad you didn't," Joshua said, liking the warmth that had come into her green eyes.

To Ethan's mind, the tidy house in Tampa looked as if it belonged to a retired army brigadier general. Sherwin Hood had never really approved of his daughter's choice of husband. That she'd gone off to Amsterdam on her own and was killed there, was, in her father's mind, Ethan's doing.

But some of the older man's hatred and anger had dissipated, the hard edges of his grief worn down to a sense of loss that he'd fought learning to live with for as long as he could, until the memories of his first-born daughter had forced him to smile again.

At least, that was how he told it to Ethan over iced tea at the pool.

Felicity, Char's younger sister, who

hadn't gone into the military, was a different matter. "There's no good ruining your life because Char's gone," she said, following him out to the driveway. "She never hated you. She was an army brat, a career officer, herself. She always understood even when the mission came before her."

"Felicity —"

"Don't pretend now that it didn't come first." But there was no resentment in her dark eyes. "I wish I could blame you. It'd be easier somehow. But I'm living each day to its fullest. That's what Char would have wanted — for both of us."

"I'm sorry, Felicity. If I could have saved her —"

She smiled sadly. "You can't save everyone. It's been a year, Ethan. Love again. If you need my permission. If you need hers."

On his way out, he saw Char's picture on the living room wall, smiling, alone in her wedding dress. He blew her a kiss and said goodbye.

His brother in Texas called him on his cell phone at the airport. "Your marshal is here," Luke said. "Deputy Longstreet. She says she's on business and watching for snakes."

"My flight's boarding now."

"Good. I'll stall her until you get here."

Twenty-Three

❧ 🕉 ❧

Juliet had to use her badge to get herself past the Carhills' security people. She'd all but had to shoot Luke Brooker to get off the Brooker ranch. He'd tried to stall her with iced tea, the grand tour, the piano and small talk about snakes and quail-hunting before she finally told him to give up. "Don't you want me to show you Ethan's baby pictures?" he'd asked with a glint in his eye that reminded her of his younger brother.

If he'd been there, she'd have taken Ethan out to see the Carhills with her. Since he wasn't, she went alone.

She loved the Brookers' corner of west Texas. The grandness of the landscape, the big open sky and the sense of space and possibility. But Luke had said they'd known when Ethan was four that he wasn't staying on the ranch. Juliet figured that was when he'd jumped out of his first plane.

Faye Carhill brought her into a formal living room decorated in shades of cream

414

and gold. Juliet sat on a lush vanilla sofa, feeling inelegant in her functional skirt and jacket. "How's Ham?" she asked.

"Oh, fine, fine." Faye smiled nervously, smoothing her St. John Knits pants as she sat on a wing chair in a gold-and-cream brocade. "He's here — out by the pool," she said, casually, as if he weren't recuperating from a horrible ordeal.

"Your husband?" Juliet asked.

"He's in his library. He has calls to make." She added awkwardly, "Business."

"Is this where you got the ransom call — here at home?"

"Deputy Longstreet, is this an official visit? Should I have my attorney present?"

"You can have your attorney present if you want. Ham asked me to stop by some time and see him. I figured I would."

"I'm sure you want to see Ethan, too."

"He's not in town." There *was* a town — Luke Brooker had offered to show it to her. Juliet told him seeing a hunk of the Brooker ranch was enough for her; nonetheless she'd enjoyed his company. She returned her attention to Faye Carhill, and said, "I'm here about the five-million ransom demand that Matt Kelleher made."

"You haven't caught all of his accomplices —"

"We're working on it." Juliet leaned back into the soft cushions, studying Ham's mother for any sign of discomfort, but saw none. But she did see a resemblance to her son, in her eyes, around her mouth, that might have surprised, even dismayed, her. "Ethan's told the authorities everything, Mrs. Carhill. You told him that you didn't pay the ransom. The five million."

She shifted on her chair. "I asked him to keep our conversation private."

"Well, then he'd have been in trouble with the FBI and the United States Marshals Service and, maybe worst of all, the Vermont State Police." Juliet kept her tone light, but Faye didn't smile. "Mrs. Carhill, you lied to Ethan. You paid the ransom."

"Deputy Longstreet, I think you should leave."

Juliet ignored her. "I'll bet Kelleher was thrilled. His original plan was to use Ham to lure Ethan into his orbit and convert him to the cause or kill him. He hooked into your son because of Ham's friendship with Ethan."

"If you're implying my son bragged about his friendship with a Special Forces officer —"

"I'm not. Kelleher could have found out on his own. Ethan had his name in the papers in the spring, not long before Kelleher hooked Ham up with his friend in Washington."

"I hate this," Faye said tightly, in a low voice. "Ham should have known better."

"From what I understand, he did a lot of good." Juliet gave his mother a chance to say something, but she didn't. "He also was on to Kelleher's smuggling operation. Kelleher knew he had to do something. He just didn't know what."

Faye turned away, refusing to listen.

Juliet sighed. "Ham knew he was in over his head and came to New York to find Ethan. That's just what Kelleher wanted. He followed your son and saw Bobby Tatro sneaking around — which is how he got involved. At first, Kelleher didn't want Ham putting the pieces together about the smuggling, but he could have just shot Ham and been done with him. What he really was after was a way to get Ethan to Colombia. That's why he put out word that Ethan could identify your son."

"I don't want to hear this."

"I didn't, either. I keep picturing your son getting grabbed in Colombia." But that, she knew, wasn't what his mother was picturing — Juliet guessed that Faye Carhill could only see herself and her husband and the disruption to their quiet, private lives of tremendous privilege. Juliet went on, "Kelleher did as much manipulating and maneuvering as he could. Then he called you."

Faye spun around in her chair, her pale eyes shining with tears. "What would you have had us do?"

"I'd have had you call your local FBI office. Instead, you paid the ransom. Then, when you realized your son was safe, you took it away."

"How could we —"

"You're wealthy, very well-connected people, Mrs. Carhill. You found a way to get your money back out of Kelleher's account. Maybe that was the right thing to do — that money sure as hell wasn't going to a good cause. But if you'd told people — if you'd told your own son —" Juliet sat forward, half wishing she'd stayed at the Brooker ranch and looked at those baby pictures of Ethan. "What Kelleher did isn't your responsibility. But what you did is. Ham thought the emeralds were the ransom."

"He wanted to make it all right," Faye whispered. "That's my son, you know. He always thinks there's a right and a wrong choice."

Juliet got to her feet. "May I see him?"

She nodded, exhausted, and pointed vaguely out toward the back of the house.

A uniformed maid with a pleasant smile showed Juliet out to the pool. Ham was there, sprawled on a lounge chair in the sun. Juliet grinned at him. "You're going to be a wrinkled-up old man one day."

He grinned back. "I hope so." He squinted up at her. "Am I in trouble?"

"Nope. I'm just visiting."

"Did my mother tell you she and my father paid the five million, then took it away? It explains why Kelleher turned on Mia O'Farrell. Why he went crazy with his conspiracies. He had five million in his bank account one day, and the next day — poof. Gone."

"He figured only a conspiracy involving a high government official could explain what happened."

"And me — I was already a traitor because I was so close to uncovering his emerald smuggling." He sat up, crossing his legs. He had on swim trunks, and his ribs showed, but at least the bites and bruises had healed. "I joined the Marines."

Juliet looked out at the warm, rippling water of the kidney-shaped pool. The air was warm by her standards, but cool for

419

bony Ham to be out sunning himself, although he didn't seem to notice. "The Marines, huh?"

He nodded.

"Well, you're a genius, right? You'll have considered all the pros and cons. You tell Ethan?"

"He says I'll last twelve hours before they kick me out."

"And you plan to show him."

Ham grinned. "Yes, ma'am, I sure do."

Juliet winked at him. "You hang in there for the thirteen hours, Ham. After that, you'll have proved yourself to Brooker, and the Marines'll make you a general."

When she left, she had him laughing. But she didn't see Faye or Johnson Carhill on her way out, although the maid gave her warm almond coffee cake wrapped in aluminum foil. "For Ethan," she said.

"He's not here —"

"Oh, yes." And she nodded, smiling, toward the driveway. "He's here."

And he was, sitting behind the wheel of her rented car. She pulled open the passenger door. "What did you do, parachute in?"

"Luke."

"Ah. The co-conspirator."

But it'd been three weeks since their

night on the lake, and Juliet couldn't hold back her pleasure at seeing him. "Ethan. Damn." She climbed into the passenger seat and kissed him. "I'm not sleeping in a tent here. Not only do you have poisonous snakes, you've got wild hogs. I hate snakes — poisonous or not — and I don't plan on running into any wild hogs. I want a bed."

He smiled at her. "A bed."

"Your parents — I met them. Very nice people. They want you to be happy again. However, if getting a bed requires —"

"They've gone to San Antonio for the weekend. Spur-of-the-moment trip."

"San Antonio?"

"It's another city in Texas."

"I know —" She sat back in her seat, noticing he had the air-conditioning turned on — a good thing, because she was hot. "That means we get the house to ourselves."

After they made love in the guest room and took a long, soapy shower together, they poured wine and went out into the backyard and watched the west Texas sunset. Juliet had never seen such a glorious sunset, deep, rich, fire colors with sparks of lavender and a soft glow, here and there, of pale pink. "I've taken a job in Washington," she said. "Nate Winter offered it

421

to me. I'm joining a special joint task force to find Kelleher's vigilante cohorts."

"D.C., huh?"

She nodded. "I start next week."

"Where are you going to live?"

"Mia O'Farrell has offered to sublet her apartment in Georgetown to me. She's on a leave of absence, or that's what she's calling it. She and Joshua —" Juliet, who'd gone home to Vermont last weekend, pictured her brother walking up to the apple orchard, Mia on one arm, his daughter on the other arm. He'd never seemed happier. "They've hit it off. She's spending the next few months in Vermont."

"You'll like her apartment."

"You've been there?"

"I'm living there. I moved in last week." He glanced sideways at her, his expression impossible to read. "She's subletting to me, too. These devious Beltway types . . ."

Juliet gave him an amused, suspicious look. "I smell a conspiracy."

"The thing about stopping to see Nate and Sarah, you never know who's going to be eating fried pies on the back porch. I ran into President Poe two weeks ago. He asked me to come work for him." Ethan shrugged. "I'm not used to telling the commander in chief 'no.' "

"Well, I should warn you. I bought a fish."

"Juliet —"

"I love you, Ethan, but I know you've had a difficult year. We can take this a step at a time. There's no rush. I'm not going anywhere." She looked at him. "But that's not a promise you can make."

"I can love you forever."

"*That's* a promise you can make."

"Juliet . . ." He tucked his hand into hers. "You didn't buy just one fish, did you?"

She smiled.

About the Author

Carla Neggers has been writing since she climbed a tree with pad and pencil at age eleven — now she's the bestselling author of many novels of romance and suspense. An avid hiker and kayaker, Carla lives with her family in Vermont, where she's hard at work on her next book. You can visit her at www.carlaneggers.com.